μ

Rattlesnake

a novel by

ARTURO ARIAS

Translated by
Seán Higgins and Jill Robbins

CURBSTONE PRESS

A Lannan Literary Selection
with Special Thanks to Patrick Lannan and
the Lannan Foundation Board of Directors

Printed on acid-free paper by Transcontinental/Best Book
Cover design: Stone Graphics
Painting: "Conversations With a Snake" by Norman Catherine,
2002; oil on canvas, 30.5cm x 40.5cm.

This book was published with the support of the Connecticut
Commission on the Arts, the Lannan Foundation, the National
Endowment for the Arts, and donations from many individuals.
We are very grateful for this support.
Printed in Canada

Library of Congress Cataloging-in-Publication Data

Arias, Arturo, 1950-
  [Cascabel. English]
  Rattlesnake / by Arturo Arias ; translated by Sean Higgins and
Jill Robbins.— 1st ed.
     p. cm.
  ISBN 1-931896-01-1 (pbk. : alk. paper)
  I. Higgins, Sean, 1961- II. Robbins, Jill. III. Title.
  PQ7499.2.A73C3713 2003

  863'.64—dc22

                                                    2003016402

published by
   CURBSTONE PRESS 321 Jackson Street Willimantic, CT
                            06226
       phone: 860-423-5110   e-mail: info@curbstone.org
                      www.curbstone.org

I would sincerely like to thank my loving wife, Jill Robbins, for taking time off her own very valuable academic work to work on this translation. I especially thank her for her acute critical eye. Para siempre, hasta siempre.

Part One

The Unsuspecting Fisher of Dreams

CHAPTER ONE

1

The squealing of the car tires told him that the driver had taken the first curve way too fast. Jerked abruptly by the unexpected whipping of the vehicle, Tom Wright held onto the door handle in a desperate effort to keep his balance. A more tolerant Captain Pacal simply let his body weight shift gently in the front seat until he was pressed against the door. As he leaned against the window the sunlight hit his face, highlighting countless scars. A sallow, purple-lipped soldier with a singularly small forehead was driving. Mute, not moving a single muscle as if hypnotized, he stared straight ahead to where a yellow line should have been painted at the center of the road. The smell of burning rubber hit Wright's nose.

It was a solid car. Bulletproof, without a doubt, with tinted windows. They'd taken every possible precaution. On the rear window, there was a sticker displaying the triangular head of a venomous snake within a red circle. On the outer part of the circle, in black letters, it read, *"Only the winners have the right to live."*

A scraggly white mutt with brown spots, its ribs amply visible from a considerable distance, crossed the road. To Wright's surprise, the soldier picked up speed. The dog hesitated for a second. It raised a forepaw, then an ear. At once it bolted to the left, with difficulty, as if it had arthritis in its hind legs. The driver cut to his left and sped up even more. Wright closed his eyes. *It is the cause, it is the cause, my soul*. He heard a dry thump, like a sack of potatoes falling from a truck, followed by the pained howl of the animal. It began as a sort of high-pitched ambulance siren, then decreased gradually like a TV set when turned off by a remote control. The driver gave a slight grunt as if his hoarse laugh were stuck in his throat.

Pacal turned back to look at him with a mocking grimace. Wright felt uneasy. He'd known for quite a while that the country had strange customs, but this? He had learned about Guatemala long before, amidst the brimming joy of youth, when a candied voice as thick as peach flesh told him all about it. A voice whose fidgeting sweetness still choked him up.

He would have preferred to sit up front to take in the landscape, to see all the motion of these short, gloomy, stiff people and the savage awkwardness of traffic, to take account of the whole situation, and to admire the smoking volcanoes whose steamy allure imprisoned the entire city, an anarchic, overgrown, erratic, modern metropolis struggling to evade its volcanic suffocation by extending itself through every nook and cranny, turning, teeming, sweeping everything away. But he said nothing.

Pacal addressed him. "So, these are the ones I was telling you about. And just so you don't think we don't know what we're doing, we have it from a good source, a very well-placed one, that they're the terrorists who have Mr. Gray."

Pacal passed him a dossier, referring to it with the English word "folder." Wright didn't bother to mention the dog incident. He was still somewhat upset, an emotion which he would have preferred not to reveal. Inside the folder there was a manila envelope holding an array of glossy photos, all 8x10's. Most of them were head shots facing the camera. Some in profile. All black and white.

He didn't like the idea of dealing with Guatemalans. He'd had one experience before and that was enough for him. He didn't even know Gray. His mission was vague, with confusing and contradictory instructions. But overall there was his memory of her. In spite of all the years that had gone by, she still hung over him like a dense, spring fog that blocked the sun's rays, the slender shoulders and fine head still fueling his lust. He hadn't seen another Guatemalan since that cocktail party in Washington, where he met that corpulent fellow with his expression of bemused indifference and curly hair—Fuentes something-or-other. They'd talked candidly about Mitterrand, avoiding extreme views. He closed his eyes and let himself be lulled by seductive images of an orange skirt swaying, kicking and whirling in the wind.

The afternoon sky was completely clouded over. Regardless of the country's famed colors, everything seemed hazy and dull, as if cloaked under a veil of mist, giving it the appearance of a grainy black and white photo. Only the tremulous, melancholic image of the woman, idealized by the long separation, stood out in vivid color as the car moved erratically in the direction of his nondescript hotel, as impersonal as any other.

"They're ugly. Like characters in some cheap flick."

He voiced this with coldness, just to make conversation. Wright couldn't focus on anything beyond the pile of photos, a series of unknown people whose faces he didn't like—flat noses, thick lips, slanted eyes, long curly hair—like dark angels hovering over America's placid safety. The pictures were an excessive repetition of unattractive anatomies. The only thing clear in his mind was the fading image of the woman. She was the only reason he had to come to this inhospitable place, but the agency had no idea of her existence. Well, almost the only reason. This job could be the ticket to his promotion, so he could avoid these dreary jobs and move up to a place where he could simply catch his breath and his guts weren't in a constant state of turmoil from the frenetic pace of the action. Not to mention a decent paycheck that would let him put his kids through college. But life is full of traps, he thought.

Pacal kept talking. He had a metallic voice, whiny, bossy, and monotonous all at once. Just one more bit of cloying excess on his part. Wright took scant notice but pretended to listen, keeping a warm, shy smile in his face all the time, occasionally uttering the conventional indicators of interest. Pacal's ceaseless drone was giving him a headache. He wished he had a couple of Tylenol, or a scotch on the rocks, preferably both. If only that voice would be still, but Pacal kept going as if he'd been given complete license.

"This is the one we saw nosing around the International Exports office, where the Nugan Hand Bank office is located. We suspect he's the ringleader. He commands the urban front for the Guerrilla Army of the Poor. We just refer to them by their Spanish acronym, EGP, for the *Ejército Guerrillero de los Pobres.*"

Wright was just listening passively, but soon he would have to say something so Pacal would not take him for another stupid *gringo*, and so the image of the woman would disappear from his head. Or at least to make that desire for scotch and Tylenol disappear. Why should he care who the head of some terrorist organization was? Those details were unimportant. Why not just implement a total cleanup and be rid of them all? The whole world had gone rotten. His face took on a curious expression, a sort of disenchanted frustration, and he said with hesitation: "Yeah, what's his name?"

"His code-name is Kukulkán."

2

The Mayan Golf Club, she once told him, is an extremely selective, exclusive club, the most difficult to join in the country, even if it does overlook one of the most polluted and filthy lakes on the continent. The club itself was located high enough up the cliff, however, to escape the putrid odors of the malevolent green heaps of garbage carried by the Villalobos River from the poorly-planned, overpopulated capital to this lake that fifty years ago was General Ubico's private playground, but now was just a silent, wretched shadow of its old self. The country club was reserved for a self-selected elite, though, in any half-civilized country, its building and grounds would have been considered strictly middle-class. But in life, everything's relative. Even more so in a small Central American country where most people had not yet begun to live, and even the moderately well-off thought that the squalid capital was the most important metropolis of the isthmus, and that Miami was more interesting than Paris.

Sandra belonged to that club, but, as she loved to say, she didn't take it seriously; she didn't take anything seriously. The only thing that mattered was the abject delight of playing with her life and those of others because, the way she saw it, there wasn't any better orgasm than the one you got risking your frail neck, dissolving your wide-eyed fear in the liquid invisibility of eroticism. She couldn't care less about the rest. Her goal was to take care of her interests—not her family's, but her own. She complied with the wretched social formalities to appease the obnoxious circle of fat, old, puckered biddies and to avoid the inevitable gossip that would really anger her authoritarian father-in-law. She considered herself smarter than everyone else, and, in an extreme case, she could use her golden face, her hypnotic gaze, to defend herself. She knew full well that any whim could be fulfilled by manipulating the lustful dictates of male desire, whose melodious symphony she conducted to perfection, so her occasional concessions to this sordid reality didn't really worry her much.

It started to rain. She had to go back to the city soon. There was a delicate matter to take care of. In fact, was it time? Yes, indeed, time to go. They were waiting for her on

El Camino Real. She thought briefly about the matter and smiled to herself thinking about what her husband and father-in-law would say if they only knew.

3

If any drivers were to pass by it on the badly named "El Salvador Highway," in reality the entrance to the Eastern suburbs of the city, they wouldn't even know that there was a mansion a short distance from the Muxbal exit because it wasn't near the road. You had to drive up a narrow, muddy path that gave the impression you were approaching some backwater dive or beggar's settlement. If you didn't know where you were going, you would never guess that you were headed toward one of the most luxurious houses in the country. If by any chance you did wander through the potholes and mud puddles that served as natural speed bumps, you would come across a high adobe wall—or at least it looked like one—brownish, dull and sad, like one you might find anywhere in the country, except for two things: it was much higher (also thicker, with steel framing, but you couldn't tell that at first glance), and it had electric barbed wire on top. Behind the wall you could make out a dense row of trees. Diligent cypresses formed a woodsy barrier. Beyond them came the terraces, the intensely green grassy lawn, trimmed so smoothly that it looked like a carpet. The elegant house was at the end, beyond the long terrace. It had red bricks and Doric columns at the entrance, and a tile roof, so that just about anyone would have taken it for a cross between the Tara of *Gone with the Wind* and the Tzanjuyú Hotel in Panajachel. The final result was as strange as the mere notion of such a singular mix, typical of this country's artistic expression.

Generally there wasn't much movement in the ample

gardens, except for that of the German shepherds, two or three morose gardeners yanking some stubborn weeds out of the flower beds, and bulletproof cars with tinted windows coming and going on a regular basis. But inside the house, noise and commotion were the rule. People came and went, uniformed servants went to and fro with trays of ice-filled glasses. At the entrance, there were at least three bodyguards on watch at all times, their Uzis standing up against the wall and their automatic pistols bulging in their pants like some kind of phallic deformity.

The metallic opacity of the rainy afternoon made it difficult to see the wall at the entrance from the living room windows. The noise and commotion were even more intense than usual despite the inclement weather, which had kept away any visitors, be they family, government officials or foreign businessmen. The problem was Don Leonel's molars. He was a man in his fifties used to elegance, money, and the power of having grown up ordering colonels to do whatever he pleased. He still gave the impression of being *"muy macho,"* able to have all the women he wanted, and of being unafraid even of God Almighty.

Don Leonel always dressed in black. He'd dressed the same ever since he was taken as a boy to see Saint Simon of Zunil. He had been impressed by that image and decided that he would be Saint Simon when he grew up. So when power finally came his way, after his father's death, he began dressing strictly in black. Even his sunglasses were black, and he never took them off, not even in the house. He'd walk around with a cigar in his right hand, which lit up an enormous amethyst ring that he flaunted on his index finger and created white whorls of cigar smoke around him, as if incense were permanently being burned upon his passage. The only thing he stopped wearing as time went by was his black cowboy hat, although he would still put it on when he went to the countryside or horseback riding. But ever since the country had begun to fall apart, those outings were less frequent and more difficult. Now he could only visit the ranch by private plane, and, at his age, he couldn't get over his fear of those rickety little contraptions. He hated anything that evinced weakness, and, since the worst humiliation he could think of was to show fear, he preferred not to fly and even less so on days like this, when the temperature changes could shake the plane like a tiny insect.

The maid gave him the wad of cotton. He chewed on it, allowing the mentholated vapors to reach up to the top of his head where he was starting to go bald. Then he let out a piercing howl that forced him to shut his eyes and feel the hugeness of the bags hanging under them. Finally, he spit out the chewed-up cotton ball, as one would an orange rind, wetting part of the finely trimmed mustache under his hawkish nose. The maid gave him another cotton ball, and then, disregarding her intense lower back pain and the descending inguinal hernia on her left side, she squatted to pick up the discarded ball now on the floor and deposit it in a bowl full of other bloody cotton balls smelling of the abattoir, as if they were a sacred offering that would be burned for the many idols that decorated the gigantic living room.

Alvaro, Don Leonel's son, insisted that they leave immediately for the dentist.

"What, so the guerrillas can kidnap me? I guess I have to remind you what Richelieu said about the male virtues of making decisions ra-tion-al-ly. It's a hard word to pronounce, I understand, but you have to use big words if you want to play with the big boys."

He actually knew that his chances of being kidnaped were minimal. The guerrillas lacked operative capabilities, plus they already had their hands full with that banker, Gray. The last thing they could think about right now was picking up a well-to-do man like him to finance their operations. He was old, but he wasn't an idiot. It just gave him a perverse pleasure to contradict his son. He liked to show that it was men like himself who were worthwhile, not assholes like Alvaro, who were ruining the country and letting their women run the family business. He was a fool for having had only one son. At least only one that he recognized as his own. But it wasn't his fault. It was his wife's fault for giving him a bunch of daughters. Women only gave him problems. More so these days. Things just weren't the way they used to be.

4

The car slowed down.

"Are we there already?"

The driver looked back at Captain Pacal with a pained expression but without saying anything. The latter turned toward Tom Wright and lowered his eyes.

"No. Traffic's backed up because of a demonstration."

Wright tried to lower the window to see what was happening. An expression of panic came over Pacal's face as he shook his head and frowned.

"Don't even think about it, for your own sake…"

Wright obeyed reluctantly, grappling with perplexity. He pressed his face against the glass to glimpse what was happening. A column of impatient men—very young-looking—was marching in an orderly fashion. Their foreheads shone, and their wide cheekbones made their faces look chubby. Some had beards and longish hair; others were clean-shaven with brush cuts. All of them were all dressed in blue jeans or other casual clothing, with low-heeled shoes, generally sneakers. They were shouting with determination. Men and women with red armbands marched beside the demonstrators, gripping each others' hands so tightly that the veins on their arms stood out. It was obvious that these were the ones in charge of keeping order, and they didn't want the situation to get out of hand. For the most part, they were an ugly lot, but they seemed polite and cordial, even with their crooked smiles and twisted teeth. Pacal was nuts. Wright lowered his window.

In spite of the rain and the grayness of the day, he was dazzled. The color of the jagged mountains in the background—a shrieking green that almost grabbed you by the lapels and slapped you in the face—was delirious, as if from a drug-induced dream. In combination with the crystalline brightness of the sunlight and the conical perfection of the majestic volcanoes, it made everything seem overexposed, so the primary colors stood out even more. The hallucinatory effects of this scene made him think of visual defects, an obsession of his ever since those horrific childhood nightmares about eyes. He thought suddenly that everyone in Guatemala seemed to suffer from strabismus; people were always averting their eyes to avoid eye contact.

Against that intensely green, damp background, the glaring red banners were even more striking. They read, in Spanish, "For a people's government, by the people and for the people." He had to laugh. That came from his own country's constitution. "We want democracy." This was an irreproachable slogan as long as it wasn't a bluff. Leftists always used it and later forgot about it. But these people looked innocent, even if they were out of order. So different from other young people he knew back home. They seemed almost to create their own environment even as they trudged uphill, avoiding the little puddles created by the rain pouring off the tree branches, the brownish mud, and the accumulated trash that kept the rivulets of stagnant, smelly water from flowing freely down the cluttered gutter. "We, the workers, demand a patriotic, popular and democratic government." That sounded a little more aggressive, but the people carrying that banner didn't look any angrier than the rest. Perhaps a bit younger, but with the faces of good citizens. "Blood is not forgotten; the massacred will be avenged." These were

Indians, you could see it from a mile away. Their colorful clothing almost slapped you in the eyes with its audacity. Besides, their slogan was painted on a *petate,* a straw mat they used for sleeping. The men wore hats, and the women, *huipiles* of every possible color and design, patterned skirts and long braids decorated with ribbons. They were all dark, famished birds, although none of their features differed significantly from those of Pacal or his driver or the people in the photos that he thought he had memorized. They weren't exactly a beautiful people, a sensual people. Their bodily movements were mostly brusque. Everything was short, blunt, and graceless.

"There they are. Look at them."

"They look young and easy to handle."

"Appearances can be deceiving. Don't be a *gringo* asshole like the ones in the cigarette ads."

"So why don't you, you know, *liquidarlos?*"

"Liquify them?"

"No, you know, liquid, liquidify—liquidate them."

"What? Just get rid of them just like that?"

Pacal started to laugh loudly, revealing a gold tooth in his left upper jaw that made him look like some cartoon tough-guy stereotype. It was actually only half a tooth, so it looked like a shiny triangle stuck in his pink gums.

"Get with it, man. You have to know how to operate around here. *El que se va con la finta cae con trompa de baboso y el que se mueve no sale en la foto.*"

Those expressions were too colloquial for Wright to catch their implications, so he limited himself to answering with a thoughtful diplomatic phrase.

"Exactly. Nothing is what it seems to be."

And it wasn't. Central Americans' excess made it hard for Tom Wright to sketch characters in his head, do away with the stereotypes, and jump ahead to a place where he could bring together the solemn rhythm of wisdom and cold-blooded calculations.

5

Sandra walked swiftly toward her beautiful, white, shiny BMW and started the engine. When she shifted into reverse, she almost sent the car phone resting next to the gear shift flying. In the rearview mirror she saw her bodyguards run to their vehicle, to follow her every move. She hated the fact that she couldn't go where she wanted without them following her like faithful dogs. But what could she do? In the current climate, there was no choice She had to put up with it.

She tore out. Through the smoke of the burning rubber, she saw that she'd left her bodyguards behind and decreased her speed slightly. It was raining harder. The luscious, trembling green-green landscape so dear to her could barely be seen through the dense languor of the loitering fog. The windshield wipers—back and forth, back and forth—hypnotized her with their metallic sound. That, along with the unending cobalt gray of the wet road. Everything was gray. Cold wetness, lifeless colors. The only vivid colors were on the slogans painted on the inside surface of the rolling hills through which the road had been cut. "Long live the EGP." In black and red. "Military assassins." Mostly in red, though some letters were blue. The sight of them amused her. She imagined the nervousness of the restless young men in a nocturnal lightning operation, sweating, reeking of pure adrenaline rush. You could see the tension and the haste in the crooked letters with dried paint dripping down to the ground. They couldn't live too far off. Maybe they were from Villa Nueva, right nearby. It made her laugh to think what her father-in-law would say if he knew that she thought about these things. She imagined herself participating in one of those operations. Overall, she admired their audacity. Then, she thought of her brother, which made her frown and wrinkle her brow, until she was able to force her memories back to the sweet innocence of the serpents, as her father would say.

At the turn of a lazy curve that ended in an abrupt winding that led to the top of a plain hill, Sandra ran into a military roadblock. Scowling fiercely, the taciturn soldiers, all with Galils, ordered her to stop. There was a pickup just ahead of her. They had the men out of the vehicle, in a line, with their hands on the hood. They were frisking them to see if they were armed. It amused her to observe maliciously how one of the soldiers kept his hands a minute longer than necessary on the butt of a skinny, beardless man who pulled back a bit in disgust and fear. The roadblock looked like a horse hurdle, which reminded her of those endless lessons at the *Hipódromo del Sur*, learning dressage, jumping, and the difficult English mounting. She got to the roadblock. The soldier saluted her, then ordered between his teeth in a deep hiss:

"Documents."

Sandra pulled her ID out of the glove compartment, moving slowly, as he looked her over from head to toe. She gave him the documents, smiling just enough so that the poor idiot felt a chill at the base of his spine and a pain in the pit of his stomach, but not enough so he would confuse it with condescension. She kept him at a prudent distance. He had bad breath.

"Those guys back there are with me. Please treat them nicely." Her melodious voice sounded as if she had perfumed honey drops in her mouth. The stammering soldier took the documents, barely flipped through them—just a formality— gave them back, and signaled to let her through. She pressed the button to close the tinted window. Through her rearview mirror she saw them let her men through quickly and she grinned at the thought that she could very well be a member of the EGP. They would have let her go through just the same because of her manners, her wealth, and her class. She remembered her brother. The military was made up of a bunch of idiots, she thought. What's more, other than Arbenz, there had never been a good-looking officer in this filthy country.

6

They arrived at El Camino Real. A uniformed employee with white gloves ran out obsequiously to open the door. Tom Wright got out without letting go of the folder that held the manila envelope. He did let them take care of his luggage, however, then walked with Captain Pacal to the registration desk. Wright observed that Pacal had some kind of foot deformity, that one of his shoes had a higher sole than the other, and he walked with a twisted foot, limping as if he were bow-legged. Still, he disguised it pretty well. You could hardly notice it as he moved. Pacal felt Wright's stare. A curious expression appeared on his face, a mixture of self-doubt and uneasy pressure.

"War injury. We're not war-room officers here."

Wright pretended not to notice the insult. He concentrated pointedly on the halls, the bars, the exits, the personnel, and the people, who came and went as if the hotel were a shopping center. He did notice the absence of public phones, which surprised him in a hotel of that size.

Absentmindedly, he pulled out one of his passports—he knew by mere habit that it was the right one—and handed it to the employee behind the desk. Effortlessly, he filled out the registration form, writing the name and address corresponding to the passport he had pulled out smoothly, without a single mistake. Pure habit.

Once this formality was finished, he tilted his head slightly to the Captain, watching his stern profile curiously while trying to force a very faint smile upon his lips that only those who knew him well would have understood as such, and not as a sign of disapproval. A veteran reader of subtle signals, Pacal immediately picked up Wright's meaning and lightened up his darkly bitter profile.

"I recommend that lounge. It's quieter. There aren't any young people, because they don't play loud music and sometimes you can find a well-built woman all alone."

He chuckled, showing his gold tooth. The Captain has elegant manners, Wright thought, but the vulgarity still shows. My entire relationship with him will be a long and boring series of commonplaces and nervous laughter. They went out and turned right into a small, dimly-lit room with few tables. A waiter came up immediately.

"Double Scotch on the rocks, please."

"Mine with water."

The waiter left. Wright pulled the pictures out of the envelope and reexamined them with great care. He took out a note pad and began to scribble on it.

"So let's review this once more."

"As much as you want. But don't forget, Guatemala's the far side of the moon"

"What does that mean?"

"A one-of-a-kind, opaque country. Nothing is what it seems..."

"Enough. I like order. I do this to help build a protective world around America. Let's get down to business. Gray came to Guatemala about three months ago."

"Yes, he did. Right."

"He proclaimed very publicly that he was looking for areas to invest and insinuated that he was backed substantially by his Australian business associates."

"Right."

"What the fuck is an Australian doing in Guatemala, anyway?"

Pacal smiled and winked his eye.

"Are you really dumb, or just pretending to be? They told me you were a personal friend of Michael Hand, the ex-Green Beret, and that you were sent to Lithgow to investigate when Frank Nugan was assassinated last year...." Wright said nothing. His face remained blank. Fearing he had committed a *faux pas*, Pacal added: "Anyway, if anyone asks you in Spanish, say: *¿Qué putas estaba haciendo un australiano en este país de mierda?*"

"Okay: *¿Qué putas estaba haciendo un australiano en este país de mierda?*"

Pacal laughed in his characteristically excessive way, his eyes shining as he spoke.

"Well, just imagine. In the midst of this craziness, churning waters make for easy fishing. And if you snooze, you lose."

They both laughed now. The Captain kept his laughter within the bounds of moderation this time. The waiter came with their drinks. At last, thought Wright. He needed a drink so badly he was getting light-headed and starting to nod off. With a shaky hand he grabbed the glass like a cat nabs its prey. The Captain raised his glass.

"To the far side of the moon."

"The far side of the moon? Too dark and spooky there. Why not to our survival?"

He felt the burning whiskey eating away his esophagus, the shock effect only slightly ameliorated by the cooling effect of the ice cubes. Closing his eyes and clearing his throat, he tried to soak in completely the swift reaction of his relieved body coming suddenly back to life, reawakening. Now he could think. Putting the empty glass on the table, he signaled with his fingers for another one and began to go over his notes.

"So then...Gray was interviewed on TV and in the newspapers. Right?"

"Yeah, everything was very public. Very visible...."

"*Dios mío*, either he was a complete idiot or bait for the guerrilla. And in that case..."

Pacal smiled, nodded, as if driving his point home a little deeper, and shrugged his shoulders in a gesture of "who knows?", dramatizing it with a gesticulation of his hands. Wright thought that the Captain either knew more or sensed more but wasn't willing to share it. Maybe he was also limited in his range of expression and lacked words for what he meant. He acted servile, like a well-rehearsed acolyte who respects his superior, but he seemed very clever. Wright would have to find out through other channels.

"Okay. On the morning of February 5th at about 7:20 a.m., he was in bed reading the newspaper. One of the maids came to tell him that two gentlemen of the Defense Ministry were looking for him."

"That's right. And then..."

"Dressed only in his robe and slippers, he went down to see what they wanted. Instead of officers, he found two polite, well-dressed young men."

"Wow, you memorized the report. You have an undeniable genius for this..."

"I read it who knows how many times on the plane. After all, my mission is to rescue him. But I need to verify all the facts."

"Hurry up then, before your drink gets warm. I have an appointment at the Ministry in..."

The captain looked at his watch pointedly, long enough to let Wright see that he was sporting a luxurious Rolex with all the exotic options possible in such a fine machine, now gleaming through the forest of hairs assaulting its delicate face.

"...an hour and ten minutes."

"Don't tell me that Guatemalans are punctual."

"A lot more than most *Guanacos* and Nicaraguans. You'll see. We're still the center, as in colonial times, in many ways. The great metropolis of Central America. Our situation might be unenviable now, but one day we will find our way back to the center with or without your help. We have long memories." He said this softly, ironically, but with a smile still on his lips.

"Yup. I've already felt the unbearable heat of the kind of tropical paradise you're talking about. Let's finish."

Pacal again let a malicious smile escape.

"One of the young men held a gun to Gray's head and yelled to him, 'This is a kidnaping! Don't move or you're dead!'"

Pacal raised his voice too much as he dramatized the young man' words. The few customers in the bar at this time of day turned toward them with a look of panic on their faces, which immediately changed to puckered mouths of silent indignation. Pacal turned red and gestured to them in apology. The tips of his moustache became damp with the tiny drops of sweat that were rolling down his face. Spittle appeared at the corners of his mouth. Wright didn't change his expression and kept his eyes on his notes, continuing as if nothing had happened.

"He didn't resist. They led him to a car waiting for them with two other young men disguised as MPs. They ordered him to get in the back seat and quickly left."

At around this time, Sandra reached the hotel. Her appearance was striking enough that passersby took her at first glance for a movie star. Any careful observer would throw out that hypothesis after spotting the wrinkles around her eyes, the large pores on her nose, the prominent veins on her hands. But the aura persisted. At any rate, no one in Guatemala had the faintest idea of what a real actress looked like. On the other hand, her clothes were always practical and sporty, yet stylish, leaving no doubt as to her exquisite taste and buying power. A silk scarf complemented her outfit, protecting her neck.

Her entrance was melodramatic. She roared in speeding and then squealed her brakes loudly. The doorman ran to open the door to her BMW, almost at the same moment that her bodyguards showed up, struggling not to lose her, squealing their brakes with the same unseemly noise, like actors uncertain of their part waiting in a fever of anxiety for their director to reappear. The bodyguards' car had barely stopped when two of them jumped out, armed with Uzis. Another one ran to open the door and check the lobby while the doorman parked her "Beemer." Then she entered, her long hair and perfume wafting through the air. She always walked briskly, with the agility of a gazelle, almost skipping, with her weight on her toes. Her mouth was half-open, smiling, and her eagle eyes registered every single thing around her, computing who was there and what they were doing. She tended to the task in front of her while allowing the onlookers to admire her majestic body as she moved along the hotel carpeting like Nefertiti herself.

In the small bar, Tom Wright and Pacal shook hands to say good-bye. Wright was tired. The trip had been long and tedious. The lack of moisture in airplanes always affected him and, despite the open bar policy, the service left a lot to be desired on those flights to Central America, what the stewardess called "those Mexico countries down there." What's more, the confounding contradictions of the operative itself were wreaking havoc with his gastric juices. His headache hadn't gotten any better. The vein in the middle of his forehead and another one at the base of his head were beating like the insistent drumming of a rock-and-roll band. To top it off, his sinuses were congested. All in all, a terrible way to begin an adventure in a country whose name alone evoked dread, agony, and melancholia in his head, washing him in despair, despite the haunting brilliance of its natural tapestry. He turned to watch Pacal leave, and it was at that moment that he saw her pass down the hall, with an air about her that took him a full second to process.

He couldn't believe it. He thought it was a ghost, a vision, a hallucination torturing him from deep inside. At that moment, his knees buckled, and he felt an urgent need to use the restroom because a sharp abdominal pain made his sphincter react immediately. It was her. It had to be. He ran to where he perceived her silhouette in the air like a perfumed aura. A bodyguard intercepted him. The thick, mustached man with a sweaty forehead, a tic in the corner of his eye, flared nostrils and an acid smell, was prepared for anything. Pacal noticed and ran over to cool things down with savage awkwardness.

"Stop! This man is with me! Ministry of Defense!"

"Well, teach that idiot to be careful who he goes after." His high-pitched, staccato voice didn't seem to match his body and gun.

The bodyguards moved away quickly, turning around constantly as if they were dancing a melodious rumba, switching partners all the time. Pacal didn't take his eyes off them.

"Is that how you plan to find Gray?" Pacal was taunting him in an amusing, aggressively underbred fashion.

"Who was that woman?"

"That's all I need. Don't tell me even you *gringos* go crazy when you see a piece of ass like that." He had a comical look of seriousness on his face, as if trying to show some sort of mistrustful admiration.

"You don't know."

"I don't know! As if I didn't know how to scratch my own balls."

"*¿Quién era?* For Christ's sake!"

"Someone too powerful and wealthy even for you, mister. She's from one of the wealthiest families in the country." He said it with a mixture of assertive authoritarianism and shame-faced awe, both tones singularly mixed in a bumbling, longing voice.

"Name?"

"Herrera. She is one of the Herreras."

The woman and her bodyguards had disappeared. Everything went back to its normal everyday rhythm. People came and went hurriedly, with cool efficiency, the men in their suits and ties and the women in elegant dresses, though, interestingly enough, without jewelry. He kept staring insistently in the direction she had disappeared, and asked himself if he had dreamt it, if it came from fatigue, the drinks or just his silly, elliptical fantasies. It was her. He had no doubt. It was her. But...maybe it wasn't her. He probably thought it was her because he wanted to see her and because he came to look for her and because he had to admit that he was still obsessed with her. He'd come for her. Now he knew it. He'd come for her.

Slowly he walked to the elevator. He hadn't noticed which room he was in and only now looked at the key. 312. Here they were still using keys instead of computerized cards. 312. It was a multiple of three, three times 104, or 26 times 4 times 3. There was a series of possibilities. As he was thinking about them anxiously, the elevator door opened on the right floor. He was now walking slowly, as if sleepwalking, weighing mystical numbers in his head. He opened the door. Immediately he was dazzled by the light of the sun setting on the horizon and covering the white walls with a copper-red color as it disappeared with the same slowness as lustful desire. Squinting his eyes, he lowered the shade, twisting his mouth in the process as if the effort required took all the remaining energy out of him. Gasping, he noticed that everything was white. There were some folkloric decorations on the walls and a wide double bed. Taking off his jacket, he hung it carelessly on the first hanger he found in the closet. He then undid his uncomfortable tie and threw it carelessly on a chair. A hoarse moan escaped him. After taking off his shoes, he let himself fall like a heavy bundle on the bed, bouncing lightly with the impact. He still felt as if an electric current ran through his body, flowing into his muscles, his loins. Panting, he whispered through his teeth, "It has to be her. I couldn't be wrong, even after all this time." He then wrapped himself in the blanket, sobbing in a harsh voice like a wounded animal.

CHAPTER TWO

1

Captain Pacal had an ache in his left thigh. He had tried to play tennis for the first time since his accident at the officers' club, in an attempt to impress a sweet young thing who could have given him a sensuous weekend in Rio Dulce. However, even though his deformed left foot was well trained and he had learned tricks to move about with apparent normality, he pulled his muscle the first time he ran on it, abruptly changing his funny scrambling motion to simply a clumsy pathetic one. The laughter it provoked bothered him. What's more, with his short legs, he looked like the roadrunner in those cartoons, with his back straight and his small legs turning like propellers. He rushed off of the court in a lousy mood. The young thing had laughed in his face and found more appealing company. Four days had passed but he was still upset. When he got to the Minister's office, he slightly favored the bad leg before sitting. Lieutenant Alpírez, the Defense Minister's private secretary, ran solicitously to help him.

"It's nothing, Lieutenant. Don't worry."

"Rigors of combat, Captain?" His eyebrows went up significantly, as if fishing for malicious gossip.

"Rigors of foolishness."

They both laughed. Alpírez returned to his seat and the Captain made himself comfortable on the sofa. He mustered over his impending interview with the Minister. They had to report on important proceedings. He would explain Wright's arrival. The Minister would comment about Castañeda. On his way downtown from the hotel, Pacal had found a large deployment of the Model Platoon and the Commando Unit Number Six. The Rubicon had been crossed. He thought of Wright, of Sandra Herrera and how she had annoyed the *gringo*. He was amused.

"Ay, *Gringuito*. If you only knew..."

"Sir?"

"Nothing, Lieutenant. Talking to myself."

"Be careful, Captain, people have been thrown to the lions for less." Pacal turned pale with rage, but he tried not to show it. The corner of his nose pinched in, his ears moved back like those of an alert dog. This little lieutenant thinks he's very funny but he's no more than an imbecile, Pacal reflected. He immediately began imagining ways to have him posted up north on a tour of duty in the Quiché, so he could see some real action and sleep outdoors in a tent. That would make a man out of him. They make all the fags office clerks, he told himself, knotting his hands.

Suddenly, the door opened. He stood up automatically. He felt the thigh muscle pull almost immediately, bringing a grimace to his face.

"Go in, Captain. And take care of yourself. You're going to become a rickety old man before you make lieutenant colonel."

Alpírez chortled quietly, with a sort of asthmatic whistle that sounded almost like a hiccup, satisfied with his joke. Pacal went into the Minister's office swearing that that little lieutenant would end his days in the Quiché.

"Good day, Pacal."

"Here I am, always bothering you, General."

"It's nothing, nothing. Sit down then."

The Captain looked at the desk. A dirty coffee cup, a smelly ashtray full of cigarette butts with ashes scattered around it, piles of papers, some with little dust balls. Most of them had the official seal of the Republic. Some bore the letterheads of clandestine organizations from the extreme right or the extreme left. Several telephones with a wild hullabaloo of little lights that turned on and off amazed him. On the back wall was the Minister's latest toy, an array of small television screens that cast all types of information simultaneously. On one of them Pacal already saw what the Minister was going to tell him about.

"This is the televised segment," the General said. "They're going to edit it to show on tonight's news." The General walked like an old man as he snorted in the direction of the appropriate TV set.

The camera focused on the Central Park Amphitheater, a much smaller version of the Hollywood Bowl. The demonstrators were holding a meeting. They were all gathered around the stage. Above, a speaker. It was that Castañeda guy. Young, with glasses. He had on a very light beige sweater. The shirt collar could be seen above the sweater, the shirttails over the slacks. The kid was unkempt. He spoke with passion, widening his eyes as if the power of speech came from them. The image was silent but Pacal could make out the gist of what he was saying because of his histrionic movements. Suddenly, Castañeda turned to his left, and it seemed as if the electricity had been cut off. People started to go crazy, running in the opposite direction. They crowded against each other in their desperation to escape, like horses running from a fire.

"The best part's coming up." The General spoke quietly, contenting himself with adding a few details. Pacal listened gravely, eyes glued to the set.

The camera moved very quickly, as if it were vibrating. It was hard to see clearly. Some men in civilian clothes with their faces covered and Uzis in their hands ran toward the stage. There was no one there. All of a sudden, Castañeda reappeared running down the street in the opposite direction from the crowd.

"Look at that motorcycle."

Sure enough, an almost imperceptible motorcycle was visible, with two riders. The one in the back was standing up. A slight reflection on the motorcycle chrome revealed another Uzi. Castañeda saw them at the last minute. His face contorted as if some terrifying scene were taking place beyond where the cameras could reach. He made gestures to the crowd so they would move away. The image was vibrating, showing black horizontal lines. Castañeda bent over and fell to the asphalt. The motorcycle driver stood up now, and walked closer to the body. He pulled a gun from his belt and fired the coup-de-grace at point-blank range. Slowly he walked back to the motorcycle. The image dissolved.

"You're going to show *that* on television?"

"Don't be an idiot. I told you it hadn't been edited yet."

"And who's going to be blamed for the crime?"

The General smiled. He returned to the desk and dug around among his papers. He raised two of them. One had black letterhead with very small letters, the other had thick blue letters.

"Let's see, which do you like better? The Anticommunist Secret Army? Or Jaguar of Justice?"

"The blue lettering is prettier."

"That one, then. And look...I want you to help me write my speech promising that the armed forces will work tirelessly to clear up this heinous crime."

"Very well, General. Just let me inform you about the *Gringuito*..."

2

A long line of cars raised a dust trail as they rolled to the mansion hidden in the overgrown vegetation. Abandoned and peeling, porous adobe walls lined the narrow path on which the vehicles had to pass. On one wall, toward the right side, was written in clearly-lined black letters: "Citizen, defend your army." On the left side there were two other messages made just as carefully but in blue letters: "Guatemala is peace and development" and "The army is peace, country, order." Above this geometric lettering, perfectly aligned with the same size letters, someone had hurriedly written in red, with thin, shaky letters painted diagonally and barely in a straight line: "Long live the EGP."

The cars reached the gate and stopped. It opened electronically. A careful observer would have seen the television camera hanging from one of the gate columns. The parade moved on until it reach the main door of the mansion. When the first vehicle stopped, Jonás, the butler, appeared condescendingly at the entrance, opening the door. Alvaro exited. He and Jonás helped to extract Don Leonel and plant his feet firmly on the ground.

"There, Dad, see how easy that was?

"Easy, my foot. For you, life's always easy."

"Well, the pain is gone, right? Don't you feel better?"

"If feeling better means being left with a contorted smile like a penitent man after carrying a saint in the procession, then, yes, I feel better...."

"Sir, by the way..."

"What's the matter, Jonás?"

"The Minister called. He said he's coming over here."

"Damn! What a pain! They think they're God's gift. Why do we have to have one more private conversation with him? It's only to his advantage. And how did he know I was going to be home anyway?"

"It's just that they know everything, sir."

3

It was a modest home in a lower-class neighborhood of the city, where people would step outside to gossip as the fading sunset blazed upon the iron-framed windows, turning them to silver before the haunting mountain darkness fell suddenly, like an unsuspecting pedestrian stabbed to death in a dirty alleyway. The houses were constructed in the old Spanish style, with a balcony facing the sidewalk, and defended by thick rails that reminded one of prison gates or the pearly gates to some inner sanctum. The balcony of this particular home had been modernized and painted in a light gray color, with rust spots ascending from the bottom corners. Aside from that, it was a typical house from the beginning of the twentieth century, with high walls, yellowed and peeling, and cornices bordering the roof, displaying blackened moldy bricks that served as the only decoration, like fake pearls around the neck of a haggard old woman.

Inside, the house was a disaster. It hardly had any furniture. Wooden crates, scattered in a disorderly manner throughout the various rooms, functioned as tables. They were all covered with papers, dirty, abandoned coffee cups, spoons, pens, matches, ashtrays that had never been emptied, scattered books. The whole atmosphere was laden with the acrid smell of cigarette smoke covering all the available surfaces like an ancient potion from some mythic past. Thick dust balls gathered at the corners of each room and occasionally displaced themselves to the center when nudged by the point of a shoe or encouraged by a slight breeze. A bright red EGP flag adorned with Che Guevara's black, hypnotizing gaze, was hanging from two shiny thumbtacks in the middle of the wall that divided what, in a normal house, would have been the living and dining rooms. The house, though, was full of movement. Men and women, dressed for the most part in blue jeans and tennis shoes, came and went with surprising speed. They picked up or dropped off papers, wrote down notes, busied themselves in almost inconceivable small ways. Occasionally someone would go to the sink and light a paper on fire.

There was only one real table in the entire house. It was

a rough, unpainted pine table sitting forlornly in the middle
of the back room, which had exits to both the back and the
front courtyards. The doors and window facing the hall had
been sealed off, leaving the room submerged in an artificial
darkness that required the constant use of electric light. Three
people were seated around the table studying various
documents: two men and one woman. The man sitting in the
middle was of medium build, but with an obviously well-
developed physique. He had short black hair, a bit in the style
of the 50's, and he was clean-shaven. Slightly olive-skinned.
His nose was a bit wide and his lips, thick, like an Olmec
sculpture. Technically, he was not handsome. Still, he seemed
attractive because of the extraordinarily intense strength of
the gaze coming from his enormous eyes, like those in Greek
frescoes, and the electricity that his twitching body
generated. He had a wide, strong neck like that of a fighting
bull and broad calloused hands. When he gave orders, he
barked like an army officer. In contrast to his military
counterparts, however, he did listen very carefully when
spoken to, with a sense of sureness, almost of beatitude, that
virtually absorbed the speaker with its intensity. Though he
was a master of irony, and sometimes spiced his speech with
old-fashioned jokes that made young feminists cringe, he had
a generous manner, and he knew how to be grateful when
someone made him see something that had not yet occurred
to him.

The other man was slightly taller, but he appeared smaller
because of his yogi-like thinness. He had a beard and
mustache, and the combination of curly hair worn slightly
long with his sharp Roman nose made him look like an El
Greco figure. Although his skin was darker, his eyes were
watery blue, and they shone like stars that illuminated any
dark corner where they rested. He talked nonstop, always,
whether seriously or in jest, rolling his eyes as he did so.
When he spoke, drops of saliva escaped from the corners of
his mouth, which seemed forever dry and chapped.

The woman was short, but, since she was on the thin side, she seemed taller than she really was. At any rate, in this country of midgets, her height was already above the national mean. She had long, black hair that was gathered up in a ponytail bound by one of those cheap elastic bands with silver ornaments that you can buy on the street. Even though she did not use makeup, and her shirt and pants were too baggy to show off her figure, it was evident that she was a beauty. Beyond her appearance, however, her dark appraising eyes revealed that she was a woman to be reckoned with, though she seemed to speak less than either men.

There was a knock at the door. Everyone looked up with dazzling speed. The thin, bearded one, whose pseudonym was "Vallejo" in honor of the immortal poet, stood up and cracked the door open. Outside someone leaned closer to whisper something in his ear. His expression tensed up immediately, and the veins on his forehead popped out furiously, as if he were having a stroke. He nodded affirmatively and closed the door.

"Oliverio Castañeda has been murdered!" The faces of the other two fell as they registered this devastating news, and their disconsolate eyes closed in pain.

"But he was at the demonstration, surrounded by people!"

Vallejo nodded.

"Yes, Ariadne. He was shot in public. In front of everyone. In front of the television cameras and the press. It's as if they wanted the entire world to know it, and couldn't give a damn."

He started to explain in an accelerated voice what the informant had just told him, but Ariadne kept interrupting him, until the two of them were speaking at the same time like a wildfire entirely out of control. They raised their voices, almost screaming at each other while the third one absorbed it all like a sponge, squeezing in his hand a little cardboard figure in the shape of a star. Sinking back into his chair, he finally spoke, hiding his chagrin and discomfiture as best he could. The others became suddenly quiet.

"Enough. Castañeda's loss is regrettable, but that's how it is. There's nothing we can do about it. He was not a member of our organization. Moreover, from what we know, the overall situation has not changed. The balance of power has not changed. The elements we analyzed are still the same. So let's leave it at that and concentrate on our task because we have two huge operatives in front of us. Don't forget that Gray's return depends solely on us. Who, when, where, are Nugan Hand's emissaries going to be contacted?"

"Kukulkán is right," the woman stated.

"But we don't even know if they've received our demands."

"They received them."

"And how do you know? If they haven't called..."

"He knows, Vallejo."

"Let me tell you something that I just told Ariadne. Harlequin reported the arrival of a *gringo* at the airport. Nugan Hand knows we have Gray, and they've already sent someone."

"Oh, please. *Gringos* arrive every day by the bunch, don't mess with me. Don't start seeing things that are not really there."

"Man! You don't even believe in your own shadow. This one was special. Harlequin knows what he's talking about."

"But they haven't contacted us!"

Kukulkán felt a sympathy in the warm pressure of Ariadne's hand on his elbow as he picked up his coffee cup. He let his lower lip drop with deliberate cynicism to underline how boring it was to have to give an anatomy class every time someone sneezed.

"The agent himself will bring the bank instructions. They know the game. They also know Nugan's money is embezzled. They'll pay, but they'll also try to catch us at the same time. You have to be able to read the signs in politics."

"If that's the case, why are we even talking, big shot, since you're the only one handling these contacts, I suppose. We shouldn't even waste our breath on it. Let's get going with the Sololá thing." They returned, downcast, to their notes, talking in low, pleading tones and leaning forward from time to time to embrace each other, while working deep into the night.

4

Don Leonel looked at the beer bottle on the table. He did not like it because of the memories and nostalgia that it brought back even now, and he reacted with a gesture typical of him.

"Jonás!"

Now that he was an old man, he couldn't work as much as he used to, but mentally he remained a path-seeker. It was while he was on the move that hidden possibilities appeared to him, indicating new directions to follow: new investments, how to move money around, ways to get around taxes, means to introduce new export products to the U.S. with a little help from friends of his who knew how to wear the cloak of patriotism and stretch it in various ways.

"Sir..."

"Take away this bottle of beer, for God's sake."

"As you wish, sir."

The butler had just left when Alvaro made his entrance. He smiled and moved with familiarity. Was it possible that his good for nothing son was finally learning the business instead of fucking every woman who crossed his path? Or was it the good influence of his daughter-in-law, who was a diamond in the rough? Among the young members of the family, the women were better for business than the men. They worked harder. Looking up, Don Leonel perceived, in the midst of the hubbub in the living room, the movement of several people in the hall who came and went, glasses in hand,

33

talking, laughing grotesquely as they told each other dirty jokes. Sandra was with them, moving about with an enviable ease and smile, displaying her power with secret pride, enhancing rather than disturbing his relations with the outer world.

"Do you have Scotch here, Dad?"

"In the cabinet. What's wrong?"

Alvaro moved in the direction of the cabinet. All the crystal glasses were lined up on top. They were off limits. Only Don Leonel could use them occasionally. Not only were they delicate and frightfully expensive, but they were keepsakes from a youth that Alvaro imagined legendary. On the middle shelf were the bottles. Campari. Vermouth. He found a Johnny Walker Black Label and took it out immediately. Don Leonel had several glasses and an ice bucket in front of him on the table. Bottle in hand, Alvaro fixed himself a Scotch on the rocks.

"What's going on? Tell me, Kid."

"Nothing."

"Nothing, my ass. Tell me."

Alvaro took a sip of his drink. He felt the relaxing warmth in his throat and the chill down his spine. He fixed his stare so he could look his father straight in the eye.

"Just that I have to go out on the plane."

"Oh sure. Then, *business is business* as the *gringos* say endlessly." Alvaro made a face that could have been mocking or anxious. He gave his whiskey another sip. He looked at his father from the corner of his eye, his grayish figure drinking with his head back.

"Yes...The business has to be taken care of at all costs."

"I've never heard a *gringo* say that."

"That's because they talk funny."

"How's that?"

"They spit infinitives dripping with stumps of broken phrases."

"Be careful..."

"But I'm not criticizing them. They're our market; they always pay on time, their cash is good. But that's no reason for me to always have to dance to their tune."

Don Leonel felt he was falling asleep but he did not want to show it. He sat stiff and silent, allowing the strength of his personality to fuel his son's anxiety, his fears, his prissiness. Thank God he had a beautiful daughter-in-law. That was the only thing he envied him. That and his age. How he would have liked to take the plane and receive the shipment personally. That's how this country was formed. By real men with hair on their chests, like him, trained to work together from childhood, instinctively responding to each other's unspoken needs and desires, moving up to support each other without asking questions. Not like now, with all those *parvenus*...

"You look like a pillar of salt. Why don't you go lie down?"

5

The sun forced you to squint even with your sunglasses on. It burned your naked arms, and you could feel it penetrate your skin and come to rest on your muscles like fleas. On your back. On your neck. But especially on your back. He had just stepped outside in his bathing suit, but Tom Wright felt that if he didn't get in the water right away the heat would be unbearable in a matter of seconds. The sweat on his forehead had already dampened his glasses. He took them off and left them with his towel and the room key on a table by the edge of the pool and dove in.

In contrast to the sun, the water was cool. He felt as if a giant hand were massaging his body, squeezing him softly and rubbing him with oil. The relaxing freshness was overwhelming. He came to the surface, and the shimmering reflection of the sun made him close his eyes immediately.

Barely making out the end of the pool, he stroked and kicked, enjoying the movement and feeling the pleasurable working of his muscles. He raised an arm and sank it in again deliciously while his long legs hit the water's surface. He counted the strokes, as he always did. Automatically. One, two, three, four. He thought of the multiples of those numbers. Counting was another way to erase reality. Almost as relaxing as swimming. Occasionally, life seemed like intervals to be filled between strokes. He knew few pleasures as grand. To clear the mind, relax the body, flee from reality, allow oneself to be enveloped by a watery silence and a bluish, chlorinated imagination. Swim, think, get away from others, uneasiness diluting into silence, far from everything. Block the mind with number games. 405 was a multiple of nine because its sum equaled 9. It was 3 times 135 or 9 times 45, 27 times 15...and on he would go. Total escape in a spiral form.

Almost reluctantly, he let the palm of his hand touch the edge of the pool. He was finished. He thought about doing one more lap, weighing the tranquility of fleeing from the world against the pleasure of lying on a lounge chair and being bathed by the sun while his mind wandered aimlessly, his muscles relaxed. That tipped the balance. He got out of the pool, and went back to the table where he had left his sunglasses. Collapsing onto the lounge chair, he closed his eyes, feeling the immense joy of the water's freshness mixed with the stinging of the sun, much like a battle between two forces to possess him. It was a delicious moment in which he didn't have to ask himself whether he was going to get to the end of the road, or think about his suspicion that, no matter what he did, nothing would ever change. That was when he heard the unforgettable, silky voice at his side, near his ear, guilelessly talking to him in English as if emerging from a hidden spring of secret warmth.

"Tom. It is Tom, right?"

It had to be a dream. But it was all too real. He feigned

indifference but it wasn't possible. He opened his eyes. She was standing in front of him, her face near his, preserving all its graces.

"Sandra!"

She made an endearing, coquettish gesture that left him feeling naked, literally and figuratively. In the depth of her eyes, he saw a whole past life that had just returned to assault him with an uncontrollable force after such a long time, and he felt like a little worm about to be devoured by a bald eagle. She read the surprise on his face and swallowed her laughter.

"So, you haven't forgotten me after all these years..."

"Sandra! How could I...?"

"Not even a small detail? The smallest?"

"Nothing. I have forgotten absolutely nothing."

"And nonetheless...time has passed."

"Time always passes. It has been..."

"Fifteen years. And eight months."

"Oh my God! You really do remember!"

"Of course, silly. Did you think I was acting?"

"No...it's just that..."

She smiled again. He did, too. Once again, he let himself be seduced by her smile. The eyes and memories of both intertwined, and he felt, in a paradoxical way, that Guatemala could not have come alive for him until he had seen her, for she represented the magical landscape, the mythical dimension of the reality he was about to experience. Desiring her and remembering her intensity, how that smile transformed itself when she desired him, like a window fogged up by sea breath.

"Come. Come with me to the restaurant."

"Sure."

He got up from his chair. She slipped her arm under his, making his entire body tingle with her warmth. It was an infinite, genuine pleasure, desired, dreamt about, to be with someone who truly knew how to use her body and provoke torturing frenzy and desire with the smallest of gestures, the slightest pressure, barely grazing the skin, making men vaguely helpless, pleading for more.

"So you are now a He-rre-ra, right?"

"Oh my God. You found out already?"

"I'm in the business of finding everything out."

"Of course."

"You are, then? An He-rre-ra?"

"But you already know I am. Come on, Tom. You didn't think I was still the timid, provincial schoolgirl who spoke with an accent and was impressed by everything you knew..."

"Fifteen years and eight months ago."

"Yes."

"No, Sandra. I didn't think that. I didn't expect anything. I didn't expect to see you at all. I didn't know if you were even going to be here."

"You at least remembered that this was my country. Or did you forget even that?"

"I never forgot that. I never forgot you. Never."

"Just the name of my country."

"I didn't meet you in your country. I've never even been here before. I met you on the Tulane campus. But I remember that your father studied snakes. Does he still study snakes?"

"And raises them like a good herpetologist. And your sister? Is she still in sociology?"

"My sister! She's now a professor at some miserable little school in the Midwest and doesn't even speak to me."

"She finished then? And why doesn't she speak to you?"

"Political differences. Let's leave that subject alone."

"All right, but remember that we met thanks to her. My dear roommate. Tell me then, would you have called me if I hadn't found you first?"

"Please. This is a business trip. Very serious matters."

"I see. The white Anglo-Saxon Protestant takes his business so very, very seriously that he doesn't even remember that the woman he claims never to have forgotten lives in the same town he's operating in. It would be better if you told me the classic lie that you had been waiting for me all these years."

"I have been waiting for you all these years. And I wish you could tell me there was no other man."

"I wish. But we'll always have New Orleans."

He smiled shyly, which brought out of her an unforgiving, mocking smile. She avoided offending him, by transforming her expression halfway into a comic, peevish gesture and turning her thoughts inward, to her father. She visualized thousands of jars, perfectly ordered, covering the four walls of the room, each with a snake inside, each perfectly labeled and sealed, all of the snakes staring at the center of the room where she caressed a thick python measuring several yards in length, wrapped entirely around her body. Her father had explained to her that, during the classic Mayan period, stone jars carved in the shape of pythons were used to collect the blood from the sacrifices or to store hallucinogenic potions that induced deliciously tormenting visions. That explained why nothing was what it seemed to be, and even less so when it came wrapped in ceremonial pomposity, which was nothing but a more subtle form of Carnival.

CHAPTER THREE

1

The Minister's office was spacious. It didn't seem excessively luxurious, and it was more cluttered that he would've expected. There was too much furniture, all of it inordinately heavy. There were too many papers. Too many phones. Too many bookshelves full of old, insect-eaten papers. Too many tasteless pictures on the wall. Too many television monitors behind the desk. There were few books, few windows, and the paint was peeling off the walls. Maintaining the infrastructure was not the regime's strong suit. On the positive side, the thick carpeting did reduce the noise considerably, however, the silence seemed more like a kind of neglect than a refuge from the buzz off the streets. Captain Pacal worried about these things. He wanted to make sure that, when he occupied a similar position and high class people like the Herreras came to visit, the tasteless decor of his office would not reveal the humble origins he had worked so hard to disguise. He stood still for a moment, deeply puzzled by his class confusion. Cautious and suspicious, the Minister of Defense barely lifted his head with a slight questioning gesture and shot off a single word.

"And?"

"No news, General. Everything's under control."

The Minister observed Pacal reflectively. The Captain's innate leadership qualities, combined with his knowledge of local politics and his high-society contacts made him a rising star. In other words, a dangerous man. He still didn't know if

Pacal was trustworthy, so, although he smiled and greeted him warmly all the time, that was as far as he went. Of course, his doubts stemmed from every politician's assumption that deep down no one can ever be really trusted.

"Don't let him get the upper hand. Understand?"

"No problem, General."

The Minister stared at Pacal, realizing that he didn't feel at ease in his presence. Using an overly hearty tone, he said, "You're the man, Captain." He endorsed his words with a nod.

"I don't understand, General."

"I mean, you're the man to make sure the *gringo* doesn't pee outside the bowl. What did you think I meant?"

"No, well, you know. One tries to guess. But you're right."

The General smiled maliciously and winked uncomfortably, to underline their alleged complicity, trying to disguise his own unease. Pacal remained silent, submitting to rank. He felt a slight shiver go down his spine. "I have to improve my relationship with the General," he thought. "His instinct is giving him signals and that's worrisome. There are never enough rocks to hold on to when the river runs wild." He opened his mouth in a servile smile, revealing his gold tooth.

"Tell me, what if the *Gringo* finds the banker?"

"I've already found a way to delay him a bit, General."

"Very good, Pacal. That's what I like. Efficient as always."

"Yes, sir. At your service."

"Dismissed."

He stood up and saluted. He made a half turn and headed toward the main door. As soon as he exited, Lieutenant Alpírez, ingratiating as ever, ran solicitously up to him, half-whispering in his curious slushy voice.

"Is there anything I can do for you, Captain?"

You could, Pacal thought, but I don't trust you, asshole.

And in this business, opening your mouth was the same as cutting your own throat.

"No, thank you, Lieutenant Alpírez. See you tomorrow."

"See you tomorrow, Captain."

Pacal noticed that there was an unusual amount of security. At the main door at the end of the long hallway, everyone held machine guns. He turned right, heading to the side hallway instead, which led to a simple door that opened inconspicuously to the back alley. This way he avoided being seen or disturbed coming in or going out. Once again he felt the secret, proud satisfaction of being part of the select group that enjoyed this singular privilege. But at the same time he worried over the phrase the General had used. "You're the man, Captain." The words danced like dark shadows in his ears, launching a sudden stirring of discomfort.

2

The mountains were radiating a brutal green tonality on that morning under a raw sky well beyond blue. Tom Wright felt he was in a Van Gogh painting, such was the scrambling intensity of blues and greens, the ardent sunshine and the rolling hills, not to speak of the dewy vegetation oscillating in the light breeze. He could just relax and enjoy the scenery because Sandra was driving. He let his eyes half-float in the muddled wilderness of the multicolored scene, drooping at the dazzling intensity of it all. But his instinct for watching everything from an operative point of view came back to him right away. Check out the side roads, people moving along the curbs, the amount of vegetation at the edge of the highway, which the army had obligingly trimmed to avoid potential ambushes. He looked at her, his eyes meek with gratitude and affection. He still couldn't get over his surprise over their encounter after so long, the pleasant bewilderment her presence generated, or even how irresistible her arms still were, with their light hair that made them seem to shimmer with gold dust and nearly forced one's own arm to rest right next to them and feel their heat. As he turned to get a better view of her, he saw the bodyguards' car following closely. He wasn't in the habit of being guarded, much less trusting his safety to others. Distrust was the hallmark of his trade. The mole could be hiding anywhere.

"Do they follow you everywhere?"

"Everywhere."

"Isn't it a pain to have them following you?"

"It's better than being kidnaped."

"Yes, I see your point."

The car glided down the highway. On the outskirts of the city, people wore colorful indigenous outfits that further accented the expressionist impact of the scene. The outfits dripped reds and oranges, yellows and purples, all resplendent and moving quickly, quickly, with the rhythm of a constant trot, like in silent movies. The further they got from the city, the fewer people dressed like Westerners. But the number of people did not diminish. The city was apparently small but extremely compact, like an anthill. It was ugly. Really ugly. And loud. Square cement houses, all the same and all dirty, trucks blasting diesel fumes that darkened the sky, honking everywhere, pedestrians zigzagging between vehicles, escaping miraculously from being run over and killed, mangled dogs barking and chasing ferociously anyone who passed by, street merchants selling the most unusual things (stuffed toys, plastic lizards) among the piercing shouts and screeching of brakes and foul odors, rotting trash piled up on the side of the pot-holed asphalt, blocking the water flow that accumulated in small brownish puddles. Everything was stinking movement that revolved and made you dizzy. It was a frenzy, a massive assault on the nerves, always permeated by filth, movements in which, over and above the green of the mountains, the blue of the sky, and the red-yellow-and-orange indigenous outfits, the gray and brown tones chastened any spark of happiness. And it all smelled like death. The apparently tropical bustle was a crude way of disguising the bitter suffocation of death that hung in the air. The car continued distancing itself from the noise, escaping the brownish climate, melting into the pure green of the countryside.

"It looks like we're getting even further away."

She smiled and looked over at him. Her teeth, a bit on the small side but not disproportionate, tempted him to a sweet nibble. Her thin lips were slightly parched now that they weren't covered with lipstick, her eyes dancing like wanton gypsies. He automatically tilted sideways to see if she wore contact lenses. She didn't.

"Yes."

"I thought so. Didn't you say we were going 'just over there'?"

"That's true, but afterwards it dawned on me that I could take you to the lake!"

"But Sandra! I told you I had to meet Pacal!"

She smiled as if what he'd just said didn't have the slightest importance.

"God, you just got here. The Captain will understand. Besides, you have to get to know the place a bit before you can work, right?"

She laughed mockingly, and that annoyed him. He felt manipulated, and he hated feeling that way. He looked at her with his eyes bulging, noting her slender wrists. He was thinking furiously. Suddenly distressed, he said in a soft, quivering voice: "No, I don't have time for tourism. Turn around or I'll get out of the car."

Sandra burst out laughing, which finally pissed him off. Now she was openly laughing at him. It reminded him of moments from 16 years back that had angered him with the same grotesque intensity. Her smug laughter was like a stone thrown at a frog, and he was the frog. With a tad of condescension she said softly: "Tom, I'm doing more than a hundred right now, don't tell me you're going to..."

Suddenly, he pulled the emergency brake. The car zigzagged violently, sending the phone flying into the back seat. Sandra hung on to the steering wheel with an uncharacteristic look of panic, almost biting herself as she clenched her teeth. In a matter of seconds she regained control and stopped abruptly by the side of the road. The bodyguards' vehicle braked right behind them. The doors flung open in all directions as the men armed with Uzis ran to the BMW. Sandra was trembling, both furious and surprised, but regained her composure as soon as the bodyguards looked in through the car window. She shouted at them: "It's all right. Calm down. It was nothing."

They checked the tires, made sure there was nothing loose underneath, and went back to their car to wait for orders. Sandra opened the compartment dividing the two front seats and took out a small flask of Scotch whiskey. She unscrewed it and took a long gulp that slid down her throat, scratching it and giving her a start that he enjoyed watching. She had raised her head to drink so he could clearly watch the alcohol descend tempestuously down that marvel that had startled him awake on more than one night.

"Want a swig?"

He shook both arms in the air: "No, thanks. What I want is to see Pacal."

Sandra pounded the dashboard, practically dropping the flask. "I left because of this kind of attitude, you know? You're so...!"

"Professional?"

"No, Tom. You're a terrible actor. Stupid. Impulsive. Boring. Square."

She would have continued with the string of adjectives if the bodyguard hadn't knocked on the car. Disturbed by the interruption, she violently pressed the button to lower the window. Instead, by mistake, she unlocked the doors. Irked, she silently cursed the electronic controls before finding the right one. The window slid downwards, half-blinding her when it let the gush of silvery light in.

"Ma'am!"

"Yes?"

"The patrol is here."

An army jeep full of soldiers had stopped just behind the bodyguard. The soldiers stayed inside, aiming their weapons at both vehicles in an agony of impatience. The sergeant got out with his weapon in hand and walked slowly toward her.

"Let's see! What happened here?"

"Nothing, Officer. Just a mechanical breakdown, that's all."

"Papers!"

Sandra cursed again, as if she were being fried very slowly in olive oil, and looked at Tom sideways as if to suggest that this annoying problem had been all his fault.

He held his laughter while he took out his passport. She turned to the back seat, pulled her bag forward, and searched for the documents with total nonchalance, mumbling softly, shaking her head wearily. Finally, she found her ID and handed it to the officer along with Tom's passport. The sergeant checked both documents carefully, with the concentrated effort of someone who still has difficulty reading. At some point the social importance of these two characters seemed to hit him fully. He raised his eyebrows and threw his head slightly backwards as if to verify he had read correctly the names of the bearers of the documents, and then he instinctively brought his feet together as if coming to attention. Mentally reviewing the etiquette manuals he had studied during basic training, he modified his gestures and tone of voice. All signs of arrogance had vanished.

"And may I be of some service to you?"

"Oh, don't bother!"

But Tom Wright was not willing to let go of the

opportunity. Almost climbing over her, he leaned toward the window and asked: "Listen. I urgently need to see Captain Pacal at the Ministry of Defense. Could you take me there?"

"Of course, *mister*! As you order."

"In English, when you don't use a person's last name, you don't say 'mister,' but 'sir.' Got it?"

"Yes, *mister*."

Sandra was livid. She turned incredulously and said forcefully, while grabbing his sleeve: "Don't be a fool, Tom. I'll take you, if that's what you really want."

But it was too late. He headed for the door handle. She instinctively reached for the electronic controls, but his feet were already on the ground, letting the bright light fill the car's interior. He slammed the door, plunging her into solitary darkness, the silence of her lonely car. Her melancholy, smiling face was completely untouched by self-pity. He walked around the car until he was standing next to the sergeant, leaned toward her through the open window, and whispered in English: "It's all right, dear. Don't get stressed out. Please go on to the lake without me."

He blew a kiss off the palm of his hand and turned to leave. The sergeant, solicitous, dared to ask: "Where were you headed?"

"To the lake."

"Atitlán? No! Don't even go near the lake, ma'am! It's full of guerrillas! Today they took Sololá. We're going to cut off the road to see if we can round them up by Los Encuentros."

Tom Wright tensed up at the news. He nervously opened and closed his right hand. Pretending a calm he didn't feel, he bent toward her and said in a mechanical voice:

"You see, dear, it didn't make sense to go to the lake today. So, just go home, behave yourself like a good housewife, and call me tonight at the hotel. I'm going to take care of my affairs!"

Sandra pursed her lips in a gesture of both displeasure

and an agony of impatience. Anticipating this, he surprised her with a kiss and ran rapidly toward the jeep after the sergeant. Before she could react, he had jumped inside the vehicle, which had already started to move and was turning around, kicking up a cloud of dust.

She was stunned at what had just taken place. Just a few seconds ago she was taking Tom to the lake, where they would have undoubtedly fallen in the hands of the EGP. But she didn't know they had taken Sololá. She only knew that Pierrot was aware that she was planning to take Tom on a trip to the lake. Had they planned that operative with Tom in mind? Or was it a coincidence? It had to be. It was impossible to prepare that kind of operative in such a short time. But the other one who knew was Pacal. Did Pacal want the EGP to grab Tom? There were so many possibilities. The only clear thing was that whoever made the first false move would be bitten as if by a rattlesnake, and the bite would be fatal. She was furious at her own perplexity.

"Is something wrong, ma'am?"

"No, nothing. Let's go home."

She started the car and made a U-turn. Through the side mirror she managed to see her bodyguard run back to the car behind her and take off with the doors still half open. She smiled at how stereotypical it was, like a scene from a B movie. The inability to escape mediocrity nauseated her. Anyone could fall, her husband, her father-in-law, her brother, Tom, even she could. Like a risky investment or a shady business deal, the political game—with its high-stake risks— produced an exciting anxiety that left the nerves raw. As long as she lived, that's what kept her going. It was the only justification for remaining in this country where fate had decreed she be born, and it was the most important thing she had learned from her distracted father while he milked from his frenetic snakes the venom that could kill with a single drop.

While she was stopped at the first intersection, she saw a swallow come in suddenly from a wheat field. It made a turn at great speed and, just before hitting her window, on a hunch, it stopped its curving flight in midair, changed direction, took a sharp turn to the right and landed in front of her windshield. There it stayed, unruffled, for at least a minute, before it disappeared as fast as it had come. Smiling, she waited until it got out of her way and followed its flight with a look that was more like a tender caress.

3

The view of the cobalt lake from Sololá was wonderful. On clear days, or in the morning, it gave the impression that the hill fell vertically from the main square straight down to the lake, several hundred feet of brilliant green rolling downhill, pressed as close as a scabbard to the cliff, until it touched the nippy, gem-like water. The square turned into a scenic lookout from which the three volcanoes surrounding the lake assaulted the viewer, drowning him in brightness as the turbulent paradise galloping smoothly towards the Pacific Ocean visually unleashed itself. They seemed so close that you were tempted to reach out and touch them. On market days the resplendent and wavering color that crept up from the square was as magical as a rainbow. The vendors from all the nearby villages, in their multicolored outfits, blocked cars bouncing on the cobblestones of the main road as they bartered their food and all unimaginable kinds of products with rapid-fire, firm movements. No one stood still for a second.

On this day, however, things were different. People had run to hide in their houses. Streets were deserted. The only things scurrying about were men and women dressed in olive green with different types of weapons in their hands. There was a rally taking place in the main square. A woman, also dressed in olive green, with long braids falling down her back, was speaking Cakchiquel through a loudspeaker. Almost a hundred expressionless people were listening to her, all squeezed together, feeling a profound mixture of fear, resignation and consuming world-weariness to the circumstances which had befallen them. There were more armed men and women around the square. Some ran up and down the streets leading up to the bank and the town exit. Once in a while, there were gunshots and explosions that made everybody jump and squeeze more closely together, their extremities out of control like loose bags of jumping beans.

There was nothing going on at the square except the rally. In an attempt to create a festive mood, a young man climbed the church tower and started ringing the bells at full blast. At the entrance to the street that led from the square to the bank, Ariadne and Vallejo flailed their arms and shouted firmly and frenetically in all directions. Had someone not known that they were barking orders to different units, they would have thought that they were simulating a comic drunkenness. Suddenly, an old indigenous guerrilla turned the corner carrying a sewing machine. Vallejo saw him and walked fast to confront him.

"But what the fuck...! Take that back!"

"Look, here, *Comandante*!"

"There's no excuse, take it back!"

The old man's face changed from anger to resignation in a matter of seconds. Unsmiling, without another word, he started to turn around to go back where he had come from.

"Wait!" Vallejo cried sharply.

The old man stopped, still holding the sewing machine. There was no excitement in his face. Vallejo walked slowly over to him and placed a hand on his shoulder, to disguise his own unease, saying with false, paternalistic jocularity.

"Remember. We took the town to show our political

strength. Not to loot. We only take weapons from the enemy and money from the rich. The rest we don't touch."

"Yes, *Comandante*."

The old man's face fell again. He was too tired to smile.

"We have to set an example of moral conduct. They can't see us steal anything. Otherwise, how are we going to build a new society?"

"With sewing machines!"

Vallejo gave him a harsh look, sighed, and said something inaudible. The guerrilla pretended not to notice and went back where he had come from. Vallejo followed him with his gaze, feeling ebbing and flowing in his veins. Ariadne came running up a few moments later.

"What did you tell him?"

"That we had to set an example of moral conduct!"

"You, who used to smoke grass by the pound even when sitting on the toilet and swore that salsa was more important than Beethoven?"

"Shush, don't start with that shit now."

"Now you're a reformed man who doesn't even drink anymore."

"Instead of nagging me, tell me. Is there any resistance left?"

"They're all hiding in the Military Police headquarters. They're not even returning fire anymore."

"Then, what was that shooting?"

"It's just that we can't get in. The walls are about this thick! Can you imagine? We could only tear them down with mortar shells, and we don't have any."

"Damn it! And that's where all the soldiers are holed up?"

"Except for their two casualties. The rest ran inside."

"So then we didn't get any guns."

"Only the ones from the casualties."

Vallejo pressed his lips together and looked down. With a guarded expression on his face, he started walking around in small circles. He would have liked to say some simple and concrete words, but his own moral strength ebbed now and spluttered. He turned pale.

"Without mortar shells, what are we going to do?"

Vallejo continued walking in small circles, his bright feverish eyes looking backward in time. The church clock struck all of a sudden, driving away his lassitude.

"Fine. Give the order to stop shooting. We have to save ammunition. Especially if we didn't get any."

"All right. Do we also give the order to withdraw?"

"As soon as the rally ends."

The rally continued. The speaker gestured with great feeling and encouraged the public to participate. The women, who in the beginning were farthest away from the speaker, had squeezed up closer to where the guerrilla with the braids was speaking. When she said, "Are there any questions?", no one dared to say anything. The women started whispering among themselves, smiling and making comments in low voices.

Finally, a young, toothless woman raised a finger timidly. The speaker gave her the platform. The woman felt embarrassed when she noticed that everyone was turning to hear what she had to say, but she finally mustered the nerve to ask: "*Compañera*, when the revolution triumphs, are women still going to have to keep washing and cooking and taking care of the children, or is our life going to change, too?"

The speaker took advantage of the question to start another speech about equality for all, an equality not only among Indians and persons of mixed race, Catholics and Protestants, workers and peasants, among Indians of different ethnic groups, but also between men and women. When she said that, it was the men in the first row who started murmuring and looking sideways at the women with anxiety. But the speaker did not give them a chance to say a word. She skillfully intensified the tone of her speech and hung on to the microphone like an evangelical preacher, raising the tones of her discourse to such a point of quasi-mystical fervor that the entire audience, illuminated, repeated at once, "Ever onward to victory!" raising their left fists in the air (some of them got confused and raised their right fist, but they raised a fist anyway) and shouting like they were possessed, "Ever onward to victory!" "Ever onward to victory!"

Vallejo saw that the rally was ending and hurried to issue instructions to the various guerrillas coming to him. As soon as they understood what they had to do, they ran off in the opposite direction. He walked uphill toward the town exit. Unexpectedly, he heard an ambulance siren. He turned around, preparing his Galil for any unexpected situation. Sure enough, the town's ambulance was coming slowly his way, with the siren blaring. He stopped at the edge of the sidewalk, leaning against the wall with an expression of doubt and anxiety flitting across his face, and watched how calmly it went on until it reached him. Only then did he realize that two *compañeros* were at the wheel, young and happy as larks, blaring the siren.

Following behind the ambulance was a bus full of guerrillas. The ones celebrating and singing inside recognized him and saluted him through the windows, greeting him and shouting, "Ever onward to victory!" Vallejo exploded in a fit of laughter. Almost parodying them, he charmlessly raised his left fist toward them, in a dry, wax-sculpture-like gesture. The ambulance and bus continued uphill, blaring the siren and shouting, "Ever onward to victory!"

"It's crazy, huh?"

He was surprised that he hadn't heard Ariadne coming until she was right next to him.

"These guys sure, oh, jeez. Let's see. Quick, let's go after them before they cause some trouble down the road."

Ariadne signaled to the driver of the car with tinted windows parked in the main square. The vehicle approached them, and they both quickly jumped in the back seat. The car kept going uphill. In a matter of seconds Solulá returned to its previous tranquility. Aside from the hundreds of bullet holes in the outside wall of the Military Police headquarters, no one would have known that guerrillas had just taken the town. The sun was shining brightly, the lake, deep blue. On the southern shore, all three volcanoes stretched up, threatening to cross the entire surface of the lake, grab the cathedral by the bell tower, and shake it like a rag doll. There was no one on the dusty cobblestone streets, littered with stale, decomposing fruits.

On the highway, however, the calm had not returned. Vallejo and Ariadne's car met up with several columns of guerrillas on the side of the road, and they had to stop to give them instructions for retreating. The same thing happened with local paramilitary groups whose security had to be assured so they would not be detected, since they still lived in their towns of origin. When they caught up with the ambulance and the bus, they had reached Los Encuentros.

The vehicles were waiting for them on the side of the road. The policemen from the sentry box had disappeared. The ambulance was still blaring its siren, and the guerrillas in the bus were still shouting and singing. Hundreds of vendors had gathered around them nervously offering food, drinks, even handicrafts. The guerrillas were eating tacos, enchiladas and tortillas with beans and salsa while they shouted, "Ever onward to victory!" The vendors laughed nervously and passed food and drinks through the bus windows, gleefully repeating, "Ever onward to victory!" More and more vendors were arriving, running down the hills with their short little steps, followed by children shouting in Cakchiquel and small dogs with slanting ribs barking furiously. One boy was flying a blue and orange paper kite. There was even a Chinese magician threading needles with his mouth while standing on one foot.

CHAPTER FOUR

1

HEADLINE: EGP OCCUPIES SOLOLA! Beneath it was a fake photo of men moving around in camouflage, Galils in hand. The caption implied that the scandalous paper had an "exclusive" photograph of the town's occupation, taken by a photographer at the local market. Tom Wright did not have time to be seduced by the newspaper's provincial grace. The quality was worse than that of the most mediocre small town newspapers in his country. It looked more like a supermarket tabloid. It didn't go under only because it subscribed to international news agencies, whose dispatches it reproduced in horrendous translations on the inside pages.

He knew that, in the duel beginning to take shape with another mind whose identity was still a mystery, the occupation of Sololá was a giant move. He had to decipher it, think carefully. Preferably after wetting his dry brain with a glass of Scotch on the rocks. His right hand opened and closed nervously, anticipating the glass's icy perspiration. However, this was also a game against time. And that was a luxury that he did not have. How many days would he have? Eighteen was a multiple of nine, three times three, cabalistic luck. It was *his* problem, because the number was *him*.

The phone rang. Before picking up the receiver, he sat down, knowing that he was pressed to act, smiling a strange, private smile.

"Hello?...Yes..." he said curtly. "It's me...Sure...I read it, sir. That's just what I was doing. I know, I know, I'm not an idiot. That's why I came. Exactly. Listen..."

He held the receiver in his hand. He had anticipated everything, except that they would hang up on him and leave him like a fool, listening to the melancholic pitch of a dial tone monotonously mocking his predicament. Smiling grimly, he hung up with enough force to discharge his anger but not hard enough to really damage the phone and put him in the embarrassing situation of having to request another one from the hotel, which would also attract attention to him. He threw the newspaper on the bed. It floated lightly, falling open at the middle and leaving the inside pages askew, showing a large advertisement of Maidenform bras modeled by an unattractive local girl with sad pretensions of looking like a small, immature Bianca Jagger.

Wright still didn't know his contact. He knew he was disguised behind a secondary post at the embassy. He also knew that the moment would come when they would have to operate together. Ideally, when he had liberated the banker...and/or captured the guerrilla leader who kidnaped him. Then he would settle accounts and take the first plane out of this damn, repellent country where the cold, cruel smell of death was even stronger than the lustful beauty.

But that was too simple. Besides, his contact, like any specialist on the subject, had to be able to provide disinformation, had to be able to keep certain news out of the headlines. But, then...he knew that the takeover of Sololá was real. He didn't know its true dimensions. But why had it appeared in the paper? Wasn't there censorship? Wasn't it forbidden to mention subversives in the press? Who had authorized the article? His contact? The Minister of Defense? Both? And of course, this led to the next question...why? What was the goal of letting that information out? To prepare the people in the capital for something? A power struggle between his contact and the Minister of Defense? A conspiracy with the business sector that controlled the press? He had to figure it out. His next move depended on that hidden element.

There was a knock at the door. Gravely, he got up to answer, but only after the third knock. He intuited that his decision, though not yet formulated at that very moment, would have something to do with what was waiting on the other side. He opened the door. A bellboy with dark, composed features, impeccably dressed, waited expressionless, holding a tray in his right hand. On the tray was a folded a piece of paper.

"Urgent message for Mr. Wright."

"That's me."

He took it. Struggling briefly when his hand got caught in the front pocket of his pants, he managed to free a few coins. The bellboy's expression did not change in the slightest. Wright closed the door behind him and opened the card immediately. It said "Dearest: I have important news for you. Meet me at the pool at ten. Kisses. Sandra."

A cloud of contempt covered his face. It was not what he had expected. He crumpled the paper into a ball and let his anger flow freely. He threw it on the floor, stepped on it, groaned pitifully. Yes, he wanted to see her. But, it was another snake on the road. He could not be distracted now. However, he had no clear clues, and he was pressed for time. Sandra was a Herrera. Maybe she could shed some light on this newspaper business.

Having found the right excuse to see her, he allowed his chaotic emotions about another encounter with this woman to envelop him softly like a perfume cloud. He was preparing to go down when he remembered the paper. Picking it up gently, he put it in the ashtray and set it on fire, watching how the flame rapidly consumed the little ball until all that was left was a pile of fine, gray ashes. He emptied them into the trash can and hurriedly left the room.

2

"We're not still mad at each other, then, my dear?"

Sitting in front of her by the edge of the pool at a small, white, metal table, he repeated her words softly to himself before responding curtly:

"Serious things are happening in this country."

"No kidding."

She turned her candid eyes to him and gave a little laugh. He thought she was as beautiful as ever, before correcting himself. She was even more beautiful than the day before. Her black hair fell loosely down the length of her back and a slight breeze from the pool lifted it just a bit, creating the illusion that it was floating slightly, just enough to force him to struggle against the growing powers of his lust. She looked at him intensely with those large, almond eyes that could disarm him with just a glance. Her endearing mouth, whose trembling lower lip seemed like a great, ripe strawberry, expressed an unimaginable mixture of hardness and the most seductive, slender of smiles, both gestures intertwined with each movement of her glorious lips. She leaned slightly to one side when she spoke, as if wanting her shoulder to touch against you, and the temptation to get close and let her do it was maddeningly overpowering. The first button of her blouse was open. A thin blouse. When she leaned over to make shoulder contact, it showed the swell of her breasts, barely covered by a delicate, transparent demi-bra. He blinked, blaming the morning sun's reflection off the water in the pool, but it was an uncontrollable reflex rising from the luxurious strain of having to move his slipping eyes away from the delicate blouse that was paralyzing him like a mouse before the cat's final pounce. As if hearing himself say something out of place, he asked:

"So you know?"

"Don't pretend, sweetie. Families like mine survive because they know everything that's happening, so they can use it for their own benefit."

There was a silence as thick as black fumes. He felt ridiculous. Besides, he would lose a staring contest with her in a matter of seconds. To break the tension, he awkwardly took her hand between his, pressing it to his cheek softly. The inelegant gesture almost made Sandra laugh out loud but she suffocated her cracked laugh so as not to wound his fragile male pride.

"Okay, forgive me. What is it that you know?"

"That's the only thing that matters to you, right?"

"I didn't come down just for the pleasure of it. I came down here on business."

"You people aren't human. You're like robots."

"We're persistent. Sometimes we're lucky. But, above all, we're professionals. Anyway, you make your own luck with hard work."

With that, Sandra exploded in bitter laughter so strong it rocked the table. She licked her finger and marked the point he'd scored with an imaginary line in the air.

"Sure. We'll give you a point for that profound insight, my dear professional."

He did not understand the reference, and he was feeling too tense to let her teasing amuse him, draw drops of humor as the dentist's drill drew beads of sweat. Noting his tension, she pressed nearer and nearer to his body, whimpering with weariness.

"My father sends his regards."

He remembered the old man vaguely from when he had visited his daughter at the university. They even did a walking tour of the French Quarter. Not very tall, thin, balding, white moustache. A shy, introverted man.

"Thanks. How is he?"

"Older than when you met him."

The banal response was typical of her. Unforeseen and

59

evasive, slightly mocking, she always sidestepped serious issues as she lay in the crook of his arm, until he was distracted or exasperated enough to make a false move. Then she pounced.

"Enough of that now. Let's talk business."

He pulled away, staring at her through his clear eyes with a tiny, almost imperceptible cringing that seemed out of character. She didn't say a word. He felt that each second stretched out interminably, like an empty universe. It was slow torture, like running uphill carrying a heavy load under the implacable, tropical sun.

"Well then. I don't have all morning."

"Of course not, dear. Time is money to you."

He stood up. He felt a sharp pain in his liver as if his belt had been tightened more than his neglected belly would allow. At the very moment when impatience was winning him over, and he half-turned to leave, she grabbed his hand, as if uncurling from a deep sleep.

"Wait. It's serious...sit down."

He sat down again. She leaned toward him once more with a gesture of melodramatic complicity, and glowed like someone tasting a magnificent wine.

"Tom, my trusted sources have informed me..."

"What?"

"That the EGP has plans to kidnap you."

The news struck him like a knockout blow. It felt as if the entire hotel had just crashed on his head. But only for an instant. He didn't say anything. Whenever he received bad news, his face remained expressionless until the adrenaline flow diminished, and the rational, logical process could begin once more. He called it creative construction.

"Did you hear me?"

"I heard you."

She whispered those words blowing air through her teeth and over her tongue like a serpent's hiss. He had forgotten some details over the past fifteen years.

"So what? Should I go hide under my bed?"

Sandra appeared to be upset. She turned her face brusquely in the direction of the pool. He noticed her lips were trembling slightly, pouting just a tad.

"No, but..."

He couldn't sit still. A myriad of emotions overtook him like bubbles in shaken champagne. He felt inside himself the stirring of a great discomfort, and thought that, methodically, step by step, she was overturning his world with a fierce, cold, torturing device: her charm. He felt as if he were already locked up in an enchanted castle, but when he noticed her troubled expression, his old instincts still managed to resurface.

"It's a way of finding Gray quicker."

He raised his glass of Scotch and soda with several floating ice cubes and made the gesture of toasting to her health.

"The banker? That's why you're here?"

She creased her brow, crumpling her nose. He laughed nervously, gazing distractedly at the pool, then played the pathetic clown to distract her from his slip with mock gestures of fear. After that, suddenly chastened, he put on a blank face, and took another quick sip of his drink.

"It doesn't matter why I'm here. I'm *not* on vacation."

"You came to rescue the kidnaped banker, right?"

"Maybe I came to kidnap an EGP commander..."

He sighed with some degree of boastful satisfaction when he saw that his improvised words had the desired effect.

"What! You're ...!"

Her surprise, though, worried him. Instinctively he looked around to make sure, once again, that nobody was listening or paying the slightest attention to them. Sandra hit her forehead to dramatize the lunacy of the idea. He took her hand to force a reaction of complicity.

"Shhh! Please..."

"But, do you realize what you said?"

He laughed again, this time sharply, denoting a new air of uncertainty, as if he had just realized he had not bought enough time to soak the weariness of his bones.

"I said 'to kidnap an EGP commander.' In this country and in this job, anything is possible, my dear."

"Why did you tell me?"

"Because I haven't told anyone else."

"So? What does that have to do...?"

"It means that if I later pick up this rumor amid the gossip that circulates around this city that adores...how do you say it?"

"*Bolas*..."

"...*bolas*, then there's only one person, only one, who could have started it."

He laughed mockingly, his eyes fixed on her, drinking once more without thinking, before placing the glass back on the table with a slightly trembling hand. She signaled with her finger for him to move closer. He leaned as close as possible to her face.

"Dear..."

"Yes?"

"Fuck you."

"Now that you mention it, isn't that what we did fifteen years ago?"

Sandra arched her lips in disgust. She sprang up, hesitating for the slightest instant while her quivering lips revealed a suppressed impulse to scream. Turning, she walked away furiously. Tom Wright banged a double fist into the palm of his hand as he experienced a sudden vision of that same scene, fifteen years earlier, an adolescent memory that now hit him like an ocean wave. Her long, decisive steps charged with sudden energy as if touched by electricity, arms swinging rhythmically beside her curvaceous waist, her hair floating lightly with the soft breeze like a sudden flight of birds, while the melodious tenderness of her unforgiving behind forced him to run after her like a sleepwalker begging for forgiveness.

3

"Kidnap an EGP commander? Are you crazy?"

"Not at all. But you're the second person to tell me that."

"Oh, shit....It's dangerous that someone else knows about this. Aside from that, though, how the hell do you plan to pull off such an exploit?"

Pacal spoke self-importantly, trying to keep his tone grave, sympathetic. He turned and started walking down the Ministry hallway. The yellowish light and lack of windows created an atmosphere of forlorn narrowness, highlighting his uneven steps. The strange claustrophobic echo sounded off the ceiling, like a boom-box. Wright explained in a slightly annoyed tone:

"Nugan Hand is going to demand, as a condition for paying the ransom, that a commander be present when the money is handed over."

Pacal cleared his throat. He seemed tired. Wright kept going round and round with what he had just stated, more and more enthusiastic by the possibility of the idea.

"So then? You grab him just like that..."

Pacal pretended to grab an invisible object with his hand and cover it with the palm of the other. He looked at it with a fixed gaze and a slight expression of scorn barely detectable at the corner of his mouth. Wright hesitated, then continued breathlessly:

"I'll give you the details later. Trust me."

"Your last president said the same thing and let the Sandinistas take power."

"Well, let's not exaggerate either. But think about it. If we grab a commander, you wouldn't have to be humiliated again, like yesterday."

He let those words go with a clear purpose. He was fishing. Gasping in fear that he had gone too far, he still wanted to know how Pacal would react to the loaded insinuation. The Captain turned briefly pale, stared at him and in a hundredth of a second, the expression in his eyes melted from an intense and unerring hatred to a gentle, ironic smile, muttering:

"You know that Sololá doesn't count. We let them operate in order to finish rounding out our information so we can destroy them as soon as the rains are over."

"Maybe..." added Wright, who had recovered his demure official pose. "But it came out in the newspapers. It creates panic in the public opinion and makes you look incompetent."

"The Minister already explained that to the leadership of the Chamber of Commerce."

"And the public? The people on the street?"

"This is Guatemala. Things are handled from above..."

"Why did you let the news come out in the papers?"

Pacal didn't answer. He made a quarter-turn and raised his glance with infantile concentration as if he were a ceiling inspector. In profile, the scars on his face shone more than usual. Wright felt a mounting indignation that his mission could be torpedoed by such a flagrant mistake, at least in his eyes.

"Do my people know...?"

"This is a sovereign country. The Embassy knows what it needs to know. Read the signs."

Wright cauterized his fit of fury with a smothered laugh that failed to hide his discomfort.

"Tell that to Gray...or to the press."

Uneasy, Pacal lowered his head and indicated with his hand that they should return to his office. He had hit an important nerve.

"The only way to eliminate the threat once and for all is to kidnap the brains of the operation. That way you can obtain all the strategy, the plans, and they will crumble like mud dolls. The weakness of these organizations is their vertical structure. Everything depends on the head. The militants don't have a clue, no margin of autonomy. They're like the classical Mayas. Their priests would be captured and their followers would surrender without a fight. Or, they would flee not knowing what to do, like chickens with their heads cut off."

"If it's so easy, why didn't you win in Vietnam?"

There was a long silence after his impertinent remark. Wright was aghast. Nonetheless, he felt that, in order to regain his trust, he would have to answer the thorny question.

"That was different. For starters, there was the whole problem of the drug business. Some feared that the end of the war would mean the end of the heroin business, and, hard as it is to admit, some of our own officers in high places were profiting from it. Then again, hard-line Vietnamese officials were also a problem. They were more interested in their personal quota of power than in winning; to top it off, some important families also profited by doing illegal business with the economic aid we sent them and didn't want to see that umbilical cord severed or lose their earnings, and..."

"You're so smart, I'm truly impressed. Of course, we know that none of that happens here, that this is an easy war to win. Right?"

"Does that happen here?"

The Captain straightened up. He let out his classical laugh, whose hypocritical echo resounded like a slow collapse down the hall. His gold tooth shone with a yellow light, reproducing his image like a mirror, giving the impression that Wright was the prisoner of a monstrous tooth. It made his flesh creep. Pacal put his arm on Wright's back a little brusquely and led him inside his office.

"Of course not, Mr. Wright. This is strictly an anti-Communist crusade. Good versus evil. Simple. That's why your Southern fundamentalists love our cause."

"And you believe it?"

"What I believe is irrelevant at this point."

After concluding his last little touch of irony, Pacal cut off his vexing laughter abruptly, deciding that it was not in his best interests to push the issue further. He ducked back tactfully, said his goodbyes, and retreated hastily to the inner sanctum of his office.

4

With an air of gravid solemnity, the bells of a nearby church began to toll. Thick, humid air carried an acrid stench as oppressive as the discolored rain floating down from the sky. The rain brought to mind childhood memories—the pleasant scent of wet soil, the gleeful ringing of the bells—but these could not erase the desolation Vallejo felt at having to render his report regarding the recent operative in that small, peeling room.

"So only two weapons were recovered in the action?"

Vallejo felt like an imbecile. He held back his answer as if to reexamine it before hurling it out on the table.

"You know that's true, so don't bust my balls."

Ariadne rubbed her hands nervously. Every time she was anxious, she spoke rapidly, without pausing.

"We feared your reaction, *Comandante*, because we thought you were going to say that it was a wasted effort with the columns we mobilized and all that blown ammunition on those huge walls, a yard thick, that weren't even tickled..."

Ariadne hesitated When Vallejo noticed that her soliloquy was losing its rhythm in a sea of useless emotional descriptions, he thought it fitting to jump in:

"Remember, you old fool; we insisted we needed

mortars. Here's tangible proof that we won't get anywhere without them."

Vallejo felt his heart beating in his temples, particularly when he saw that Ariadne's transparency was evaporating and rapidly turning into a meek, sad-eyed nervousness. Kukulkán pulled his pipe from his shirt pocket, filled it slowly with tobacco and lit it. He remained expressionless. Standing up, he inhaled deeply, then exhaled rhythmically, animated by the burning tobacco which gave his spirit time to settle, and his rationale, time to get going once again. Speaking in a surprisingly calm tone that contrasted sharply with his tense muscles and hard stare, he said:

"The mortar business is an old story, but you know that Cuba gave them to the *Guanacos* instead of us. I told the Commander-in Chief that I'd get them on my own in Panama, but the National Directorate gave me their same old shit, and the priest we had just named to it damned me again for not believing in God. I think that...that someone was jealous, an asshole *comandante* from a certain front I cannot name, who controls his territory like a feudal lord and personally checks out all the young girls under his watch."

A sepulchral silence fell. Kukulkán inhaled the pipe again with somber deliberation, his eyelids half-closed. The other two waited for him to pick up his train of thought, without daring to add anything, feeling disoriented.

"Now, having said that, I think the action was a success."

"A success! Go tell that tale to your nanny!"

"Of course that is what we're going to say in our press release, but I think it's dangerous for us to fall into a false sense of triumph with all the ammunition that..."

The harsh eyes silenced Ariadne.

"A success indeed."

"Don't invent things, you asshole."

Kukulkán sank into silence again. His face hardly moved. He appeared indifferent but his eyes and his jaw muscles, which seemed to be perennially chewing a tough piece of gristle, completely betrayed his apparent calm. His gestures were a mixture of the fifties-era *pachuco*, a military cadet in civilian clothing, and a generous country doctor.

"The army is not going to tell the *Gringo* from the CIA how many losses they had and how many weapons they lost. And if they do, the *Gringo* is not going to believe them because it'll seem so exaggerated that he'll think they're pulling his leg, and he won't trust them. The action was to impress the *Gringo*. And the army itself was interested in impressing him. They let the news come out in the papers. While they were at it, they lost the *Gringo*'s trust. Now the *Gringo* is going to want to get the banker back more than ever. As a matter of fact..."

"Yes, boss?"

Vallejo's touch of humor fell flat. Ariadne barely disguised a grim smile. He always regretted mocking Kukulkán like that, but it was a reflex he couldn't quite control.

"He'll want to capture whoever collects the ransom."

"Really? It just seems...harebrained..."

Ariadne rarely questioned anything, so much so that Vallejo would tease her mercilessly, saying that it'd be militants blinded by mysticism, like ' ɛr, that would organize "Red Sundays" and voluntary workdays when the revolution triumphed. The few times she expressed disagreements, she did it with a fresh-faced girl's little voice.

"You'll see. Just wait."

Vallejo began to consider the hypothesis. His brain was running like a motor, nearly giving off sparks while he explored alternatives and variables, posed different possibilities.

"Well, so then? We could...uh...mount an operative..."

"That's what you get for being such a pothead, you idiot. Your wires are all crossed and there's no damn way to straighten them out."

"Shit. You guys crossed them with the fucking things you

did to me in Mexico after leaving me hanging on the island for a couple of years..."

"Fuck that. You became neurotic all by yourself. Remember what the Commander-in-Chief told you, that in a single year you'd left your father's house with a pool, married an older woman, had a son and left to receive military training in Cuba, that it was no wonder you went a little crazy?"

"Fuck, there you go again with that psychoanalytic shit."

"I was just reminding you."

"Besides, in those days I didn't even smoke yet, idiot, that was later..."

"After your Troskyite deviation."

"Lay off. And we were so serious before."

The conversation eliminated all tension from the air. Sighing, Kukulkán let them get back to the subject. However, a slow smile of cunning crept to his mouth as he let Vallejo think out loud, his eyes glinting with energy. Kukulkán enjoyed watching him talk at a thousand miles per minute, while pacing the length of the table. He simply sat back, inhaling his tobacco, chewing on the tip of his pipe, his eyes fixed on the wall where there was a poster with Vallejo's face, underlining his public importance as a sort of underground rock star. He nodded gravely from time to time. Vallejo often said whatever came into his mind, but his evaluations were on target most of the time.

"We're going to have to prepare a surprise party."

"For me?"

"No. For the *Gringo.*"

When he turned to Kukulkán, Vallejo ended up confronting his own replica. It wasn't the first time he'd seen the poster but it never stopped being a surprise to see his own eyes staring back at him, through him, as if he were an image forged by himself with the ability to unfold his personality both as a dramatic character and as a sort of artistic creator. He felt like the author of his own persona. The paper was beginning to yellow but the eyes were as

69

penetrating as ever. Looking at himself in the poster was like standing before a concave mirror.

In reality, it wasn't a poster. It was a centerfold page of the newspaper, *Prensa Libre*. At the top, in bold type, was his legal name: Gabriel Augusto Fuentes Paz. Then his photo. Immediately below the photo, in a slightly smaller type than his name, it said "Member of the EGP." There was a small space and then a text that he almost knew by heart and had repeated more than once in his dreams: "Gabriel Augusto Fuentes Paz, alias 'Vallejo,' is a young Guatemalan man who, rather than taking advantage of the privilege of his university education to study a profession for his own benefit and that of his countrymen, dedicated himself to organizing the violent student group called FERG, through which he committed acts of terrorism in the capital city, as well as in the interior of the country; acts that he now continues to carry out on a larger scale as a member of the extremist band of Communists called the EGP. As a result of his subversive acts, Gabriel Augusto Fuentes Paz, alias 'Vallejo,' represents a danger to you and Guatemala." There was another blank space and then, "Call with information on his whereabouts to the following numbers: 37-04-95, 20-2-21/26 or to your local authority—NSO, National Security Organization." It concluded with NSO's slogan: "Defending peace is also your business."

Kukulkán had put it up on the wall some months back, telling him, "When you were a teenager, you wanted to be a rock-n-roll star and see your face on a poster. You've done it, baby. Here you are! Look at yourself; you really look handsome."

5

It was a small and crowded office. A tiny box in a modern building constructed on the cheap with low ceilings. The only window was sealed, but, to the side. There was a section with narrow glass slats that opened and closed like a Venetian blind. Its singular pattern made it difficult for a bullet to enter from the street, but it also made the air oppressively hot. The air conditioning worked poorly. Piles of papers could be seen everywhere, forming bizarre geometric structures. They seemed to resemble triangles because, as they greedily marched up in their race to graze the ceiling, they leaned slightly toward one another, maintaining a precarious balance. On the top part of the walls still visible behind the piles of papers, all types of posters could be glimpsed, including the ones that security had published about local terrorists. Tom Wright recognized the photo looking at his eyes as one of those that Pacal had pointed out on the route from the airport to the hotel.

"I am Behemoth. Thit down."

The man neither stood up nor extended his hand. He barely signaled with the tip of his chin in which of the two chairs in front of his desk Wright should sit. *Bad sign*, Wright thought. Fine way of meeting.

"After your telephone call I thought it was urgent that we meet to avoid misunderstandings."

Behemoth didn't seem to listen to the last words.

"I have all your paperwork here. I feel ath if we've known each other for a long time."

The man spoke with a strange lisp, as if he had a lip or tongue deformity, but it seemed to become selective if he didn't pay attention. The distinctive trait countermanded his fatherly and authoritative tone. He read the papers for a while in stiff silence.

"The idea of a kidnaping wath a thtupidity!"

His gray moustache gave him a domineering air. The roundness of the face revealed his love of fine food, and his growing baldness gave him an air of serene authority betrayed by his trembling lips and his plump fingers stained with nicotine.

"Sir, I think the information we could obtain..."

But the man had not called him to his Embassy office to listen to arguments he already knew too well.

"We have enough information about thith organithation, thankth to the fileth that Náscar captured in Mexico in 1976. At thith moment, that ith not what we need!"

He did not know the person to whom he was speaking, but it was easy to figure out the nature of Central American mission directors. No matter how stinky this dirty war was, they had to sweep the garbage under the rug with the gravity of a mute and leave the air odorless and shining in case a congressional junket delved into their ties to military figures like Pacal.

"And still, when we were finally able to see the papers that the Guatemalan army captured in December of '80, it was clear that it was no longer the same organization as in '76. It had grown. They had changed their tactics, developed a new policy for dealing with the local population..."

"Now they're on the defenthive. They've lost the initiative."

The selectiveness of his distinctive lisp was clear.

"They occupied a regional capital yesterday. They've kidnaped an Australian banker and they still have a lot of sympathy..."

The man opened his desk drawer, let his fingers forage around for a few brief seconds and extracted a worn pack of unfiltered cigarettes. He took one out for himself without offering one to Wright and lit it with shaky hands. He inhaled deeply and leaned back in his chair, losing his balance for a fraction of a second, as if he suddenly felt very old and frail.

"Lithen to me, Wright. I'm telling you. They have loth the initiative. Time will prove that I'm right. Bethides, the only thing you want ith to take the head of a commander to Langley so they'll promote you."

His tone had relaxed during his smoke. He had gone from

bossy to professorial, with a metallic tone that grated on the nerves.

"Frankly I don't understand your logic at all. What type of information do you send to Washington? Up there we haven't..."

"Don't thtart getting me angry, Wright. Bethides, in case you didn't know, you and I work in different departments."

He was surprised but tried to mask it. The man had the upper hand and allowed himself a cynical smile as he displayed knowledge Wright didn't have.

"Yeth, Wright, we're not in the thame structure. Therefore, you have no reathon to know what type of information I thend to the company, and, as for the other matter, if you want your commander's little head, go, look for it and get it. The Nugan Hand operative ith completely in your hands. Or not?"

The man stood up. Shorter than Wright and broad-shouldered, he was dressed casually. His shirt opened to the middle of his chest, displaying a thick gold chain and a mass of gray hairs.

"My instructions were to consult with you."

"Your instructions were to liberate the banker thafe and thound, not to capture commanders. Right?"

"My instructions *are* to liberate the banker safe and sound through whatever means I consider suitable without excluding any option or alternative. I have freedom to act in that regard."

"Then, exercise it."

"I'm doing that, sir. I'm doing that by consulting with you, which was also part of my instructions."

The man stared at him as if he were a horse for sale. He walked around him and looked at him from behind. Wright turned to confront him, and got smoke in his eyes.

"I thee that we are novices at thith..."

"I've been in for ten years!"

"Anyone can push papers at Langley. What is needed here is cleverness. Astuteness. Roguery. Do you know that one of the Central American thubverthives stated that for the revolution to triumph, they needed Marxthithm and balls? I thay almost the thame thing. To prevent it from winning, we need cleverness and balls. We have to do things with a lot of inthtinct, with a very fine thenth of thmell and with disdain for the little manuals from Washington. And you, my dear Wright..."

"You offend me sir."

"Well, then, be offended. Ath long as you react."

"I only came to see you because my instructions said..."

"There you go again. I know, I know. Well just tho you know, mine say that I have to listen to you...but not to tell you what you should do."

"You said the kidnaping idea was stupid. And that the information that was available..."

"Thothe are my opinions, Wright. Are you an imbethile, or what? That ith what I think. But they are not orders. I'm not authorized to give you orders. Only advice. Only opinions. A rain of ideas. Protect you if it were to become nethesary. Thupport you operatively if you blow it and get into trouble. But nothing more. Nothing more. *Entiendes*? People like you are the ones that make *Chapines* think that we're foolth."

"It is not exactly like that, sir."

"Yeah right. Like hell it ithn't. Nothing ith ever 'exactly like that.' And he who believes, *creer*, that it is, is always nailed for being a moron."

"You're tough, sir."

"I've been here for years. More than you can imagine. And I hate it that they thend me clean and pure *gringuitos* who really believe that thith ith a cruthade, a holy war, and that nobody ith going to try to fuck your woman up there while you thave the free world in the dark tropical forests..."

"Sir!"

"Wake up, Wright. Thith shit is *jodido* and no one who gets in comes out clean."

"I see where you're coming from, sir. Enough. Enough already!"

Behemoth sat down again and breathed through his nose. Wright closed his eyes and tightened his fists. He grabbed on to the image of his childhood home in the Nashville suburbs as if it were a life jacket. A bright, clear, spacious, airy, above all, airy, house, and him playing with his two sisters, both wearing bright shorts, in the large roomy garden, large and scented with fresh grass, very roomy, where their father had built an atomic bomb shelter. The refuge had turned into his favorite hiding place, into his sisters' doll house, into the place where he would run from the power of a mother bereft of seductive and magical qualities, from the indifference of a father ashamed of his son's physical weakness, a factor guaranteeing that he would not make the football team, from his sisters' tyranny. But, he would save them when the atomic attack came. That had never happened, but now Guatemala would see who he was.

As if to distance himself from the superficial aspect of his fleeting weakness, he quickly erased the childhood memory of a father with opaque gray eyes set in a freckled reddish flesh and transferred all his attention to Behemoth. The man's pretension of disassociating himself from "*Gringos*" was also a mask, as ridiculous as his own. The shirt opened to mid chest. The whole country, Sandra, Pacal, the mythical guerrilla fighters—it was all just a great costume ball, a masked fiction where everyone pretended to conjure up secret powers that none of them had. Arrogance tempered by sentimentalism. In that regard both the *Gringos* and the locals were a lot alike.

"One last thing sir. And I will leave you in peace."

The man laughed out loud and his eyes narrowed but shone more brightly.

"Go ahead, Wright. I'm here to therve all the young new arrivals like you."

"Is there any possibility that Gray was sent to this country as bait so the guerrillas would kidnap him? Could he also be working for us?"

The man furrowed his brow. A gray cloud fell over his face. He teetered lightly in his chair, thinking. Then with a histrionic snap, he slapped the desk with the palm of his hand. With the same speed, the color returned to his face. He turned up his lips into an open smile and said with unusual warmth:

"Get out of here, Wright! You know I can't anthwer that! Beat it! Get out!"

Now it was Tom Wright's face that lit up. Smiling, he said goodbye effusively and in one movement, closed the door behind him and disappeared from the office.

6

The door to her car opened. The valet offered Sandra his hand but she jumped out ahead, ignoring him completely, and quickened her firm steps to the inside of the hotel. Her abundant hair floated like a shadow in pursuit of its owner. She made her way acrobatically to grab one of the scarce public telephones between the restaurant and the exit to the pool. Once her bodyguards caught up with her, they established a prudent no-man's-land between them and frightened onlookers. She dialed a number. Her fingers had not finished dialing and already she was getting a busy signal.

"Cheap telephones. The calls never go through."

She dialed again. On her third try she finally got a connection.

"Hello."

Three upper-crust ladies with bright patches of rouge on their cheeks, too much makeup, and pearl necklaces saw her and cried out with sharp voices:

"Sandrita! What a surprise! You, here...!"

The Maginot line that protected her opened up timidly before those ghostly faces, allowing the women to bombard her with chatter

"My, but you *are* looking quite beautiful, Sandrita, such a blessing to see you!"

"My dear girl! What a horror to have to go around like this, don't you agree? But in these times..."

Previously so arrogant and sure of herself, she cringed for an instant under the tiny kisses on her cheeks, cold as death, while she choked on the smell of perfume.

"Oh my dears! How wonderful to see you! It's been so long! Forgive me if I don't greet you properly but I've been running around like you *cannot* imagine!"

"No, my dear. Don't you worry. We know how these things are, right, Doloritas?"

The intimate gesture of pinching her cheek sanctioned the complicity implied in the phrase. Surprised, Sandra jumped back and forced a smile to forestall gossip while Doloritas stretched out her neck to glimpse the number that Sandra was calling.

"We'll leave you in peace, my dear. Just go on about your business."

Sandra patted their shoulders affectionately. The women walked away in an effervescent mood, solidly anchored in their satisfaction with themselves. They even seemed to have put on weight during the exchange. Sandra directed her attention again to the telephone.

"Hello? Hello?"

On the other end of the line she could only hear electronic noises and a heavy melancholic silence. She put her hand on the phone.

"Oh, that man. Is it possible that he's not there?"

She hung up with a barely contained violence, absolutely compulsive. Her father, a short handsome man with a moustache like David Niven's and vivid eyes, who always appeared in a knit sweater with the inevitable pipe in his mouth, was as methodical and rigorous as any good scientist—an absurd profession in a country like ours, she always protested. Who cares about being Director of the Museum of Natural History in a country where no one visits museums except for maids, and then only to make out with their boyfriends? Not her. She had always felt breathless when things didn't turn out the way she wanted. She detested it when her plans fell apart. It ruined her day and sank her into hysterical fits of anger. Her father would look at her tenderly every time she had one of her tantrums. To calm her down, he would tell her one of his favorite snake stories.

"I'm fed up with your serpents!" she would scream, while leaving the room in a pique, violently slamming the door behind her.

"Things will get better," she would barely hear over the door slamming, spoken in a philosophical tone. "They will get better."

He had explained to her the symbolic relationship that serpents had with voodoo, like the "damballah-wédo," which is a serpent god. There was the wind-serpent, the night-serpent, always like a long extension whose head met the tail, reconciling it and promoting the meeting of opposites. The serpent, he would tell her, draws near to the extremes. It penetrates and disappears in the bowels of the earth, resurfacing like the sun with ascendant motions. When it sheds its skin, it changes and yet stays the same at once. It symbolizes fertility and ancestral eternity in its function as an animal totem, as a cosmic serpent, similar to a Maya goddess called Ixchel. She bursts into the world humbled, from the land of humiliation, and wounds the heavens, where, rising and entwining with the stars, she brings about at last the great reconciliation of her adversaries, like Tojil and the Jaguar in Flames. In its symbolic polyvalence, the ophidian becomes a figure of non-subjugation, of absolute liberty, of free flight to the heavens, of the discovery of love, or the rediscovery of the primitive broken unity that will lead to the universal fraternity of all people.

She went out to the pool and looked around until she found an empty table. Turning, she noticed that her men were about to follow her. She made a rapid gesture with her chin. In the face of the derogatory looks of others walking down the corridor, they returned to the main entrance of the hotel to wait. With stealthy speed she occupied the empty table. A waiter leaned solicitously almost before she was seated.

"Scotch and water please. With a lot of ice."

In spite of the "please" it sounded more like a slap than a request. The waiter walked away hurriedly, not wanting to annoy her inadvertently.

She relaxed, shaking her head disdainfully, as if to erase a bad thought. Still attentive to her surroundings, she noticed a strange-looking fat man. Maybe he was a dealer. She bit her lip, noticing now a pair of *Gringos* speaking in quiet voices to each other at the other end. Either embassy agents or fags. A *Chapín* paced nervously from one side to the other as if his contact had failed to show up. He could be a guerrilla, but more than likely he was a militant in an anticommunist organization. Nobody noticed her except for the normal libidinous glances that she had learned to solemnly ignore. Shrugging her shoulders to nobody in particular, she closed her eyes for a very brief moment, thinking that she no longer felt anything for men.

"I thought it was impossible to get near you without being wasted by one of your gorillas."

She opened her eyes abruptly. She attempted to get up and grab her purse simultaneously as if thrust by a spring. Tom Wright was in front of her. The Scotch glass was sweating on the table. She had fallen asleep. Only for a few moments, but she had fallen asleep. Furiously, she reproached herself her for her carelessness while she mechanically put on a charming smile like rotten sweets and made a tender hopeless gesture in the air.

"They're well trained. They can tell the dogs that bite from the lap dogs."

"You think I'm that ordinary?"

"Ordinary no. Inoffensive."

She took the glass of Scotch from the table and rapidly gulped down half of it. Before Wright had a chance to sit down, she stood up and put her arm through his.

"Tom, why don't we go someplace where we can talk more privately?"

"You didn't used to be so direct when we were in college. In those days you would have blushed at such a proposition..."

She removed her arm with the speed of a coral snake.

"And you weren't so vulgar. In those days, you still pretended to respect women."

Her voice softened until it recovered its sugary tone. Putting her lips together to kiss the tips of her fingers, she placed them on his neck, directly under his ear.

"And you were a lady. You were such a lady that even the Southern belles paled at your side."

They began to walk back inside the building. She came closer with each step, taking his arm again.

"We were so young then...so innocent. It's difficult to remain innocent with all the things that go on here, Tom."

"It's difficult to stay that way as we get older."

Her snake eyes reappeared, clear irises and narrow pupils.

"Come on, Tom. You know exactly what I'm trying to say. In the United States everything was so simple, so predictable, so naïve. You can't do that here. You'd get shot, kidnaped. You can't even know who's on which side in your own family."

"Even when you're a member of one of the most powerful families in the country?"

"Especially when you're a member of one of those

families. All the little people want something from you and get angry when you don't give it to them. They all envy you and rip you off behind your back. Everyone hates you and plots how to screw you over. The blow can come from where you least expect it, from the flank you thought you had already covered."

"And then you shoot back."

"To survive, you do whatever it takes. You save money so you can get away if you have to. We're not morons. We're only loyal to our instinct for survival."

"Not even to your family?"

"To our family, yes, of course. How could you even think that? Or at least to those members closest to us."

"You say that as if you had something up your sleeve."

"Oh, Tom. If you only knew."

They were already in front of the elevator. Like automatons they pressed the button, while she brushed her hair back swiftly, impatiently, in the mirror. When the elevator arrived and the doors opened, they walked in calmly together as if they had planned it ahead of time.

"I have some gossip."

"Oh, really? Spit it out."

"Don Leonel has been buying at bargain-basement prices the houses of people on the death list who've had to leave the country."

"Could be, Tom. Those deals of his, who knows..."

She came closer, taking his arm, leaning on his shoulder with the melting-wax tenderness of a little girl and closed her eyes. He felt his heart beating faster. Taking her hands in his, he looked straight at her face while struggling to speak in a gentlemanly tone, almost whispering between his teeth.

"I won't be able to see you for a few days. I have to...export some local handicrafts."

"Is that the code for delivering Gray's ransom to the EGP?"

He shook his head, bit his lip, whispered to himself in

surprise, and leaned forward to kiss her forehead in an exaggeratedly stilted gesture.

"You know too much for your own good."

"That's how we survive. Knowledge is power. We have to be up to the minute in everything. That's why people from your country never exercise power well. They don't know what's going on. Especially in your circles. In that regard our two countries are not so different..."

The elevator door opened. She jumped out to the gaunt corridor, followed by a suddenly indecisive, hesitant Tom Wright, who said in a new voice, full of unexpected vibrations:

"I didn't know we were going to my room to talk politics."

"I didn't know we were going to your room."

She turned and looked at him with a slightly ironic smile.

"But you said..."

"Never mind. Let's go to your room."

They kept walking, and only stopped in front of the door while he rummaged in his pockets for the key. She waited with interest, amused yet disturbed by his clumsiness.

"One thing hasn't changed over the years. You're still full of contradictions."

"Stubborn, you used to call me. It occurred to you after reading that novel about the governor of Louisiana..."

"*All the King's Men* by Robert Penn Warren."

"That one."

"It's true. You already were stubborn, and now you're even more stubborn."

"I learned a lot from that novel."

"Since when do people learn from literature?"

They walked into the room. It was dark, despite the huge window overlooking the pool. A gray Venetian blind kept out all of the light, save for the elusive rays that hit the ceiling diagonally without disturbing the moldering silence.

"It's dark in here, Tom! It looks like a den!"

"Bright sunlight bothers me."

Without consulting him, she walked over to the window and yanked the cord violently. The room was immediately flooded by unforgiving light. Tom Wright squinted as the intense, annoying whiteness engulfed him. Her face became just a silvery glow.

"As for being stubborn, it's another survival instinct. You always have to contradict people, surprise them, stay quick on your feet. You exercise power when you force others to guess what you're going to do, then do the opposite. Don't you agree?"

"Very clever. Is that why you opened the blinds?"

"Maybe. But it's not cleverness. It's a sixth sense that you have, as if you had invisible antennas to help you anticipate everyone else's moves and be always a step ahead of them. It's just human nature."

"Or women's nature?"

"Maybe."

"You always had that philosophical touch."

"And you were always a hardheaded hunk. My mother used to call *Gringos* like you unsalted potatoes. You all eat your food without salt, without salsa, without chile...you have no spice in your lives, literally or metaphorically speaking. You're so boring that you're more interested in healthy food than tasty gourmet food. And speaking of chiles..."

"So, did we meet here this morning just to discuss the cultural shortcomings of my people?"

"To begin with, no, because they're not shortcomings but chasms, and I hope that you all keep your distance because it must be sad to become a vegetarian and eat without chile or salt. At any rate, we don't have to worry about our health here because no one dies of natural causes. And besides, if I bothered to look for you this morning, my dear, it was just to tell you that, when you pay the ransom, the EGP's going to try to kidnap you."

"Is that what you're afraid of? Or do you know for sure?"

"One should only fear the fakes who, when they try to take their masks off, find out they're stuck to their faces. Of course I know it for a fact. I'm a member of the EGP."

Tom Wright jumped back against the wall in an odd gesture of contained panic as if he were trying to cover his back.

"See? That's what I mean by unsalted potatoes. You believe anything anyone tells you, then panic before you think. Maybe I'm not certain they're going to kidnap you, my dear."

He had never seen her so alert, with all her intelligence suddenly displayed in her eyes.

"OK. Are you in the EGP or not?"

"Maybe, maybe not. That's a secret I'll take to my grave."

"Whatever you say, my dear Watson. So then, what do we have to do? What should I do? What do you recommend that I do?"

"I would go with Pacal and his people, so that, together, you can try to screw them when they try to screw you. We're talking about screwing, aren't we?"

"Yeah, right. In the first place, if you *are* in the EGP, you're a traitor for advising me to capture your own people. Unless this is a trap you're setting for me. And in the second, it's simply ludicrous. Do you think that if they see me coming with a thousand uniformed soldiers, they'll stay still as sparrows waiting for me to grab them? Please! Your instincts leave a lot to be desired, my dear."

"You think so?"

"You don't?"

"Go figure."

They stood facing each other. Sandra smiled slightly. He looked at her mouth, her eyes, her hair. He had a bewildered feeling in his gut. Part of it was fear. There was the thrill of action, but there was more as well. She parted her lips slightly, allowing the tip of her tongue to escape a bit between them. Raising her eyebrows, she came closer. He didn't move.

Smiling ever so slightly, barely letting the white tips of her teeth show behind her lips, she came even closer.

"*My* instincts leave a lot to be desired?"

She came closer still. He backed up against the wall, as if he were blotter paper. She continued to advance. He leaned forward and gave her a light kiss on the lips. She immediately moved back a couple of steps. Slowly and thoughtfully, she put out her hands to him. Their fingers locked and squeezed hard. Then, she pulled them away.

"Are you still unsure, love?"

She headed for the bed. Sitting down on it, she tossed her hair back once more, crossed one leg over the other and leaned back, supporting herself on one elbow. Suddenly, the daylight became more intense. Tom Wright, plastered against the wall as if he were just a figure in a vulgar hotel painting, sighed and took a couple of timid steps in her direction. He stopped halfway as if he were still uncertain, or his feet weighed a ton. She then tilted her head and allowed her hair to fall back onto the bedspread, brushing it from one side to the other as if it were too heavy and she needed to relax her neck. At just the same time, she lifted her legs even more. She was now lit as if spotlights were focused on her entire body. He said, "You weren't like that in college." His voice had weakened. It seemed to barely hang from a thread, the dying whisper of a drowning man.

"College was 15 years ago. Besides, for you it was like that. For me it wasn't. But in those days you didn't care about equality. You were like a feudal lord protecting me from what you assumed everyone else's glances were saying."

Her voice purred. Tom Wright sat at the edge of the bed with both his legs together like a woman in a miniskirt. He reached out with his arm and barely touched her legs with the tips of his cold fingers in a gesture that seemed overly clumsy from lack of practice. She didn't move.

"You've changed."

"You, too, Tom. You used to feel me up much faster."

He felt as if he'd been suddenly shocked and immediately pulled his hand away. Looking at the palms of his hands, he stood up in a muddle, terrified, recognizing her power for the first time.

"Don't tell me that the old fire that made you jump every woman on sight has gone out already?"

She then stood up and, without taking her eyes off of him, hugged him and put his head on her shoulder, rocking him sweetly to scare off the few remaining fragments of irresolution. With the same sweet and paralyzing gesture, she squeezed his arms, compressing his ribs gently until he felt that he had lost his breath, trembling submissively, weak, as if abandoned in the middle of a burning desert. The light in the room had gone out, and he was being crushed by rose-colored tentacles.

CHAPTER FIVE

1

The pine table was the neurological center of the urban front's directorate. The vortex of activities taking place every day in the city were planned there. All of them were rigorously compartmentalized. Only Kukulkán and Vallejo participated in all decisions, glued to the table, sorting a myriad of papers. Not even Ariadne was allowed to do it, though everybody knew she was capable. If something ever happened to either one of them, she would take his place, even if the Commander-in-Chief didn't approve.

"That son of a bitch, the only reason he wants women in this organization is to serve him his coffee nice and hot while he's thinking. Or to get rid of his hangover. When they turn out to be tough like the *Bruja*, he leaves them, even if they are the mothers of his children and the godfather of his eldest happens to be Che. He can't deal with ballsy women."

Aware that sooner or later she was going to be the first woman to reach such a high rank, Ariadne balanced her behavior between a tried-and-true toughness and a flattering, accommodating posture that bothered even her, but that was something she couldn't help, her face always wearing a brilliant look of false innocence.

Every time he sat down at the table, Vallejo placed himself in front of the poster with his own face. The eyes in the picture jumping out in his direction reaffirmed the distance traveled since his years in school, dedicated to pursuing rich girls like Carmencita Fischer, swimming and swimming in his pool until he almost became a national crawl and butterfly champion, and organizing excursions to the Agua and Pacaya volcanoes for his Liceo Javier classmates. He did a lot of that. He remembered his crazy years in Paris a little before '68, where, for the first time, he met people from the EGP and thousands of organizations from all parts of the world: Basques, Palestinians, Eritreans, Irish, Uruguayan *Tupamaros*, Argentinian *Montoneros*, and the thousand variations of Marxism and Marxism-Leninism that have ever existed. It was the period of his "Trotskyite" phase, of the unending discussions over the "Document of March 1967," written by the now Commander-in-Chief. Those were the days when he would drink with Roque Dalton, arguing with him about whether or not *Bola de Nieve* had a better voice than Benny Moré, discovering Elena Burque's passionate bolero singing, and when, after several hits of opiated hash, he would swear that salsa was more important than Beethoven. He recalled that insomnia would always hit him in the early morning hours, when he was utterly alone in his Parisian hole-in-the-wall after drinking several bottles of cheap wine, and he'd get up to scrawl lousy, sentimental poems to erase the biting nostalgia for the girl who had abandoned him.

"Don't look at me with that face; I haven't said shit against the weaker sex! Oh, fuck, that hurts! Don't punch me in the arm!"

After that he returned, but this time to organize hiking groups that little by little did more than just climb mountains, gradually getting more and more involved in the movement. Now he was there, in front of his own image, seeing his other eyes looking back at him, re-imagining him, but also looking up as if contemplating the blue mountains appearing unfailingly on the horizon. "*Oh, azules altos montes*," as Juan Diéguez Olaverri put it in his famous poem. The important thing was never to stop laughing at yourself.

Ariadne watched him carefully. His intensity was what

made him attractive. The enormity of that ample forehead on which were drawn a thousand thoughts flowing simultaneously along its length and width with a direct connection to his mouth, which mumbled incessantly about the transformation of the planet from a bipolar world to a globalized one, about the implications of a new international economic order for Central America, or about the need to outline a program to give a more partisan aspect to an organization that was still no more than a wide and heterogeneous movement.

"I punch you because you drive me nuts, and you're foulmouthed to boot."

Ariadne was also from the capital, but she was middle class. She had no swimming pools or trips to Paris. She did study in a parochial school, and lucked out there. The nuns became radicalized, and she got caught up in it all. If it weren't for that, she would be some boring man's housewife, knitting and attending tea parties or baby showers most afternoons. The irony was that now she was doing that anyway. It was one of her jobs, so she could find out what those young wives married to the up-and-coming executives who presently controlled the Chamber of Commerce and Industry were thinking. She detested it, it bothered her, but she was conscious of the valuable information she was able to pick up. By simply gossiping and trying to impress their friends, all those ladies loosened their tongues and always said more than they should. That's how she had gotten wind of Gray.

Kukulkán came in last. By then Vallejo was finishing his first cup of coffee and lighting his second cigarette.

"Too much smoke in here, *Compañeros.*"

"Ha, who are you to talk? What about your pipe?"

"Well, my pipe isn't as bad for your health as that shit that you smoke. They're not even real cigarettes."

"You're just dying of envy, asshole. This is the last pack of Gauloises that 'The Lizard' brought me."

"Oh, I see. By the way, what ever happened to 'The Lizard'?"

"He's off in Mexico interviewing Angel Face, but he published our communique in *Le Monde Diplomatique*. The idiot cut out a couple of paragraphs, but it turned out all right."

"In Spanish?"

"And in French, too, what do you think about that? It's not as if I were...."

"Well, keep talking it up. And let's get to the meeting, because I have to make a contact in...less than an hour."

"Well, get going. It's not like anyone's stopping you."

"Shh. Shut up, both of you. Men are impossible. Get serious and let Kukulkán speak."

"Are you going to take notes?"

"My sad destiny as a woman. I don't even want to talk about it with you two macho men. Just go on. Let's start."

"OK. I spoke this morning with Harlequin. They're going to pay. The contact has already been arranged. The *Gringo* is going in person."

Ariadne lifted her eyes from the paper.

"Are you also planning to go in person?"

Kukulkán made an affirmative movement with his head and took a big gulp of coffee.

"OK, this is the code. When we speak on the phone we should talk about it as if he were buying, and we were selling, Maya textiles."

"Answer me directly, please."

"You know I have to go."

Vallejo cleared his throat and joined the conversation with an air of deliberate calmness.

"Ariadne is right, *Comandante*. We said before that they're going to try to grab whoever makes contact with them."

"That's what they want. That's why I have to go. Harlequin..."

"Who's in charge of this organization, Harlequin or you?"

Kukulkán sat stunned by the unacceptable tone of Ariadne's reproach.

"That's enough, *Compañera*. I recognize the risk, but I know what I'm doing. We didn't get involved in all of this to chicken out and avoid risks at all costs. We have to be daring when we plan our operations, yet execute them with a high degree of prudence. Let's move on now. Back to the code, '*huipil*' means ransom."

"In past years, this organization was run by two men, a sophisticated intellectual and a risk-taker. Now these traits have been blended into one single individual, but the result has not been a synthesis but a short circuit of sorts."

"That's enough! I don't want to hear another word on this matter!"

"When a decision is made, I obey. But in the meantime I have a voice to express my thoughts and opinions. And I don't like you to scold me as if you were my father. If I said what I said, it's because you didn't pay attention to what Vallejo or I said, and it's a real concern, not just something we're emotional about."

"Calm down you two, time's ticking. Say it clearly, Kukulkán. Why do you think that you have to be the one to go?"

"Because I'm the bait that will make the mouse fall into the trap."

"But the *Gringo* can also be the bait that will make you fall into theirs. Didn't you talk openly with Harlequin about that?"

"Certainly. That's the way this business works. There always comes a time when you're face to face with the enemy, and both parties have to risk it. Like a bluff in poker. This is one of those moments. That's why we're going to plan with extreme prudence. But we're still going to take calculated risks. Got it? Now let's leave Harlequin out of it and study the situation."

He was no longer speaking with that annoyingly calm, somewhat metallic voice infused with a touch of diplomatic gravity that he used when pondering an adequate reply, but rather with a light, lilting one. Still, he did not lose his slightly military attitude, typical of one used to giving orders.

"I hope the bluff works because, if we lose this bet, we're screwed."

"Better yet, the three of us should go. We can't leave the *Comandante*'s safety in someone else's hands. We'll make like the three musketeers."

2

The hotel room had lost its luminosity because it was noon. The sun's rays no longer came in diagonally through the window. Sandra was lightly covered by the fine cotton sheets, her body's perfection acquiring a new clarity under their whiteness. Her jet-black hair sprawled across the pillow contrasted markedly with the bedspread's virginal timidity. It was like the satisfied head of the Medusa, convinced of her power to dazzle her timid Perseus.

Their savage and exultant kisses had saturated one another's profoundest desires with the violent affirmation that only the proximity of death, or the sensation of loving and resisting at the same time, can give. An embrace charged with desire and nostalgia for an idealized adolescence had brought with it the joy of conquest and submission to a relentless destiny. It had been a confrontation of wills, a duel of wild animals that, utterly worn out by the fight, eventually gave themselves over peacefully to the inevitable without losing an ounce of pride. Later, after dozing briefly in Sandra's arms like a rag doll, Tom Wright suddenly jumped from the bed and ran to the shower. She remained perplexed but beaming.

She called to him from the bed:

"There's a *huapango* song that I like a lot, you know? Or is it a *huasteco* song? It's all the same. It's called *'Cascabel,'* 'Rattlesnake.' Do you want me to sing it to you?"

"If you want."

"Ok, here goes. Pay attention. The words are important."

"It's hard for me to focus on those things."

"Your problem. *Te lo perdés.* Here it goes."

When he came out of the bathroom he already had his shirt and underwear on. She saw he was mumbling under his breath. Still under the spell of their complicity, she asked him in her hoarse voice, her features totally composed:

"What are you saying?"

"Nothing."

"Don't play around. Tell me."

"I had promised to myself that I wasn't going to let this kind of thing happen."

"What kind of thing, dear? You're being very indirect."

"*'Let me not name it to you, you chaste stars!'*"

"Oh my, aren't we literary? Is this perhaps some psychic metamorphosis? Have you turned into the prophet-philosopher who preaches renunciation but speaks with Eros's accent?"

"Oh, Sandra! You knew I had commitments. I'm running late..."

"What's that saying of yours? *'The best laid plans...'*"

"OK, that's enough. Get up quick. *Tengo que irme.*"

"Why don't you just speak to me in English? I hate that Mexican accent dripping out of your mouth like half-eaten taco sauce. Everything in due time, my love. Relax. And remember. I like it nice and slow and delicious and wonderful, none of that fucking and running as if you were from Cobán, *los que sólo comen y se van....*"

"Oh, come on. I'm in a hurry. OK?"

"I recognize that, my dear. What I'm saying is that you could be sweeter, more sensitive, tender....After all it is the first time in fifteen years. Or doesn't that matter to you?"

"*Sí*, Sandra. It counts. Forgive me."

He sat down on the edge of the bed with his pants halfway on, then leaned towards her, placing his hands awkwardly on her shoulders. She sat there looking at him with those clear eyes tranquil like deep water massaging his longing, eating him up with their gaze. She was enjoying the tranquility of one who has plunged into a spontaneous act of love capable of polishing even the rays of the sun, and now she was relaxing drowsily, remembering dreamily an old *bolero*. She gestured with her right arm that he speak in a whisper, so as not to violate the bedroom silence still coolly protecting them from the vibrations of the afternoon heat. He said:

"*Escucha, querida*. I'm not trying to be an idiot or anything. This matters to me. It has always mattered. I have always thought about you."

"Even on your wedding day?"

"Especially on my wedding day."

"Why did you get married?"

"Because I detested loneliness. And it was in my best interest..."

"Not for love."

"No."

"Nor because you loved fucking her."

"Even less."

"You needed someone to stick your food in the microwave for you."

"I needed family, attention, to feel myself recognized."

"You thought about me all those years..."

"I thought about you every day."

"And yet you never wrote me, never sent a postcard, never called..."

"I couldn't, dear."

"Did you want to forget me? Remove me from your life?"

"Maybe to get the obsession out of my head."

"But today you forgot that you had forgotten me?"

"Relax. *Es solo que...*"

"Let's not get melodramatic. Perhaps just the discreet charm of fucking? After all, you've been so busy lately that you haven't had time to sow your wild oats. And your faithful wife will never imagine that her husband could do such a thing, right?"

He stood up as if he had been unfairly reprimanded. He walked in the direction of the window, contemplating the hazy afternoon. With bitterness he remembered in fragments the few nights they had shared in other climates, other worlds, when he was still unaware that happiness evaporates with the speed of a mirage. The moments of peace, he knew now, were brief and left little more than a bitter taste in your mouth. But pride always remained, the self-respect of a white Southerner grotesquely reliving his tragedy of conquered conquerors.

"Well, yes! If your highness is interested in hearing about it, it has been important to me all these years. I thought about you..."

"You never wrote."

"*Mierda*! Men never write letters."

"Oscar Wilde wrote letters."

"Oscar Wilde was gay!"

"All writers write letters."

"All writers are gay."

"Hemingway was gay? Faulkner? You used to like Dylan Thomas in college. He wasn't gay. One time you repeated from memory some lines from..."

"They were drunks! Deep down it's the same thing! They're weak! And after a few drinks they become sentimental, nostalgic, and they write rhapsodies in bad taste...."

"You used to like drunken poets. You're just like them. You get sentimental, too, after a few drinks. You even write when you're fucked up. One time I caught you, but you tore the papers from my hand and hid them quickly."

"*Chingar*, Sandra. I don't drink so much."

"You drink. You did already when we were in college."

"*Mierda*, I was just a kid. A boy."

"You still are."

"That's not true! Now I'm..."

"A CIA agent. It's the same thing. Besides, you're all eternal children. You never grow up, like Peter Pan."

"Fuck! That's enough! Enough!"

He turned and walked back to the bed. The room, whose clarity and cleanliness were his only refuge from the threatening, stinking city, had suddenly become more terrifying and scathing than those noisily narrow streets full of puddles with rotten weeds, than those men with confused looks, dark, ugly, short, with curly hair smelling like rotten fruit. He stood in front of her. His body trembled as if he were about to suffer an epileptic seizure. Almost crashing into her, he grabbed the end of the sheet and violently pulled it to his feet as he hysterically yelled out:

"*Vístete*! Right now! I have to go!"

Sandra's eyes opened wide. Her heart raced. It was a wild horse jumping into her throat, biting her, and she exploded with bitter bile as if punctured with a Maya sacrificial knife. In one single gesture she jumped from the bed as a raspy scream emerged from her throat. She spit in his eyes and bit his hand with her teeth. She grabbed the sheet from him and wrapped it around her body as she bombarded him with shouts.

"*Imbécil*! The hell with you! This is what pushed me away from you, mister asshole! You think you're a big shot because you've seen James Bond movies and you're a real Anglo, a real redneck, but you're nothing more than a poor devil, a cheap cog in a machine that you don't control or understand, poor bastard! *Comemierda*!"

He backed up against the wall, casually rubbing his hand

after cleaning his eyes. He felt his blood coursing through him and a throbbing in his temples as if someone were whipping him, as if he were trapped in a bubble.

"Fuck you, Sandra. You married a rich macho man, a He-rre-ra. Don't talk shit to me now."

"You guys are such assholes that you have no clue what happens here or why we do what we do! You think we still take *siestas* under big *sombreros* and live in trees! Meanwhile we stick our fingers up your asses, and you don't even realize it."

Her cascade of words fell on him like blows, one after another. She felt her anger drown after her last remark. Jumping up swiftly, she ran to the bathroom. He stood where he was, flabbergasted, until she turned on the shower, and the steam gradually invaded the room. As if he were learning to walk all over again, he moved to pick up the rest of his clothes, but his numb hands and legs began to shake. He had to sit back down on the bed. His clothes were sticking to his body, still wet from his shower, the cold sweat of tension, and the steam that ruthlessly invaded the room.

"Fuck you Latins. Fuck this country. And fuck you."

He was still tying his Rockport shoes, the widest ones (she once said, more than 15 years ago, that they looked like *tamales* spread on a banana leaf), when Sandra reappeared like a mirage from amidst the steam, her wet hair hanging over her shoulders. He felt a shock in the creases of his will power. She gazed at him and said, without the slightest aggression:

"As far as fucking, you also leave a lot to be desired."

In an instant she disappeared again in the bathroom steam as if she had been little more than a fleeting illusion. He couldn't resist a retort:.

"You didn't even know the difference at Tulane. I guess that this torpid climate wets all kinds of appetites, which you've undoubtedly satisfied in myriad ways by now. That Catholic upbringing you used to avoid fucking with me back then is obviously a thing of the past. Your poor husband must be a cuckold a million times over, but at least you can still enjoy his big, thick bank account."

"The truth is that I learned all these variations from your sister. I'm not sure you know everything she taught me. And besides, let me tell you, asshole, that at this point in my life they don't fuck me anymore. I fuck them. Who I want and when I want. Me!"

When she returned from the bathroom she was completely dressed. There was no hairdryer, so her damp hair hung over her shoulders, leaving a dark stain where it rested against her blouse. She stood before him, wrapped in a long silence of benevolent melancholy, shaking her head sadly.

"I'm so glad I left you. It was the best thing I could have done."

Those words once again wounded his pride. As exhausted as he was, he tried to raise his hand without deciding if it was a threat or an honest attempt at striking her, but she never wavered. Raising her left arm to block his possible blow, she landed a tremendous slap on his face with the other hand. Its echo had not yet faded when the door slammed, leaving him trembling with a rage he couldn't understand or control.

Once out of the room, Sandra stumbled to the elevator, moaning uncontrollably and struggling to regain control. She visualized a scene from her childhood. She had arrived home in a similar state after a terrible fight with her best friend. Her father, who was generally too absorbed in his work to pay much attention to her, was so shocked by her condition that he momentarily abandoned his bottled reptiles to hug her and whispered sweetly in her ear, "Don't cry, my little flower. Deep bitterness is venom to the heart."

She was still breathing raggedly, as if an invisible hand were squeezing her lungs. She was leaning against the elevator door when it opened. She stumbled into the void, feeling a sense of vertigo. She managed to land on her knees, keeping her balance by placing her hands on the back wall.

The doors closed, and the elevator suddenly began to ascend, which knocked her down completely. She would have been discovered in this humiliating position when the doors opened two stories up, but, luckily, there was no one there. She was just beginning to get on her feet when the doors closed again and the elevator began to plunge, knocking her to the floor. When she finally made it to the first floor, she was still fighting to regain her composure. A sharp pain pierced her temples like a drill.

Trying to keep all the control her frazzled nerves allowed her, she walked out, searching desperately for the public phone. She ran to it like a thirsty animal and dialed a number. Her fingers had barely finished dialing when she heard the busy signal.

"Shit!"

She dialed angrily over and over again until she finally got through.

"Hello? Is Captain Pacal in? Thanks...Captain? The big rat ate the cheese....Yes....I have to go. Goodbye."

She hung up and began to walk away distractedly. The people in the lobby and the hotel stores went by her like a fog. She punched one of the columns with her hand to recover her sense of self. Breathing deeply, she glanced at her watch. After verifying the time, she returned to the public phone. It gave her a headache just to think about calling again. Even Mexico had public telephones everywhere. The phone was still free, but there was a man standing next to it. The brutal reality that there was only one phone in the best hotel in the country made her feel small. To her relief, the man suddenly walked away. She moved quickly to the phone and visualized the page in her notebook where she had written the phone number in code. She made an effort to remember each cipher, then dialed. The call didn't go through. She tried again. She was lucky. On the second try, she got a connection.

"Hello? Is the handicraft salesman there? Let me speak to him please...Hello? Yes. I just wanted to let you know that the snake is approaching, shaking its rattles. Yes. At the moment, everything is going as planned. Be careful with Pacal....Goodbye."

She put the phone in its place and walked in the direction of the hotel door, looking for her bodyguards all the while.

3

Don Leonel's house looked like a bustling ant colony. All around the place, armed men swarmed with metal flashing, as if they were about to be attacked by a ghost army of thousands. The Minister of Defense was visiting. The Minister detested conceited old men like Don Leonel, who scolded as if there were no tomorrow, but he had to work with them. He might no longer be a servant to the rich, but he was still their partner. For the moment.

The Minister was seated on the sofa in the living room, allowing his abundant flesh to expand until it occupied every possible crevice. In front of him, Don Leonel and Alvaro looked diminished. The Minister had already begun to treat the wrinkled, dry man more like a child than a figure worthy of respect, and Alvaro, as a real child, even though he was married and had important responsibilities. He was married, in fact, to a gorgeous woman.

"It's a great pleasure to have you here, Minister. You must know, that, although I have complete confidence in you, I've heard rumors, and I'm dying to ask you about them."

"I thought as much, Don Leonel. I wasn't going to bother you with these details. You know me. We've spent all our time making plans for the future, and it finally seems that they're no longer idle dreams. Operation Rattlesnake has begun."

Alvaro's eyes widened when he heard the name.

"Rattlesnake! I didn't know that..."

"It was confidential, but now you have to know because it's underway at this very moment."

Alvaro turned to see his father's reaction. Don Leonel seemed to become rejuvenated with the news. He readjusted himself in the chair, sitting on the edge and leaning closer to the Minister. He didn't want to miss a single word. Moving closer to Don Leonel and ignoring Alvaro completely, the Minister continued:

"My agent called not long ago, and I came here right away. At this very moment, let's see what time it is, our man is en route to his contact. It seems that they succeeded in delaying him, as we wanted. Now he'll have to use the reserve contact and meet him after dark. The rest is under control."

Don Leonel rubbed his hands in juicy anticipation.

"I'm drooling like an old fart. Forgive me. I know it's not very elegant. But after feeling like I spent my entire youth fighting ghosts, I find it touching in my old age, not just to recall those youthful first steps, but to enjoy this moment, with the country in such turmoil. The dead can't be brought back, but, even if it sounds pompous, I'm savoring the triumphal moment that will give meaning to all our suffering. What remains to be done?"

"We're just waiting for the State Department to respond. We have everything laid out, but we have to abide by the answer of..."

Alvaro felt that they were speaking in a code that he did not understand. Shyly, he ventured to ask:

"To be honest, someone should explain to me what's going on."

"Oh, shut up! In due time..."

"No. It's okay, Don Leonel. Because now we're going to need Alvarito. Look. We hope that when the EGP kidnaps the CIA agent, the State Department will react harshly and commit itself to eliminating subversion in this country."

"But I thought it was in our best interest not to destroy the EGP..."

"Shut up!"

"Easy, Don Leonel. And you, Alvarito, don't worry. This isn't El Salvador. *We* decide....The Americans are going to have no other choice but to support us because they're already fucked."

"Great! And, thanks for your confidence. But tell me, Minister; are your contacts with them reliable?"

"More than you can possibly imagine, Alvarito. Much more. You wouldn't even believe it if you knew."

The Minister flashed a sharp and malicious smile that forced him to close his eyes, given the flabbiness of his red face, while he tapped the floor with his boot.

"You remind me of someone, Minister, but I can't quite place it. As soon as I think of it I'll tell you."

Outside, the incandescent afternoon sun of a day that threatened rain but would not finally release it, weakened everything around it like a subtle attack of the flu that diminished reason and created bubbles in the mind, lassitude in the muscles and slowness in gestures and movements. Flesh rotted in the sultry air that did not ventilate, but rather suffocated more, and blood evaporated agonizingly before the blinding white brilliance bouncing from house to house, calcining all colors, and glancing off vehicles like an infinity of rays converging their pointed lances on squinting pupils, leaving them blinded from such luminosity.

Part Two

A Spiral Around an Invisible Axis

CHAPTER ONE

1

Evening was falling gracefully on the city. Around the volcanoes, the sky's many-hued clouds played with the possibility of refreshing their surroundings before disappearing without a trace, lighting up the mountainous profile of the valley. As the sun disappeared, the air cooled down and, perfumed by the pines and eucalyptus trees, left a scent whose over-rich sweetness evoked sleepy memories of sentimental feelings covered by a slight coat of dust and accompanied by the rhythms of boleros with vaguely-remembered lyrics. Tom Wright didn't have time to appreciate the brilliant beauty of sunset. He was stunned by the apprehensiveness that the volcanoes' shaded darkness generated in his entrails. Darkness. Loss of visibility. Danger. He alone was to blame. His temples were still throbbing, even after his four Tylenols.

Pacal was waiting for him by the car. It was the first time he had seen him in civilian clothes. He was wearing a huge suit, which wrinkled way too much as it draped over his body. His tie was exaggeratedly wide. As much as he tried to project an image of elegance, it was evident that he was uncomfortable sporting a style that he didn't normally wear. Anyone who saw him could tell he was a cop from a block away.

Frustrated, Wright thought everything was turning out wrong. Perhaps he should find a good excuse to cancel the contact. Without saying a word, he slid into the back seat of the car. Unconsciously, his eyes stared at the sticker that seemed to bear down on him. The triangular serpent's head, the red circle, the writing in black letters. Pacal nimbly jumped in next to him, and the vehicle took off. It headed for Roosevelt Avenue and the road to Antigua.

They sat next to each other without saying a word. Outside, they passed, like a mere projection of unreal images, pedestrians, buses spitting out enormous quantities of black smoke, newspaper hawkers, gum and flower vendors, fire eaters, copper-colored faces with forced smiles of pure courtesy or hypocrisy, cars of all shapes and colors honking in unison, the pale yellow street lights threatening to come on slowly as night fell. He even thought he saw at a distance putrefied puddles in the shape of pentagons, and he heard human cries that scratched at the brownish air like nails screeching on a blackboard,

Inside the car there was a semblance of calm. Wright felt a desperate need for a double Scotch. His mouth was as dry as a squeezed lemon. The tip of his tongue was asleep. His hands—again—were lightly trembling. The pain in his neck was terrible. He would have loved a neck massage almost as much as a drink. He couldn't think straight and his headache wouldn't go away. When he tried to look outside, his eyes ran into those black letters: "Only those who win..." He closed his eyes.

"Are you all right?"

"It's just a headache. Everything in order?"

"Couldn't be better," Pacal answered. He kissed his thumb and index finger to dramatize his pleasure. "Other than missing the first contact, of course. But the backup's better."

"No, it's not!" His own violent tone shocked him, as if he had split in two, and were observing himself vent his bottled-up anger. "The contact will be at night. Don't you see? Anything can happen. The visibility will be much less, especially with this public lighting of yours. What are you trying to do, save money by using 25-watt bulbs in the light posts? I just can't forgive myself for letting this happen. Shit!"

Pacal gave a childish smile that contracted his face and punched him lightly on the arm.

"Relax, man. My people will execute everything perfectly, you'll see. Besides, I've always preferred backup contacts. They fray the enemy's nerves. And we come in more relaxed because we've gotten over our initial fears. Besides, you responded like a man with her this morning. You have nothing to worry about. I envy you. I would've liked to have been in your shoes."

Wright turned violently. "Do you know everything, Pacal?"

"That's our job, sir."

"Just so you know, I don't like it. I don't like your manner. I don't like that you know what you know...."

He exhaled deeply as if he were suddenly deflating, and gazed intently at the faded markings of the road.

"Your attitude's reasonable. I would think the same way in your place. It's the only way to survive. Trusting no one. Who knows, I might even pull the rug from under your feet, huh?"

He leaned back, sinking into the seat and tilting his neck back to let his characteristic laugh come out like an erupting geyser. The saliva arched up to the roof of the car. Wright sensed the acidic smell emanating from Pacal's pores. He thought he was probably imagining it. But he wasn't. It was really and truly emanating from Pacal's flesh. It wasn't intense enough to make the atmosphere in the car unbearable, but it was strong enough to let you know it was there. It wrenched his gut even more because he recognized it immediately as the smell of death.

2

All the houses in that middle-class neighborhood of the city were squat and square but not identical. They had been built with only two or three variations in such a way that their similarity overpowered the different colors and the elaborate diversity of their garden ornaments. On some, the garage columns had been left plain, while others were covered with ivy or some other type of climbing plant. Some had hanging plants and others didn't. Some had ivy covering the chain link fence; others had high concrete fences that kept people from seeing inside. All of them were small. They looked too close together and stiff, like when someone wears clothes that have become too small for them. The tiny gardens were overflowing with ornaments, flamingos, altars with plaster virgins, or giant cement mushrooms, swings and teeter-totters. They all had flat concrete terraces filled with every possible kind of antenna. Some had peeling white paint and were gradually becoming covered with mildew, while others had been recently whitewashed.

Out of a garage with thick columns and a metal door, came a red and white Ford Bronco with tinted windows. It backed up slowly, blocking the narrow street. The driver ran to close the open gate as quickly as possible. He came rushing back to the vehicle and took off. Once they were out of the neighborhood, three figures emerged from the floor of the car, where they had been hiding in case someone noticed the car's movements. They were Kukulkán, Vallejo and Ariadne. She wore a blonde wig and a light brown blouse, dark brown wool skirt, stockings and low-heeled, elegant shoes. Kukulkán looked uncomfortable in his suit and tie. He had a thick black mustache stuck to his upper lip. Vallejo was a lot more relaxed in his own suit, but he looked like Dennis the Menace with his red wig.

"They call me the black man from Batey..."

"Shh. Don't sing off-key like that."

"Much less a song that promotes laziness."

"Oh, man!"

The vehicle turned in the direction of the road for Antigua. Slightly before the exit, where a long line of motels begins, it turned onto a small street and stopped for an instant. The driver got out. Vallejo moved into the driver's seat. Once the three of them were alone, they returned to the highway and continued on their way, followed at a certain distance by another vehicle. Kukulkán slowly loosened his tie so he could breathe easier.

"Okay, then. The moment of truth has arrived."

"Holy shit, don't make the situation more melodramatic than it already is 'cause I'll start crying and screw up the whole thing."

"You'll get it all wet."

Ariadne turned around. With a tone aimed at humor that instead came out charged with tension, she replied: "Enjoy the sunset. It might be your last one."

"I try to enjoy it every day. Because I think that every day could be the last one. I also enjoy tying my shoes and buttoning my shirt. It could always be the last time. That's why I carry Neruda's *Elemental Odes* with me."

"Now your poetic side comes out, man."

"It had to be you saying it, the disrespectful Vallejo."

"Wouldn't you like to be able to write something like 'farewell, farewell, lonely souls of the dead moon, lofty questions of the sea light, farewell, until I lose in space what accompanied me on the journey, the light...' what else?"

"Shit, now you're going to come up with something like 'a gust of wheat and poppies.' I prefer Roque, and just so you see that I know poetry, hear me out: 'Those who filled the bars and bordellos in all the ports and capitals of the zone, The Blue Grotto, El Calzoncito, Happyland, the kings of the red page, those who were sown with bullets when they crossed the border, those who cried drunk for the national anthem under the northern snow, the forgotten, the beggars, the potheads, the *Guanacos* sons of bitches, the eternally undocumented, the handymen, the vendors, the hungry, those who draw first blood, the world's saddest, my compatriots, my brothers." Ha! What do you think of that?"

"It's as vulgar as you are. Kukulkán has better taste. Besides as long as we're talking about Central Americans, why not Otto René? He's one of ours and 'Let's Go, Country, for a Walk' could almost be another national anthem."

"Hell, Otto René is too solemn. You read him and it almost makes you want to cry. Life is too fucked up to start crying about poetry, too. That shit's too corny. That's why I only like Otto René's love poems. That whole section of, 'The Private Also Matters'—those are kick-ass poems that touch you without making you feel you have to stand up and salute the flag."

"Of the EGP."

"You like those poems because they were written for girls like you, fresh out of psychology school, all sentimental, so you'll read them and cry your eyes out and then join the movement so when we win..."

"We can organize Red Sundays."

"Or plant little trees while we figure out what the fuck we're going to do with this shithole country that won't straighten out even if you beat it to death."

"Vallejo, you're not just bad mannered, you're annoying. Say something, Kukulkán, don't let him talk to me that way. And then they complain when we want to create a women's organization..."

"Calm down, both of you. There's San Lucas."

"Calmly is how we're going to get it from them. Don't forget to say 'thank you' when you feel it from behind."

The vehicle took the turn to Antigua. The car that was following them continued straight on to Chimaltenango. A gray Toyota parked in front of the food stands in San Lucas took off when it saw the cars pass by, and hurried to follow them.

"You're intolerably vulgar, Vallejo."

"Just so you know, I can even recite English texts from memory. Listen: "Yet she must die, else she'll betray more men.""

"He's insulting your sister, Kukulkán. Don't let him. That's why I prefer older men. They're not as vulgar."

"How boring, older men don't have what it takes. It's better with balls, baby, so don't say that. Why even do it?"

"Stop him Kukulkán, I can't take it anymore," she said, shaking her head in mock anger, trying hard not to laugh.

The evening had shown signs of rain, but none came. The clouds adopted an evenly spaced, bright orange formation, like cotton balls soaked in iodine, floating across the tips of those dark-hued volcanoes, a long chain of timeless red love barely showing a thin silhouette as the sun went down further into the Pacific.

Like moving black crosses, the rambling wings of birds flapping to get to countless tree tops to nest at nightfall hovered around them, submerging the restless environment in a deadly darkness that felt like a quick burning sensation on tender skin, lightly coated by the cinnamon sweetness of the emerging moon.

3

The hotel looked like a modern building with colonial artifacts. The entry-way was a narrow corridor full of 17th and 18th century decorations, dark walnut saints and iron chandeliers, pots with climbing ivy, and carpeting with rococo designs that created an artificially baroque environment highlighted by the absurd kumquat orange color on the walls. All the window rails on the outside and the inside were made of thick wood carved in spiral shapes that looked like stylized serpents slithering down the columns. The reception desk was on the right side. Further inside was the lobby. The dining room was right across from it, across the corridor. In the back was a large garden with a bright kidney-shaped swimming pool in the middle.

The furniture in the lobby was colonial style, made of wood, and a lot plainer than the rest of the decorations. There was a lot of movement going on. Primarily Americans and Europeans, young couples, and others not so young, were coming in and out slowly, already adjusted to the leisurely pace of the stone-paved city. Some wore shorts in spite of the slightly cold air. There were also a respectable number of local guests. Most of them were scattered around the lobby, reading the paper, having a drink at the bar, or just contemplating the sundown with a hint of silent yearning.

A Ford Bronco with tinted windows stopped at the front door. The valet took an eternity to walk out and open the door. The businessmen and the young woman got out and walked in naturally. They patiently let the hotel employees carry out all their appointed tasks, such as returning their car keys and bringing in the luggage. They took pictures of the Agua volcano with the red sky in the background, enjoying the colors on the horizon. As soon as they came into the corridor, the manager glanced up to scrutinize them. After looking them over, he greeted them politely and inquired how he could help them in a suave, professional voice.

"We have reservations under Itzam-Na Exports."

The manager used his index finger to look up the name on a typed list. His wrinkled forehead relaxed, and his face lit up as soon as he found it.

"Here it is. Suite 25. Have a pleasant stay."

He took a key from the rack where all of them were hanging in perfect symmetry and gave the newly-arrived guests a form to fill out. With a clap of his hands, he called the bellboy. While Kukulkán filled out the form, Vallejo and

Ariadne wandered discreetly into the lobby, carefully studying each of the objects that had been previously labeled in the report and blueprints they had been given. They looked for any changes that might had been made in the configuration of the furniture, chairs or sofas moved around or placed in such a way that they might block emergency exits, thus impeding a possible escape. They even paid attention to all the decorations. Noting the high number of employees, they tried to guess who might be an agent and who wasn't. At a glance, Vallejo recognized a couple of their own people passing for tourists on their second honeymoon. He looked discreetly at the time and couldn't help smiling when he confirmed that they had missed their first contact. In case anything went wrong, it would be better to try to escape in the dark.

The car that carried Wright and Pacal arrived a few minutes later. They both jumped out of it, surprising the valet, who didn't have time to respond before the car disappeared around the corner, driven away by its small, secretive chauffeur. Wright and Pacal quickly walked in. They were moving at the same speed in spite of the Captain's deformed foot, which created a funny impression, as if his whole body were shaking at once. In the corridor, Wright walked away from Pacal as soon as he could. He wanted to check all the details himself: windows, doors, people at the hotel, the employees' mood, and the places where they were stationed. Automatically he drew a map in his head to better visualize his movements in case of an emergency.

"I'll take care of the forms, Wright. If you want, go ahead to the restaurant."

It was obvious that the enormous garden created potential problems. It had dark places everywhere, and a lot of ghostly bushes. The adjacent buildings were surrounded by tall trees from which platforms for macaws were hanging. Cursing his weakness with Sandra, he hurried to study the place carefully before darkness covered it completely. He breathed deeply as he fell into the familiar and precise routine that he always followed right before a major operative. On his way back from the garden he was stopped by Pacal, who was standing on one of the steps leading inside, making him look taller for once. The weak light that bathed him made his deep scars look much bigger and more grotesque than they really were.

"All set. I told them that, if you wanted, you would go ahead to the restaurant."

"Do you want me to stay there the whole time?"

A slightly colder wind descended from the volcano with a pitiful howling. Wright winked his eye and smiled.

"And don't forget the sign. Someone will be carrying a rolled up *Time* magazine in his left hand and a carnation on his lapel."

"Rolled up, showing the cover on the outside. You think I'm a rookie. You're the one who should be taking notes, young man."

Wright headed for the restaurant. As soon as he was out of Pacal's sight, he turned and went directly for the wall that faced the garden. He checked the windows and curtains, and went over all the possibilities in his head. He looked at his watch nonstop. Instinctively he felt under his coat to make sure his gun was still there.

Wright went out again, looking at the lobby all the time. It made him laugh to see the local guests. Just like Pacal's suit, there were dead giveaways that most of them were cops. Or maybe they were EGP agents? Anything was possible at this point.

He returned to the garden. This time he started by examining the outside walls. He was checking the plant bed right outside the windows, when he saw, at the corner where the building ended and the service rooms began, two armed men speaking into walkie-talkies. He left the place without their seeing him and went back inside. He walked the entire length of the long corridor that led to the main entrance and looked out. He sensed some unusual movement. A Jeep

Cherokee Chief with no license plates and tinted windows was driving by, slowly. On two street corners—the one with the colonial ruins of a church and the one with a store selling art objects and Maya weavings—he noticed more armed men, again with walkie-talkies. The same thing was happening on the following block, where the hotel parking lot was located. The side streets were filled with gawkers, or people who might not be accidental onlookers at all. He went back to the garden. The moon was beginning to make its presence felt, and the tall trees seemed to be gesturing, as if agitated by all the commotion and shaken by the breeze descending from the mountain after sunset. The two men were still standing on the corner where Wright had left them. At that moment he heard the walkie-talkie make some noise. One of the men replied:

"The subject has not appeared. Over."

There was more noise. The man turned off the radio.

"That's strange. He says he should be sitting there already."

He turned his walkie-talkie back on and talked again.

"Blue triangle, this is red circle. Subject's presence negative. I repeat. Subject's presence negative. Operation moves on to phase two. I repeat. Operation moves on to phase two. Over and out."

He didn't want to believe the near-certainty forming in his head. To even try to imagine it gave him heartburn. He backtracked to the restaurant and continued to spy from the door. There still wasn't anyone with the appropriate signs in their. An older American couple used to early bird specials were already waiting for their meal at their table. In another part of the room a young mother, evidently a foreigner, insisted on forcing yet another spoonful of pablum into the mouth of her evidently overfed baby, who resisted her efforts vigorously in his high chair. From the door he saw the heads of the men with the walkie-talkies looking inside the restaurant.

Wright returned to the lobby. Coming in through the opposite side, from the garden door, was an attractive woman with lively, green eyes. She had a few wrinkles in the corners of them, and a mouth with sad, thin lips. She projected that feminine, almost aggressive look of professional women who laugh and cry only when they're alone. She was blonde, but her hair could have been dyed because it didn't match her dense black sideburns or her cinnamon-toned skin. Serious but elegantly dressed, she wore a light brown blouse, a dark brown wool skirt, and low-heeled shoes. She had on a necklace and a bracelet, both of silver and coral beads. A real lady. He wasn't expecting that. He hadn't even expected a woman. Nevertheless, there she was, with the rolled up *Time* magazine showing with the cover on the outside in her left hand, and a carnation on her chest. Undoubtedly she had come from the bungalows across the garden. She walked very calmly. Her eyes captured even the slightest movement in the room. It was obvious that she was headed for the restaurant.

Wright took a few steps in the direction of the check-in desk, and then turned quickly on his heels as if he had forgotten something. He tried to intercept her just when she crossed the hall on her way to the restaurant. Faking absentmindedness, he crossed her path until he almost ran into her. Surprised, she tightened her lips and glanced at him fiercely. He whispered in her ear:

"You like to read *Time*? It's my favorite."

She had everything carefully planned. She had anticipated almost every movement that could take place during her long journey through the rear of the hotel. She had come all the way next to the side wall. In this way, nobody would see her in the middle of the open yard, near the pool, nor coming in through the main entrance. She walked next to the wall that separated the hotel grounds from the stone-paved street on the other side, the one beginning at the steps of the church ruins which, according to the map, used to be

"*San José el Viejo*," old St. Joseph, and led to a small coffee plantation that, in turn, ended on the main causeway. She could easily hide, if necessary, behind the bungalows that lined the hotel wall. She could then come into the lobby from the side garden, which was less well-lit, and see who was doing what inside. She could have walked unexpectedly into the restaurant without being seen from the main entrance. But she never thought that the contact would be made with her at the exact moment when she was crossing that no man's land between the lobby and the restaurant.

She took a step back, hesitating dangerously for a couple of hundredths of a second. No one moved. Only one person looked up. So quickly that she surprised herself, she murmured "excuse me," and swiftly moved to the restaurant entrance. She sat at the first table she found, without losing sight of him. Wright stood in the middle of the corridor, glancing at the people in the lobby and the guys outside, who were barely visible because of the glare of the light on the windows. He took out a notebook that he always carried in his shirt pocket and quickly wrote a message. He immediately went inside and sat at her table.

"Do you like to read *Time*? It's my favorite."

She was still tense, due to the unexpected encounter in the corridor. She felt the restaurant was too hot, that she was suffocating. She hesitated once more, but then she did reply.

"No, I prefer *Newsweek*."

"Do you work for Itzam-Na Exports?"

"Yes, are you the buyer for NH Imports?"

"Yes. Listen and listen carefully. This is a setup. I don't know if they're after you or me, or both. But it's a setup. Leave immediately. I'll contact you again to make the transaction. I've explained it in this note. Take it and get out of here fast."

He discreetly passed her the note. She put it away immediately. By now both of them were standing and ready to leave. At that moment he perceived the surprised look of the men with the walkie-talkies. Pacal knew that he should be there for at least half an hour. But their meeting had lasted less than three minutes.

"Quick! They've seen us!"

They left swiftly, crossing the no-man's land, and headed for the lobby. Several pairs of eyes glanced up, but nobody moved. At that moment there was a commotion at the garden door. The men with the walkie-talkies were rushing in. He hid behind a pillar. She ran, trusting for unexplainable reasons that once again confirmed the eternal mystery of the world, that this *Gringo*, her enemy, would cover her back. In five very long seconds that left her breathless, she reached the doorknob, turned it, pushed the door open, and vanished under the protection of darkness. Choking and coughing as if she were snorting dust, she ran to their bungalow, trying to order her thoughts while blood throbbed in her temples.

Inside the hotel, the men, Uzis in their hands and shirts open to their belly buttons, approached the dining room performing a bad re-enactment of a *film noir*. The older couple jumped out of their chairs like puppets with cut strings, scattering porcelain and food while they cried like snared prey. They were shocked by the guns, by the round, hairy bellies of the men, and the shine of their gold chains and bracelets. The young mother feeding her child stood as if flash-frozen. The child began to cry loudly at the sight of the sweaty men with flattened noses and huge claw-like hands.

Wright took advantage of the confusion to pull out his gun. He shouted as loud as he could:

"Stop! This is a mistake!"

Upon realizing that the voice was coming from behind them, the armed men turned and pointed their guns in the direction of the lobby. Their move made it clear who was who. Everyone ran for cover. Someone hit the floor. A waiter ran outside, followed by two well-dressed men. Hysterical screams ensued, along with the sound of feet scurrying around the furniture. Several of the so-called guests, once they took cover, pulled out their own weapons. The entire lobby seemed like boiling milk spilling uncontrollably out of the pot, leaving a foul smell that lingered in the air.

There were screams in the corridor. Someone was desperately dialing out from the front desk. Doors slammed; objects hit the floor. There was yelling on the streets. Wright slid from the pillar to the side wall to cover his back in case someone shot at him. The yelling and hysteria intensified. There was a sound of breaking glass, as if a waiter had dropped a tray full of dishes in the next room. Wright took advantage of the confusion to try to find his way to the side door. He realized that getting out was next to impossible. Nevertheless he had to try. Getting down on the floor, he started crawling, pulling himself along by his elbows.

One of the men who previously had been on the phone for a long time, took his gun out and pointed it at him, but he did not shoot for some reason or another. At that moment, the men with the Uzis made it into the lobby with the speed of squid swimming at sea. The unexpected sound of a siren diverted their attention. Taking advantage of their momentary distraction, Wright stood up and made it to the side door.

He could have escaped. But just when his fingers were touching the glass of the door and he could feel the serenity of the night air, four armed men came in through that same door and pointed their guns at him. He almost laughed. The whole scene was a parodic tribute to Rabelais. Prudence was the better part of valor. Dropping his gun to the floor and raising his arms, he started yelling loudly so that everyone could hear him:

"My name is Tom Wright! I'm an American citizen! Please inform the Embassy! Call the American Embassy immediately! Let the press know of my kidnaping!"

His screams paralyzed everyone as if they had the power to hypnotize. The pause allowed him to repeat his pathetic message three or four more times, before the men, with some uncertainty, encircled him and made him feel the tips of their Uzis, combining rage with contempt. They grabbed him by the arms and pulled him. Two others pushed him from the back. They crossed the entire corridor that way.

As they came out, Wright noticed the Cherokee Chief with tinted windows he'd seen not too long before, parked in front, with its motor running. They forced him to get into the back seat. The men jumped in as well, two in front and one on each side of him. He felt their fat, sweaty bodies. Their worn-out suits gave the impression that they were about to pop open. Their double chins looked like fat greasy sausages over the rigid starched necks of their white shirts. A second Cherokee Chief came up from behind.

The onlookers followed all the commotion. Gathered at the front of the hotel were curious people of all sorts, but mostly barefooted kids, some drunks who didn't really know what was happening, maids with their respective boyfriends, and a Maya woman selling handicrafts. They almost surrounded both vehicles. The man sitting in the front seat opened his window slightly, showed the tip of his Uzi pointing at the sky, and fired a round. Immediately they all scattered, looking for shelter like roaches when the light comes on in the kitchen. The driver stepped on the gas, and the vehicle took off. Wright felt his neck snap from the violent takeoff. The second vehicle followed close behind.

4

By the time Kukulkán and Vallejo heard the noise, Ariadne was already bursting in through the door, terrified, her face turning purple. They had taken off their jackets, lowered the knots on their ties, opened the top shirt buttons, and rolled up their sleeves.

"To wear a suit and tie these days sucks. It's as stupid as wearing a suit of armor was in medieval times."

"Or wigs, stockings and makeup in the eighteenth century."

"I would've started the revolution just to change styles and not have to wear these rags again."

"The hippies were right. There's nothing like blue jeans."

"You just say that because it's your generation."

"Ha, and you're a fifties beatnik! Don't give me that bullshit! I can just see you standing in front of your high school building with one leg up against the wall, whistling to all the girls who walked by."

"I was too shy. Zurdo and Manzana did that."

"Don't bullshit me. I know what you did in Leipzig. Poor Zurdo's always getting blamed. Why doesn't anyone like him?"

"Because he's full of it, and arrogant on top of that. The Commander-in-Chief's good little boy. When he sets his eyes on power, he's more Stalinist than Beria. Maybe it's his past haunting him..."

"Then we'd all be just like him."

"Screw you. You know the military police shaved his head when he was in high school, right? But, it's not true that no one likes him. Women adore him. That's why he grew an Afro."

"He did that to cover up his premature baldness, don't fuck with me."

At that moment, their voices mixed with the desperate one coming from the other side of the door.

"It's me!"

Ariadne was breathless. Her eyes had shrunk to pinpoints, and she was squeezing her eyelids to keep tears from flowing out.

"It was a trap! They got the *Gringo*!"

While they instinctively picked up the few papers they

had scattered around, Kukulkán went over all the possible scenarios in his head.

"What do you mean they got the *Gringo*?"

"Armed men surprised us. He saved me by pushing me outside."

"Was it an operation against the *Gringo*? Are you sure?"

"So sure it'd make your head spin. I'm not imagining it. The *Gringo* got me out of there. He said he'd reestablish contact. Sent this note."

Kukulkán took it, read it, crumpled it up into a little ball and put it near where he could swallow it if necessary. Vallejo was burning another paper in the bathroom sink. Kukulkán hid the minimal essentials and passed them around. The vein across his forehead looked like it was about to explode.

"Lights!"

As if by magic, the lights were turned off. Vallejo reacted with the speed of a thin, bony sprinter trying to beat a runner at the last minute before reaching the finish line. Ariadne gulped down a glass of water and splashed some on her face. She dried her hands carefully, and she had barely thrown the towel on the bed when Vallejo was handing her a weapon, loaded and ready. At that same moment, they heard Kukulkán's voice for the last time, followed by complete silence.

"Vallejo first. Ariadne covers the rear. The contact point will be the house in front of the Calvario Plaza fountain in..."

He looked at his sophisticated watch with chronometer.

"...One hour. Eight thirty on the dot. We'll wait five minutes only, then move on to the reserve contact point. Quickly!"

Vallejo opened the door carefully while protecting himself. Fresh air gushed in. Stars could be seen in those few parts of the sky not yet covered by massive clouds threatening rain. He saw no movement nearby, but the commotion in the hotel's main building and outside it was obvious: the noise of vehicles, sirens, people shouting, bodies moving from side to side as if electrocuted. The yard felt like an oasis of peace by comparison, cut off from all that agitation.

He threw himself quickly to the ground, then leaned on his elbows. He had several grenades on his belt. Everything was calm. He knelt and finally stood up partway. Creeping along the wall of the cabana suite, which was indeed a small cabin standing by itself, he took the same path that Ariadne had previously run to reach them, bordering the hotel wall. On the other side was the street, then a coffee plantation. In the middle of the wall was a narrow, metal gate. Only the help used it. The only other escape route was to climb the wall and jump over it. But it was high, and it had glass pieces encrusted in the cement, as well as barbed wire, on top.

He moved like a crab, walking sideways with his back sliding against the wall, looking everywhere, the weapon in front of him. The night was cooling rapidly. The sky was increasingly cloudy. Even so, he was sweating. Drops fell down his forehead and stuck to his eyelashes. Every once in a while, he'd wipe his forehead with his shirt sleeve to clear his vision. He also felt the cold clamminess of the wall on his back as he rubbed against it. It was piercing the marrow in his bones. When he had covered half the distance, he saw that Kukulkán was coming out and beginning to trace his own steps.

The garden felt like a dew-covered, mystical oasis enveloped in a dim, bluish light, placid in the middle of all the noise. The screams, vehicle movements, and sirens coming from the main building were increasing. It was as if someone had left the television on with the volume set too loud in the middle of a peaceful, sleepy town. Not even three minutes had gone by since Ariadne had reached them. Unless the operation had been carefully planned by the enemy, they still had time to get out. He didn't think it was that complex, or the *Gringo* himself would have noticed the movement long before making contact with her. Unless he was part of a larger conspiracy. Anything was possible in this life and this crazy world in which they lived. Almost unexpectedly, he reached the side gate. It was closed, with a heavy chain and lock. Fortunately, it was a conventional lock. He began to work it. After what felt like hours, although it couldn't have been more than forty five seconds, he managed to open it. He didn't make a sound. Kukulkán was getting closer. Ariadne was beginning to come out the door.

Slowly, carefully, Vallejo opened the gate. He had the gun ready just in case they were waiting on the other side. He knew that Kukulkán had to survive. That was the only thing that mattered. He turned. Kukulkán was creeping along the wall. Vallejo could see the tension in his jaw. It made the muscles under his cheekbones stand out. He pulled the gate. The hinges squeaked. He kept his finger on the trigger. The noise seemed like the loudest he had ever heard, although it was only a soft squeak. One had to be very close even to hear it.

The gate was now fully open. He waited. He didn't hear anything. He breathed deeply, tensed his muscles, opened his eyes as wide as he could, thought about Paulina, a gorgeous Chilean lover he had had years earlier, and jumped into the street. There was no one there. He saw a Cherokee Chief parked in front of the ruins of the *San José el Viejo* church. The red glare from the siren of another vehicle that must have been parked in front of the hotel was also visible. But in back, nothing. The coffee plantation. The street that led to the main causeway. The shadow of the volcano. All in darkness, calm. He looked inside again to where Kukulkán waited, almost melting against the wall. Ariadne was on the floor in front of the cabana. Vallejo gave the signal. The coast was clear. He went outside.

Kukulkán moved quickly. He slid toward the door with the quickness of a jaguar, his legs jumping laterally and carrying his weight up and down, the gun facing the front. Ariadne headed for the wall. When she reached it, she turned to adjust to her new angle of vision. Kukulkán had almost reached the exit. She turned to look at the main building. At that instant she saw them.

A man had run out of the hall door that led to the pool. When he went by the restaurant windows, his silhouette was clearly visible. He was dressed as a waiter, and he seemed to be heading in the direction of the pool dressing rooms, on the opposite side. Jorge, she thought. It was one of their own guys, working as a waiter in the hotel. But immediately two men ran out the same door after him. They lingered in the cobblestone space full of flowerbeds, between the restaurant windows and the pool itself. Their heads turned in all directions looking for their prey. Ariadne knew immediately that they were going to see them.

She turned to Kukulkán. He continued sliding towards the gate. He was almost there. She was doing the same, but then stopped and made a whistling sound like a bird's scream. Kukulkán heard it and stopped. He was less that a yard from the exit. He turned and saw the two men running towards the pool. He looked to the other side. The gate was not far from the lobby. Soon, someone would come out from the side door through which Ariadne had escaped. There was no time to lose. He ran to the gate. The men noticed, and shouted.

Without thinking, Ariadne opened fire. She thought that, given the commotion going on in the main building, this interchange would go unnoticed. Feeling the hail of bullets, the men threw themselves immediately on the ground. Kukulkán was gone. Ariadne ran like crazy for the gate.

One of the men lifted his Uzi and shot. Ariadne felt as if she had been run over by a car. An atrocious force lifted her up from the ground, suspending her in the air, and she lost all notion of what was up and what was down. After turning as if floating, seeing the stars pass by, the gravel, the illuminated hotel, she fell and tasted the humid dirt in her teeth. Clods of dirt hit her eyes, her ears. She was too shaken up to know what had happened. She shook her head, tried to concentrate. The gun. It had fallen, but it was a short distance away.

Moving to recover it, she felt pain in her muscles as if they were aching from too much exercise. The man with the Uzi ran dangerously in her direction.

"Stop right there! Don't move!"

He lifted his Uzi. She thought she wouldn't have time to shoot before he did. They were going to kill her. Then, another burst of gunfire. The man approaching her leapt like a cat in the air and landed at her feet. It was magic. She didn't understand, but looking up, she saw Jorge shooting from the opposite side of the garden, engaging her would-be attacker. It was her last chance. She was dizzy and couldn't control her movements, and she felt as if her knees were unable to support the weight of her body. She was sweating profusely, but, when she tried to clean the sweat from the back of her neck, her hand came back covered with blood. Pulling herself away from the wall, and breathing deeply, Ariadne made one last effort to reach the gate. The man that had leapt like a cat started to stand. He wasn't dead. He felt around searching for his own gun.

Ariadne stopped. She lifted her gun carefully and held her breath. She let her bodily movements get in rhythm so her aim would be true. Then she fired. The man bounced from the ground to the air a couple of times. The other one looked for cover. Then he continued his standoff with Jorge. She ran to the gate. There weren't many yards left, but the time it took to cover them felt like an eternity. Her legs felt like Jell-O. The sweat on her brow clouded her vision. She trembled uncontrollably. She thought she saw more men coming from the famous side door of the lobby. Three or four. But she didn't know if they were real or if it was a hallucination. They didn't seem to notice her. She ran for the gate. She was safe.

But she wasn't safe. She had just stepped in the cobblestoned street when a Grand Cherokee pulled in at top speed. It braked so hard when she almost crossed its path, that the smell of burnt rubber filled her lungs. Had she come out a second earlier, the vehicle would have run her over. The slight delay caused by her having to aim slower than usual had saved her. But now she had a Jeep blocking her path. As if in slow motion, she lifted her gun and shot at point-blank range. She didn't even hear the burst of gunfire, nor did she bother to look to the right to verify that she was not being followed. The weapon shook; she felt the vibration shaking her muscles like an old railroad car, the blow on her shoulder and the acrid smell of gunpowder. The man evaporated. She continued shooting. There was another one beside him. Had there been two others in the back seat, they would have perforated her like a colander. But it was her lucky day. They had left the vehicle to go into the hotel. Only two were left in the car. The glass flew in all directions. The shards fell on her like diamonds reflecting the light in a thousand glimmers, an unexpected shower of sparks. With instincts that surprised even her, she painfully began to move her legs, gingerly, running in the direction of the coffee plantation.

"Over here! I'll cover you!"

It was Kukulkán's voice. It seemed to reverberate everywhere. He would cover her, but from where? She turned halfway. The Cherokee, uncontrolled, had rolled into the hotel wall. She saw sudden flashes. Someone else was shooting from the street corner. It was a new, different sound. She was standing unprotected, in the middle of the street. She turned halfway again. It was hard for her to keep her balance. She felt that she was moving slowly, but, otherwise, she'd fall. The breeze wafted through her hair, like the hissing of a cobra. It was the only indication that some bullets had nearly hit her. She moved towards the plantation, more like she was sleepwalking than truly running. She heard the snap that steel made when some bullets hit the cobblestone. She saw where Kukulkán was because of the fire from his own Galil. She was running in that direction, when she heard the roar of an engine.

"Another car's coming! Run this way!"

"This way" was the opposite side of the sidewalk from where the hotel was. She saw that Kukulkán pulled out something from his belt. Like a baseball pitcher, he arched his body and threw it in a parabolic curve at the gun-riddled Cherokee. The object crossed the sky like a meteorite before landing on the vehicle. Then everything exploded. The sky lit up, the stars disappeared, and she felt an unbearable heat as if she suddenly were no longer in Antigua at night, but on the beach at Iztapa, noontime, Easter-week. A wind lifted her from the ground, suspended her in the air, and carried her as if on a magic carpet to Kukulkán's feet. She practically rolled there before tumbling down like a drunkard.

In the growing darkness, he grabbed her hand. Another Cherokee was coming. Now there were four guys. They could be seen clearly through the windows. But the explosion from the first vehicle forced them to stop, and it cut their line of vision. Kukulkán pulled Ariadne brusquely towards the plantation as if she were a sack of potatoes. They crossed the field diagonally. On the other small street was a blue Volkswagen. It had been parked there previously by other comrades, anticipating an emergency like the one now taking place. Kukulkán had a duplicate key.

Kukulkán shook the key ring as if he were trying to exorcize demons. He opened the door, almost pulling it off. He pushed Ariadne inside, hitting her head against the upper edge. He then ran around and sat in the driver's seat. The instant he started the engine, which seemed to catch slowly, the other jeep reappeared. In the rear view mirror he saw that, a block away, another vehicle was also heading in their direction.

He took off. He was stuck on a narrow street, and he couldn't turn anywhere until they reached the main causeway. He was drawn to its yellow luminescence like a moth, feeling a natural protection while zigzagging the car on the small street so it would be a more difficult target for his pursuers.

They were shooting, but he didn't hear anything and they didn't get hit.

They reached the main causeway. He took the road to Ciudad Vieja. He passed in front of the Ramada hotel. In the opposite direction, a Toyota pickup was approaching. He allowed both vehicles to come closer. With a sudden impulse, he jerked the steering wheel. The Volkswagen skidded. He straightened out, then slammed on the brakes. The car blocked the road, forcing the incoming pickup to stop a few yards ahead to avoid hitting it. Kukulkán jumped out, pulled Ariadne, almost breaking her wrist and forearm in the process, and headed for the cabin of the Toyota. She was shaking like a plastic toy.

"Get us out of here! The police are behind us!"

While he was shouting out instructions, Kukulkán reached the cabin and opened the door on the passenger side. The driver's eyes were a sea of frenzied terror. He tried to stammer something but was unable to make a sound. Paralyzed behind the steering wheel, he let Kukulkán put Ariadne in. She now seemed to be choking in a distressful way. Then Kukulkán got in himself, slamming the door shut. The man did not even notice that his own pants got darker as his kidneys transformed his fear into urine.

"Quickly! Make a U-turn! I'll tell you where to go!"

The pickup slowly made a U-turn in the narrow street. It seemed that the maneuver lasted forever. They moved to the left. Shifted gears in reverse. Then backed up to the right. Put it in first gear again. They moved forward to the left. Then back again. Still forward once more.

They were beginning to accelerate when the pursuing vehicles appeared. Seeing the Volkswagen blocking the path, they slammed on the brakes to avoid a collision. The second Cherokee almost hit the trunk. Four, five, six men jumped out from both sides and started to push the Volkswagen, to move it out of the way and continue their pursuit. Swearing with all the curses ever invented in Spanish, they broke the window to remove the parking brake before pushing it to the edge, then machine-gunning it to vent their frustration. With this primitive and useless gesture, they lost precious seconds. By the time they were on the move again, the pickup had disappeared as if the earth had swallowed it up.

CHAPTER TWO

1

"These things only happen in Guate. Shit."

"Oh, please. Shit happens everywhere. As long as the damage is not irreparable. Mortar fire only leaves you deaf for a minute."

"Don't you find it a bit incredible?"

"Of course I do, but it just goes to show that you shouldn't bite the hand that feeds you. Do you think we could live like we do anywhere else?"

"Don't start that shit about how we live in the best of all possible worlds and if we lived in Miami I'd be working as a dishwasher or something."

"You, most of all. You'd have to change your ways. Put some order, some tranquility, in your operating style. I'd be a banker or the manager of an important corporation..."

"Like the Mafia."

"Why not? Women's lib has reached even them."

"Now you're a feminist to boot. That's all I needed."

"Life's a learning experience. Besides, I've always said that if you're clever enough you can even beat the White House at its own game, despite what the doubters say. They're content to stay within their own limits, and they'd never even believe a story like this."

"Well, we should take that seriously because they might not believe our story either."

"For once you've said something useful, even if it's not original."

"Thanks a lot. The things I have to put up with. And with no defenses. At this rate, you'll be telling me that you're in the EGP, and I don't have a clue."

"It'd all be for show. All's fair in love and war."

"What's the show about, love or war?"

"Just war, if we see 'war' as business by other means. Which is also another show, another spectacle."

"Stop philosophizing, and get back to what we were talking about. Tell me more about the wild scene at the hotel."

"I've already told you. What else do you want to know?"

"The newspaper said that the EGP came in shooting and kidnaped another *Gringo*."

"The *Gringo* isn't as dumb as he looks. He sensed they were going to grab him, and he made a huge racket."

"Pacal never thought he'd defend himself."

"Defend himself, yes. But not that he'd let the girl get away. That's where everything broke down. Pacal was caught completely off guard. Turns out that the *Gringo* was less trusting than Pacal imagined. He kept noticing little things, and that sharpened his instincts. The mind is like a little ant that keeps coming and going..."

"And to top it off, the commander escaped."

"I swear, those damn soldiers are a bunch of amateurs. Even with all their cars, motorcycles and helicopters, they still let him slip through their fingers."

"It's their fault for planning the operative at night."

"No. They wanted to do it in the dark so they could nab him more easily."

"Is the plan still in place? What did my father tell you?"

"According to him, Operation Rattlesnake is now going into phase three."

"The truth is that I just don't get what we're doing sometimes."

"You just have to try to remember who's the keeper of your darkest dreams."

"Shit! Now you're going to start philosophizing again."

"If we don't, we'll never understand anything. We risk our lives to guard ourselves from death, and face death to guard ourselves from life. Because life bores us, but death scares us. And worst of all, we're not even really preparing ourselves for death, but for the preparation for death. Time's always wasted on preparations and rehearsals. Not even performances, but rehearsals."

From the cabin of the small airplane the landscape below was an intense green with brown gaps visible where deforestation had caused mud-slides. One day soon these green mountains would all turn brown. At a distance, the thick gray clouds floated, packed with contained fury, suspended in a pre-historical time above the rickety machine that jumped and creaked among the pockets of hot air soaked in the scent of sugar cane and cows' milk. Further on, at the very edge of the horizon, the sky was clear. A shy light blue, so transparent that it almost seemed to fade to yellow, hung frailly from the cottony cumulus linking the spaces between the blackened volcanoes. It was the glow of the Pacific Ocean. On the right of the plane, the sky was a black, fulminating violence. It was horribly hot in the cabin.

Alvaro began the descent when he saw the dirt runway in the middle of the green field. The plane shook as the altitude changed but, like a well-trained horse, it allowed itself to be led in spiraling circles, slanting slowly downward, until it touched the reddish earth of San Marcos. After it hit the ground, it bounced up and fell once more before stabilizing on the runway, where it vibrated like a car on the cobblestone streets of Antigua.

Sandra turned to check that the second plane was landing behind them. She looked wistfully to see how it leaned nimbly from one side to the other before making timid contact with only one wheel, like a child dipping a toe into the pool before jumping in.

A jeep and a truck awaited them at the end of the runway. As soon as Alvaro shut off the engine, Sandra opened the door and stepped out briskly. The heat and the buzzing of insects were only minor distractions. She had the ability to concentrate with such an obsessive intensity that her arms tingled.

The truck pulled up to the plane, stopping almost under a wing. Two employees got out and began to take out small packages wrapped in burlap sacks stamped with a flour company seal and put them on the plane. Standing by the plane with his hands on his waist, Alvaro carefully observed the employees' movements. He was wearing aviator sunglasses, a short-sleeved shirt, and khaki drill pants. The humid breeze blew back his hair. Suddenly he stared at one of the workers and said:

"Now I know who the General looks like."

The jeep took them to the mansion on the estate, where Maruca was waiting for them at the front door. Her typically speckled blue striped skirt and faded cotton *huipil* marked her origins in San Pedro Sacatepequez. She looked old for a young woman, and, at the same time, young for an old woman. This was due to her large almond-like eyes and her laughter, belied by a chin that indicated an unlimited stubbornness. She smelled like wild tropical fruit.

"Whoa, slow down, sweetheart! You're going to hurt yourself like that."

The jeep had barely stopped and Sandra was already jumping out without losing a step. Three young Indian women with large ribbons in their braids came out running and talking all at the same time, causing a boisterous commotion. Sandra answered their questions affectionately. She was wearing tight blue jeans, knee-high riding boots, an ordinary white blouse, hair loose. Svelte like a tropical flower, and completely unaware of the flirtatious gestures of which Maruca so disapproved.

"Have we gotten any calls yet?"

"No, ma'am. Not yet. But what a way to..."

"And the radio?"

"Nope. You look nervous, girl."

Sandra went past Maruca like a cyclone, without kissing her forehead or patting her on the back, as she always did. Maruca didn't take it personally, she thought there must be a serious matter that had her boss so worried. Sandra almost ran in the direction of the small office full of papers and trinkets. But they weren't trinkets. On top of an old, enormous, mahogany desk, which, despite its mistreatment, couldn't hide its magnificence, there was a telephone, a telex, radio equipment, a safe and a dismantled computer with all its components scattered around. Everything was dusty and disheveled, but that was the nature of the *hacienda*. Sandra never let anyone come in, not even to clean, practically under penalty of death. As in the Ministry offices, papers grew here in unequal piles until they leaned on one another, leaving triangular spaces between them. Many were already yellowing, but they had their reason for being. Everything always had its reason for being in life as in sewing patterns, even if it wasn't clear at first glance. Appearances were certainly deceiving.

Sandra began to walk nervously from one end of the room to the other like an agitated puppy sensing an imminent storm. She quickly reviewed some papers, generating small clouds of dust every time she touched them. Maruca appeared in the doorframe so unexpectedly that Sandra screamed and jumped back.

"My God, Maruca! Why did you scare me like that?"

"Forgive me, ma'am, but I thought you might like something to calm you down."

"No, thank you, Maruca. Don't let anyone interrupt me. Leave me alone."

"I brought you some juice anyway. When you're agitated you always get thirsty."

"Oh, Maruca, you're like the mother I never had."

"Wasn't I your real nanny then, my child? Didn't I get up every time I heard you coughing at night? Same thing with your little brother; his asthma was worse than yours. I'll never forget how my little boy would be nearly choking..."

Maruca placed the glass of juice on the table and covered it with a plate to keep the flies out. Sandra gave her a slight, grateful hug, and her eyes evinced the generosity and fragility that she would have shown, if she could have allowed herself to betray her feelings. Maruca left the room trotting, and Sandra returned her attention to the papers. Only then did her sight become blurry and her pupils dissolve until they looked like narrow black lines vertically traversing her irises.

"My little brother..."

Sandra examined everything as if expecting someone to jump her from a drawer or a dark corner at any moment. Suddenly she hit her forehead with the palm of her right hand. She ran to the safe, absorbed by distrust and quickly dialed the familiar combination. The safe opened. Seeing that some of the papers were out of their envelopes, she frowned. She shuddered and relaxed after finding the one she was looking for. Enraged at Alvaro's carelessness, she let all her anxiety explode in curses. Even if only three people had access to the safe, that paper was everything. She took it out very carefully and examined it again in the light bursting in through the window.

"For the purpose of implementing development... payments are authorized...via such and such company...to be deposited in the account of such and such bank...the purchase of the necessary equipment is authorized to augment exports from the Republic of Guatemala...civil aviation equipment in Canada....Authorized. United States Government..."

And so...there it was in black and white. The document of her dreams, a paper that could tumble governments or put them behind bars for the rest of their lives. A paper that allowed her to control the Bald Eagle. Her safeguard. Her passport to freedom. Everything very clean. Legal. The government reassigning goods to benefit the private sector in agreement with the benefactor country. Totally coherent within the economic logic of the eighties. She took a sip of juice. She folded the paper, put back it in its envelope and stuck it to the top part of the safe where no one would look or feel. At that instant the phone rang, the sudden noise startling her. She turned violently, nearly spilling the glass of juice in the process.

"Hello? Fer-de-Lance! It's about time! I was desperate! You know what? It's better if you hang up and call me by radio. That way I can leave this line open in case Pierrot makes contact...okay.... goodbye. Call immediately, ok?"

She hung up. She felt slightly dizzy. She didn't know if it was the effect of the heat, the discomfort she felt in her stomach or something else. Her period. The damaging darkness over which nothing can be done. It didn't matter. She didn't like to think about that. Nothing was accidental. When you work consistently, everything has a reason. Nothing is repeated. Everything always happens as if it were new, even if it is identical to the previous experience. That's what she was thinking, as a way to drown her memories. Like the time her aunts told her that her attitude was selfish. "Well, so what," she'd replied, "I am selfish then." They slapped her face for her impertinence. Her brother laughed. That's what made her cry. She learned not to think about that, though.

Sandra walked over to the telex and wrote a message: "Bald Eagle. Confidential. I've obtained information from my sources. Prince Valiant in questionable hands. Government not responding as expected. Hard-line officers think coup. Review lunar calendar to find date. Urgently need response to said initiative. I'll contact you via appropriate channels as soon as I return to the city. Rattlesnake."

She was finishing writing when the radio started buzzing and making static noises. Pacal's voice, breaking off and returning, coming and going over the airwaves, reverberated in the office.

"Hello? Hello! Fer-de-Lance here. Over. I repeat. Fer-de Lance here. Over."

"Hello! Rattlesnake here. Go ahead, Fer-de-Lance."

The voice continued, suffused with static, broken up by electricity and echoes.

"I repeat the information. Prince Valiant is in our hands. Well treated. He had a good breakfast. He thinks he's in someone else's hands. We're stalling."

An expression of a mischievous child with, perhaps, a slight touch of remorse invaded her face. She looked at her feet. They made her laugh. She recovered a serious tone, barely masking her excitement.

"I'm glad, Fer-de-Lance. I'm activating phase three of the plan right now. I'm still awaiting contact with Pierrot. As soon as I make it, I'll return to the market to sell Bald Eagle the merchandise."

"My congratulations. Don't worry about us. Nothing's happening here. Phase three will be the charm."

"I hope so. I only hope that you won't fail again..."

"We didn't fail! It's just that Prince Valiant got smart! Maybe I underestimated him, but the point is he smelled the trap and it was hard to catch him in those conditions. Besides, the enemy isn't painted on the wall."

"Well. Let's not argue now. I'll be in touch again after meeting with Bald Eagle. Over and out."

Sandra disconnected the radio and returned to the telex. She reread her message, correcting a word or two without being distracted by the buzzing flies. The anguish of writing. Always horrible, resigning oneself that what was said, was said. She sent it and sighed, looking repeatedly at her watch. Her jaw was tense. She tried biting her lower lip with her top teeth, and inhaling deeply the air heavy with pollen, scented with mangos and cashew nuts. She made a sudden gesture of frustration and knocked the glass over, spilling the juice all over the table. She ran to the door and yelled at the top of her lungs.

"Maruca! Quickly, bring a rag. I spilled juice on the papers!"

She returned to where the stain was moving quickly, like a large yellow wave, soaking into one paper after another and dripping slowly onto the floor. She looked at the drops impotently and in disgust. At that moment, Maruca came in with a large rag in her hand and began to clean. Sandra watched her in fascination, immobile. She allowed Maruca to give order to her life and to solve her crisis like she'd always done. When she fell from the mango tree. When her father beat the crap out of her. When the nuns expelled her from school for unbuttoning the top button of her blouse in front of a boy. When her brother smacked her on the head with a bat. Maruca was part of the immutable laws of nature, protecting her and straightening up her mess.

"There, look! In that corner!"

She pointed with a shy and insecure finger while Maruca wiped the spot indicated with the rag, making the spilt liquid disappear as if by magic.

"Oh child. You're like a little snake. The way you twist and knock everything over with your tail."

At that moment, the telephone rang again. She reached for it automatically, and knocked over a pile of papers with her arm. She turned, picking up the receiver while simultaneously trying to hold up the leaning column, but it eluded her grasp and fell, the papers flying in all directions like confetti. Maruca rushed about, trying to grab them before they fell to the floor and got stained.

"Hello? Pierrot! Finally! I'm so glad! You don't know how nervous I was!...Yes....Speak loudly because I can't hear you. Yeah, the connection's very bad. Yes. I've found out everything. I was very nervous, you just don't know. I thought you wouldn't call, you don't know how happy it makes me...Yes, I know. Calm down. Let's get right to the point...Now that I know where you are, I'll go back to the market to meet with Bald Eagle and see what we can agree to…Yes. The Squadron has him. Pacal. Now they each have one. You have the weaver and they have the handicraft buyer, ha….I don't know if they grabbed him with the money or not. Let me find out….Yes. Calm down. And the girl? Did she recover all right from the scare?….I'm glad….Goodbye then….Just like we agreed. Don't worry. I may be a traitor like you said, but you can count on your Harlequin, my dear Pierrot. Lots of kisses and take care."

She hung up the receiver. Her face turned red. Now she was relaxed. Perfectly calm. She smiled. Just like when she lost her mother's ring and then found it again.

"Should I bring you another juice, ma'am?"

Maruca had finished cleaning and arranging papers. Sandra half closed her eyes as if she were sleeping. She stretched, making no effort to hide the drowsiness that invaded her as she relaxed.

"No thanks, Maruca. I'm going back to the capital."

"Oh, ma'am, but you just got here!"

"You know how hectic things can get these days. Go on and tell the guys to prepare the plane for me."

Maruca shrugged her shoulders and left running with the jubilation of a little girl willing to fulfill her master's wishes. Sandra stretched again and laughed. Alvaro came into the office at that moment, all smiles, asking in a strained and quivering voice:

"So you're leaving? Everything in order?"

"You're here? And the shipment?"

"It's all gone. No news. Only that your plane hasn't returned yet. Give it a half an hour more or less."

"Oh, damn! But it's urgent that I leave!"

"You'll get there on time, baby, don't worry. We know where it's coming from. Besides, think: this way we have half an hour alone."

He came close and embraced her. His mouth looked for Sandra's, finding instead the hardness of her cheekbone and licking her nose before getting a fistful of hair that went deep into his mouth.

"Alvaro! With everything I have going on in my head..."

He let her go. He wasn't angry. On the contrary, he smiled cunningly.

"It's never the right time for you. Being married to a woman like you is a bitch."

"Patience, pet; the night is long. We'll have time."

"Isn't that what I said then? You always put it off. If the magical day ever arrives, I'll be so tired from waiting for you that I won't be able to get it up."

Alvaro didn't say that last sentence, but Sandra imagined it after he had already shaken his head in both directions, turned and left.

2

Indifferent to their surroundings, the cameramen ran with their tools of the trade from one end to the other, accidentally hitting some transients gathered around. The crowd, buzzing like a swarm of excited bees, drowned out any swearing at the abusive cameramen, who only moved when the candidate appeared surrounded by his bodyguards.

Vallejo watched the muddled spectacle from a corner of the alley that led to the small plaza where the impromptu rally was taking place. He didn't want to get any closer. It would be full of cops. He wanted to keep his options open in case of an unexpected chase. As a matter of fact, he shouldn't even be out there. His picture had been on TV and in the newspapers. Although he'd dyed his hair and disguised his facial features, the experts known for examining eyes and cheeks would recognize him in an instant. He hadn't planned to be there, in fact. He was on his way to a safe house where he had an emergency meeting scheduled, unleashed by the Antigua incident, when he fortuitously ran into the rally. Even though he didn't agree with Manuel Fuentes Color on many issues, he respected him as a capable politician and a decent man—one of the few in the country. He was from Quetzaltenango after all.

Vallejo had originally met him at the home of the Villagra family. Meme Fuentes Color was dating Mica, the youngest of the Villagra daughters at the time, even though he was much older, divorced and with grown children. The Villagra girl had just divorced the poet Amílcar Cabral herself, and was dancing off her sadness with a rum-and-coke in hand, while the aforementioned poet ran a tab at Pinky's Bar. Mica was Vallejo's great friend. They would talk about everything informally and thoughtfully. It was she who got him interested in César Vallejo, always reciting to him, "I will die in Paris in the pouring rain, on a day that I already remember." Indeed, in Paris they drank Algerian wine with Lucho Tomáz, Neruda's ex-secretary. Vallejo would always say in a mocking tone, "humanity is a concept for onanists because there are never heroes possible when the storm occurs in a dark sea of shit."

One night Mica invited Vallejo to a party to meet her new lover. Mica's older sister and her brother-in-law were there as well. The latter was the handsome owner of an important newspaper and it was already rumored that his dream was to be President some day. Also attending the party was a young man with a small moustache, bodyguard to the patriarch of the Christian Democrats. He had a black belt in karate and played with his gun the whole time. Eventually he became the party's general secretary and aspired to more. And Meme Fuentes Color was there.

The bodyguard to the CD patriarch and the press magnate became engrossed in a tremendous discussion in the kitchen of the house, ignoring the rest of the world. Meme Fuentes Color, "fed up of talking about politics," left at some point, returned to the living room, and immediately started a discussion about politics with Vallejo. Even though he was no different, he at least recognized that Guatemalan politicians didn't know how to talk about anything *but* politics. Sometimes about women or soccer. If not, they would remain mute, drinking with a historical thirst that was never satiated. Vallejo and Fuentes Color talked about how the country might develop, about how to build a great hydro-electric dam in the west to industrialize Quetzaltenango, about the Communists' lack of a sense of humor, which led them to get drunk and cry rather than laugh. "Ché said that the Communists don't talk under torture but were incapable of assaulting a nest of machine guns. He forgot to add that they were also capable of holding several bottles of cheap liquor with little evidence but a few tears and a runny nose, yet were incapable of picking up a girl in tight pants or of dancing rock-n-roll." Vallejo tried to convince him that the electoral road was closed in the country. "Don't look for something that isn't there, man," Meme would tell him. "The only thing that you guys are going to get is all of our asses kicked big time. You have to learn that politics, as your favorite poet said, isn't any sort of heroic behavior, but rather a beautiful kind of cynicism soaked in nostalgia, splattered with beautiful words here and there, where the only thing that truly matters is that your brain and heart don't harden too much."

It was impossible to agree with someone who thought it was enough to reform the system and build democratic institutions to get rid of the military. Nevertheless, his big eyes radiated a childish innocence and human warmth. His smile, covered by a black moustache, projected a depth of feeling covered by a veil of imperturbability. After a short silence he thought it suitable to add, "Mitterrand's my man. He's the way." Vallejo rolled his eyes to the ceiling in a mocking gesture. "Goddamn, if that's the way, we're fucked."

At the end of the following year, Vallejo had already gone underground. However, he continued to look Meme up occasionally. Unlike others, Meme Fuentes Color never closed the door on him nor stopped discussing issues openly regardless of the inevitable disagreements. Now, years later, Vallejo had run into him on his way to a secret meeting, at the press conference that Fuentes Color was giving to foreign correspondents.

"It's important for the people of Europe and the United States to understand that what's happening in this country isn't a Communist conspiracy to destroy democracy! What we have here is a union of different sectors of Guatemalan society jointly opposed to a ruinous military dictatorship! What we have here is a power struggle between different death squads! Like Mafia families, they do what they want to advance their interests! They're not allies of the United States! They only pay lip service, imitating, like parrots, democracy's ideals so their aid won't be cut off! I don't support armed struggle either! However, I recognize that it's stupid to think that our guerrillas are part of an international conspiracy! This regime is like Hitler's! The only difference is that Maya Indians are being exterminated instead of Jews! That's why we should recognize those who fight, like the French resistance when it fought the Nazi occupation!..."

Vallejo looked at his watch and frowned. Walking away backwards, he noticed an attractive woman in the crowd. He thought how good she looked with filthy self-indulgence. He smiled slyly when he imagined what Ariadne would say if she found out. You had to be careful with feminists. Men couldn't just say what was going through their minds anymore.

He saw Meme Fuentes Color again. He shook his head. It was nice to hear those words in public. Weren't politics supposed *not* to be heroic behavior? Or were the thousands of deaths that heavy? Because having the courage to say that in public and to the international press confirmed his great heart, it confirmed that the man with the curly hair was a rare soul with a marvelous candor, but it also confirmed that he wanted to die from sheer distress. Vallejo still looked at him for an instant and pressed his hands against his chest until they cracked. He disappeared immediately down the narrow street, followed by a bony dog with brown spots, that limped along with rheumatic legs.

3

Don Leonel turned off the television. It wasn't clear if he had thrown the remote control against the wall or if it had merely slipped from his hand, but it almost hit a horrendous painting that his wife had purchased many years before and that she swore was very expensive. His face shone as if he were drunk, even though he no longer drank heavily since his second heart attack. His lip trembled with such force that the corner of his mouth looked like a rubber-band. He stumbled when he stood up, and nearly fell back onto the overstuffed sofa. He managed to keep his balance by waving his arms like an injured bird, but, when he stretched to reach for his cane, he shifted his body weight and floundered again. This time he did end up buried in the pillows despite the desperate waving of his impotent arms.

"Jonás!"

He heard the sound of steps on the stairs. Jonás came in running, breathless, eyes wide open, wiping his forehead with the left cuff of his shirt to clean himself up in front of his master.

"My apologies Don Leonel! I was upstairs!"

"Don't give me that apology bullshit! Things are blacker than night! Get me the telephone immediately!"

Jonás ran to the small office on one side of the living room. In the meantime, Don Leonel managed to sit up correctly. He pulled his coat from under his behind to fix his lapels. He felt around for his cigarette case and lighter on the small table next to the sofa. Jonás reappeared with the telephone.

"Get me the Minister of Defense!"

"Yes, sir."

Jonás had difficulty dialing the number. He was doing it so quickly that he would make a mistake and have to start again.

Don Leonel's thoughts slid surreptitiously back to the cloudy memory of his youthful days, when the tingling of life reached the deepest part of his heart. It did him good to remember the energy he had at that time, when he resembled a young bullfighter. He liked to show off his status in linen suits and sleek convertibles. He didn't have a great voice but played the guitar with some skill, and beautiful women always surrounded him. Back then he had racehorses in Santa Lucía Cotzumalguapa. He remembered in particular one day when his horse was about to win an important race, galloping as if possessed by the devil, and the jockey fell off. People screamed in horror but Don Leonel ran without hesitation onto the track, risking his own life. The jockey was run over and horribly mutilated by the horses that came from behind him. Don Leonel hurried over and put the jockey's head on his lap. "Hang on, Garcez," he told him, "hang on." But he didn't hold on. The jockey died in his arms before the ambulance arrived. Garcez was his favorite jockey, but, more than that, he was his close friend. They had grown up together on the estate. He, the master's son. Garcez, the son of a peasant. They were the same age. They fished together, hunted together, tamed colts together, they whored together. Now they shared death together, but on different sides of the fence. Garcez had died bravely, but he had lived plentifully before that. Both of them had. And yet, when you looked at life carefully, it was always dangling by a thread. You always desire a certain outcome, but God determines otherwise— man proposes, God disposes. They truly were nothing, nor could there ever be stability or solidity on Earth. After the ambulance left, Don Leonel, understandably distraught, returned to the stands with tears in his eyes. At the moment he sat back down, as his companion was about to wipe his tears with her gloved hands, a cornucopia of ice cream hit his face like a whip, leaving a vanilla trail on the lapels of his jacket and on his tie. "Fucking rich assholes!" An effeminate voice blew away rapidly with the wind, ruining the world's harmony.

Jonás dialed repeatedly. He had barely dialed the third cypher when the beep-beep-beep of the busy signal interrupted his effort. He started again. Once more, beep-beep-beep. He was perspiring. His eyebrows glistened as if covered by diamonds, and the receiver nearly slipped from his humid hands. Finally he smiled and relaxed. The call had gone through.

"The Minister of Defense, please. It's urgent…from Don Leonel Herrera…"

4

"Hello? Don Leonel?….Yes. I was also thinking of calling you….I still have the television on….There's nothing to worry about….It just so happens that we had already planned an operative. Mere coincidence but what he said favors us, imagine….I'll come by your house later….Calm down …We'll see each other soon."

The Minister hung up and rubbed his chubby hands together. They resembled the French bread from the Jensen bakery that, as a child, he had gazed at through the store window with unfulfilled desire. He took the remote control. He looked for a moment at the frozen face on the screen, then pushed the rewind button. The video of the speech started to play in reverse and at top speed like a grotesque, surrealistic comedy.

Pacal sighed as he took a heart-shaped chocolate from a box on the desk. He automatically looked at his Rolex.

"It's time, General. Should I call for your helicopter?"

"Don't trust appearances."

"What did you say?"

"Nothing. Call."

Pacal walked to the table where the intercom was. He ate the chocolate discretely while he looked at the General's tightened lips out of the corner of his eye.

"Lieutenant Alpírez? The Minister is ready. While you're at it, please request my vehicle immediately."

He blinked and stretched his arms with his elbows bent as if he were a fattened goose.

"It takes two wrongs to make a right."

5

The embassy official pushed the button on his intercom.

"Let her in."

Behemoth rubbed his hands together. His heart was beating like a drum. A vapid smile appeared on his thin lips. He smoothed his clothes. He looked for one of his unfiltered cigarettes and swore. The pack was empty. Suddenly, the door opened as if pushed by a ghost.

Sandra walked in smiling. He stood. She walked in with her distinctive strides and extended her hand. He took it, sliding his fingers a second longer than necessary on her skin, but she pretended not to notice. He straightened his moustache and passed his hand over his balding head.

"I received the telex. To tell the truth, it ith difficult to believe..."

"Difficult to believe?"

"Thtudying the characterithtics of Wright's kidnaping, everything would indicate that it wath Pacal..."

"That's true. But I thought that with your lengthy experience in our country you were above that..."

"Thandra. You know that you have my complete trust."

She stood as if about to leave.

"What are you doing Thandra, by god? Thit down pleathe."

"Then forget about...believe me..."

"Calm down. I am dying to hear your information..."

Sandra sat. She opened her purse to extract a cigarette. The man moved around like a top to reach his cigarette case before her, almost knocking over a pile of papers. He managed to gallantly offer her a Virginia Slims.

"Those? I smoke Marlboro..."

He blushed. He felt that he was undergoing an exotic torment that he had never had the occasion to experience in combat. He whispered, "I think in this drawer..." and started to open all the desk drawers.

"I don't have Marlboro. I thmoke without filterth but I finished them."

Sandra took out one of her own cigarettes, allowing him, very chivalrously, to light it with his lighter. She exhaled deeply and let the cloud of smoke float softly toward him.

"Oh, I'm sorry, I didn't notice that I was blowing smoke on you. You know. People have such bad manners around here, my God..."

"Thandra, please. You are such a lady..."

"To be honest, I'm not used to it anymore. Around here, all ladies have to have balls."

"I know."

"In that case, let's learn to put up with what we can't avoid. We can't fight city hall."

She smiled slightly, allowing her eyes to envelop him as if they were the open arms of Kali, the Hindu goddess.

"Explain to me then..."

"Fine. These things are serious....You don't have a microphone hidden around here, do you?"

"My God, Thandra!"

"As you know, we only say certain things when the situation has reached a critical crisis level. I'm suddenly at a loss for words, even though I've got more than enough will to say them. We only speak when we're truly convinced that saying something is absolutely imperative."

"Thandra, please! I don't understand!"

"Listen. If I say what I'm saying, it's because I'm certain."

"Thertain...?"

"Or if you prefer, I'll tell you the joke about the clown. What I meant was that I've been in touch with..."

Sandra, stretching her lips, looked up at the wall where the posters were.

"No! I thought that...!"

"Calm down, listen. Everything is as black as night..."

"You're not going to tell me you've been in touch with..."

"Don't look at me like that. Why wouldn't I be in touch with my own brother? In Guate, family is family in spite of everything."

"What are you thaying?"

"And if I dare to say anything to you now, it's only because they're planning to assassinate Manuel Fuentes Color."

"Oh my God!"

"Now you *know* I don't agree with Fuentes. I do respect him as a career politician, though, not one of those opportunists who go whichever way the wind blows, who always want to seem to be what they're not."

"Of course, of course."

"Besides, I don't even want to think about what would happen if they're successful. Can you imagine the scandal..."

"I need to call Washington immediately..."

"Yes, well. That's why I believe the Minister of Defense is right. There's no other way out."

"The coup?"

"You know very well what I mean. You yourself wrote the speech for your ambassador before the Chamber of Commerce when he said that the Department of State looked with tremendous concern at the obvious inability of a weak government to control subversion. That if said leaders chose their successors without taking advantage of the democratic process, and those chosen were corrupt, lacking the necessary qualities for such a high position, then the United States could be forced to consider other alternatives."

"It was a threat, Thandra, you know that. But you altho know that…What we wanted wath to influenth the Prethident tho that he could choothe our man as his thuccethor…"

"But he didn't choose him. Not only that. He chose a possible drug dealer, the equivalent of slapping you in the face. Maybe we're stupid or something…but in any case all of that is history now. What happened yesterday, combined with Fuentes Color's possible assassination, has changed the balance in an entirely different direction. Let's forget about elections. There will be a coup. The question is: What are you going to do? You can no longer stop it; you can't avoid it. It's too late, Bald Eagle. The man running with the ball is almost at the end zone, and there's no one left to tackle him. Are we on the same page?"

Behemoth opened his cigarette case, hurriedly pulled out one of the Virginia Slims and felt around for his lighter. Before reaching it, she'd already lit hers. He leaned his head over and allowed her to light his cigarette, and exhaled upwards, allowing the smoke to hide Kukulkán's face. She half smiled with that undecipherable air that could be sarcasm or rhapsodical parody. He nervously felt his gold chain.

"I thee."

"Of course they would rather work with you. After all, it's easier. Let's be clear about something: there's no turning back."

Behemoth choked a little on his smoke. He tried to

contain a rough cough and stood up. He started to walk from one end to the other, looking up occasionally as if he feared that the face on the wall could discern his ambivalence or insecurity.

"Thingth are not done like that."

Sandra opened her hands.

"That's how you play chess. It's a different matter if you don't like to be put in check. The important thing is that it's not check mate."

"I need to call Washington, Thandra....Right now."

"I understand. It's your duty."

"Yeth. Tell me. Ith the Minithter the brainth behind the coup?"

"And you're asking me?"

"Yeth, of courth... there ith never too much information. Now tell me. Do they exthpect an answer? From you? Do they know..."

"Relax. Of course not. They know I'm connected. How could they not know that? But they don't know with whom."

"Who thpoke to you?"

"Everyone speaks with me. Even the Minister of Defense..."

"Your brother. Where ith Kukulkán?"

"Who knows."

"Shit, don't fuck with me. You jutht spoke with him!"

He violently put out the cigarette he had barely smoked in an ashtray full of old butts and allowed himself to fall into the desk chair. His face had the same gray tone as the little hair he had left. She looked at him without losing her composure.

"He called me by means of a secret code we established a long time ago in case of emergency just to tell me that he was fine after what happened in Antigua."

"And while he wath at it, he told you...!"

"You're prying. Those are family matters."

"Doeth he trutht you?"

"Of course not, my dear. He's no fool..."

"You are thiblings, yet you betray each other."

"That's not true! I gave him information that's going to spread anyway. Besides, he knew I would do that; he knows me better than anyone. I never...I have to go now. Enough of this! It's too close, too..."

She pretended to sob. He stood and ran to caress her head and shoulders.

"Calm down. Forgive me if I had to athk all thothe thingth, but I had to do it. You've alwayth been thtrong..."

"It's family. You don't understand blood ties! You're like ice in whiskey."

"Yeth we do underthtand. It'th the job, you know. Well, we are more...Anglo, I thuppose. But it'th all right..."

"Yes, but before I leave, advise me. What can I way to the Minister of Defense when he comes by the house?"

"My God Thandra! I must...! I underthtand your point of view, of courth, but... I can't just like that...I'm thorry I didn't know about this thooner through other channelth..."

"It looks as if things were triggered by last night's events and by the news about Fuentes Color."

"Have you thpoken to Don Leonel?"

"Yep. I cover all my bases."

"Ith he in on thith?"

"You and your questions. You'll also want to know..."

"Fine I already told you I can't make thethe dethithions...."

"Don Leonel, as you can imagine, is furious with the President's treason of choothing that drug dealer as his successor."

"...and hith inability to maintain the command of the army in a counter-rebel crithith..."

"Perfect!"

"That'th not an answer. I have to conthult firtht."

"When?"

"Give me a little time. I'll call right now and..."

Behemoth stared at her. He lifted his left eyebrow and winked dreamily with his right eye.

"How about getting together tonight and I'll give you my anther?"

"I'd have to see you early."

"That'th even better. I have to dedicate thome time to think about how to get Wright out of the jam he got himthelf into."

"Don't remind me, please."

"I don't know if you knew it, but the original idea was to uthe him ath bait to capture...Kukulkán."

"It was very clear that there was something fishy."

He let out a coarse laugh like a movie extra who'd lost his director's instructions. She clapped as if celebrating his naiveté and rolled her eyes. They stood. He hugged her. It was difficult for her to extract herself from his hairy arms, but, when he felt sure he had her clamped, she slipped away as if she were covered in Vaseline. Winking, she ran to the door, closing it behind her.

6

The press conference ended. Numerous camera flashes illuminated the air as if a crazy star projector in a planetarium had begun to rotate on its axis and spin out of control. Besieged by the crowd, Manuel Fuentes Color stepped down from the podium and searched for his car. The bodyguards opened the way for him. Several journalists seeped in, sticking microphones in his face like sharp daggers. Nobody paid any attention to the curses. Sightseers fluttered by the line of bodyguards as if in some orgiastic ritual. A wonderfully-dressed television commentator with nicely-styled hair managed to sneak in under the arms of a large bodyguard and growled in Fuentes Color's face.

"What you've just said is a declaration of war."

"It's a shout of despair. I'm disgusted, you see, fed up with being ignored by the Department of State. They think everything is East and West…"

"For your safety, sir."

"I'm going to Europe in three days. In any case, I have the support of the Socialist International."

His vehicle finally arrived. A muscular arm whose body couldn't be distinguished from the crowd opened the rear door. He ducked his head in order to enter. His body was wide and appeared unable to go through the narrow opening, but with some agile wriggling he disappeared into the vehicle. Two more men got in behind him. The chauffeur began moving the car slowly among the flashes, the television camera crews and the curious people who shrieked like malnourished turkeys. The mass of humans began to disappear in a cloud of dust. The car picked up speed. A second car took off behind it. Ariadne saw them turn on the corner. She was going to the same contact as Vallejo and wasn't able to stop and take notice of the movement of both vehicles and people.

She was wearing a blond wig and a lot of makeup. Her eyebrows had been shaved, and this made her feel naked. The hairs on her arm were bleached blonde and she had painted her nails. The night before she had dreamed that the sun had disappeared. It was as if she were on an island surrounded by the sea. Suddenly the sun began to go out as if in an eclipse, and everything became dark. As the sunlight died, a gigantic hand pushed down on her chest to the point that she was no longer able to breathe. She awoke with a jolt. As a young girl she had always had nightmares and would wake up screaming in the night. Her father would run to hug her and bring her a glass of water. Sometimes he would stay to read her stories until she fell back to sleep.

Her father was a ventriloquist. He worked on the radio and performed in all the town fairs. One time, when she was a little girl, he even traveled with the national soccer team to El Salvador during the elimination round of the World Cup. His dummy, "Don Roque," was the team mascot. Her father told her that, in a lapse of attention, the Salvadoran fans stole Don Roque. The Guatemalan fans began to yell at the top of their lungs, "Give Don Roque back, give Don Roque back!" Don Roque, however, disappeared and the team was eliminated from the World Cup. Her father said that those were simply things that happened. When he got back he had another "Don Roque" made.

On Sundays the family ate lunch at their grandparents' house. There she was able to see her uncle. He was very dark, with a wide moustache, the way gentlemen wore them at the end of the last century. His hair was curly. He would always put her on his lap and call her his "little baby doll" and play horsey. He had delicate fingers like those of a woman.

Now her uncle was the chief of the secret police. However, when they caught her involved with the FERG, he had saved her. He took her out of the disgusting tiny room where they had her before they removed her clothing, and he brought her to his office. With a hoarse voice that fluctuated between calm and screaming, he really put her in her place. He told her to stop getting herself involved with bullshit or the next time he wouldn't lift a finger to help her.

"You get drunk off the pain of the poor!" he said. "And you're not poor! You've no reason to involve yourself in things that are none of your business!"

She trembled like a little garden plant shaken by a hurricane. When he could no longer say anything else, he let her go and tore up her record card. When she was almost to the door of the precinct she managed to turn around and say in a weak voice, "I am who I am, and I'll do what I have to do without anyone's help."

He frowned in disapproval and shouted to her, "Worse for you, baby doll."

She tried to hurry in spite of feeling weak. She only had

to walk a very short distance from where they had dropped her off. She watched the cars disappear like black dots several streets down. She clenched her teeth together and felt her stomach tighten. The wound was hurting her in spite of the morphine. She jiggled her bag with sweaty fingers in order to make sure, one more time, that her gun was there. Anyway, it didn't matter. As bad as she felt, she wouldn't be able to do anything should anything happen. A cold fear ran down her back like a green snake sneaking into her blouse. Kukulkán would be furious if he found out that the car had not brought her right to the door of the house, but she still thought that it would be dangerous if her collaborators found out the exact address. She had gone out only because it was a real emergency.

When Fuentes Color's car turned the corner, a Cherokee Chief without license plates got behind the second car in the retinue. The driver saw it immediately. He drummed on the steering wheel, accelerated and drove through the stop light just as it changed. However, the Cherokee Chief also went through the red light. Right away it passed them. Turning the wheel hard to the right it squeezed between the second car and Fuentes Color's car, slamming on the brakes. The second car had to stop immediately, crashing slightly against the rear of the Cherokee Chief.

Right then everyone heard the sound of a helicopter with the humming of its propeller blades like *matracas*, Good Friday noisemakers. Several people turned their heads and saw it flying low. It was a government helicopter. With the sound reverberating inside Fuentes Color's temples, his driver accelerated. All of the passengers in the car turned around and looked back. To their dismay they noticed that the second car was no longer there. With mouths agape, they saw the distant human movements behind the Cherokee Chief stopped in the middle of the street. The sound of the helicopter kept them from knowing if there had been a shoot-out.

"They fucked us."

It was incredible to think about it. It was a beautiful day with a blue sky, as if someone had repainted the scene with bright watercolors. In the distance the two volcanoes looked like two little dots of melted, colored wax. But it was no longer a normal day, unless they could manage to escape the ambush that had obviously been prepared for them. The prisoner of an agonizing impatience, Fuentes Color pushed his hands and feet into the front seat as if, with his own effort, he might be able to make the car go faster. They were about to reach the corner and were gaining speed when at the next intersection two new cars with tinted windows and no license plates appeared.

"Hit them!" shouted Fuentes Color.

His driver didn't take his foot off the gas. The heavy automobile shot forward like a meteor with such good luck that it reached the intersection when the first car without plates had already passed but before the second car could completely block it. They hit the trunk of the first car and the left mudguard of the second, twisting both cars to 45 degree angles. The vibration of the impact made the three jump as if in an earthquake followed by a dry explosion. The smashed vehicles went sideways as they tried not to lose control. Fuentes Color's car was also damaged, but it was large and had the advantage of greater momentum. They continued to the next block.

"Damn! We got through!"

His face was beaming, highlighting his paleness even more. It was as if this wasn't really happening to him but was a movie he had seen as a boy, before discovering the infinite sadness of being born Guatemalan. For an instant it seemed as if they had escaped. His men barely smiled with those smiles that masked a deep angst. They turned around. Those men had gotten out of their wrecked cars. They couldn't hear anything over the sound of the helicopter.

Upon turning their eyes to the front they saw that there

was a third vehicle at the next corner, blocking the road. The riders were all out. They were hiding behind cars parked along both sides of the street, and they had their machine guns pointed at them. Fuentes Color studied the distant curve, full of little tin soldiers, with an absent look.

The powder flashes came from the muzzles, though nothing could be heard. The front window exploded into a thousand pieces and the car swerved a little to the right. It hit a parked car and bounced back toward the middle of the street. The car again started to swerve to the right and only then did Fuentes Color realize that his driver was slumped over the wheel. His body fell on the gearshift in infinite slow-motion. They struck another car on the side of the road and bounced back toward the middle, finally coming to a stop. Fuentes Color pressed his lips together tightly. He felt a slight disorientation, as though he had fallen from a cloud. He wished he could go and hide under his parents' bed.

The shielded men advanced. They were all wearing masks. They walked slowly, their Uzis out in front. One of them spoke into a walkie-talkie. It seemed like a scene from a silent movie because of the noise from the helicopter. The closer these men came to the car, the more the helicopter descended, as if it was about to land on the roof of the car itself. Suddenly the car windows exploded outward. The shots did not come from the front. The men from the cars in the rear had opened fire. Fuentes Color's companions jumped like electrocuted dolls, as if their clothing desperately wanted to leap from their bodies. Everything was silent except for the sound of the helicopter. The men walked like robots.

Six figures surrounded the car at the same time. The windows were all shattered, glass everywhere. The other bodyguards were bent over in their seats. The driver had finally fallen fully onto the gearshift. Nobody moved. Fuentes Color, however, was still alive. His hair was out of place and there were glass shards and scrapes all over his body. He had blood on his suit, but not too much. He looked at the men with a lucid stare, his eyes wide open. He half-smiled, and winked his left eye.

"Kill me, then…assholes…"

The man with the walkie-talkie looked at him in silence and turned his radio on again.

"Yellow Triangle here…Can you hear me?…Yes. Objective wounded. He's alive…as you order. Over and out."

The man put his walkie-talkie away and took out a pistol. Fuentes Color flashed an enigmatic smile as if laughing at himself for falling into such an obvious trap. His eyes were an ocean green, hushed, splashed with dark whirlpools.

"Murderers… Every dog has his day…"

The man stretched out his arm until the barrel of the gun was resting beside his temple. Fuentes Color did not move. His temple convulsed spastically. An enigmatic look remained fixed for the last time on the image of those volcanoes, Huracán and Cabracán, which always demanded sacrifices. The man pulled the trigger.

Slowly the helicopter flew upward. Leaning to the right, it gained altitude. It crossed the sky, continued up past the volcanoes, and disappeared from sight.

CHAPTER THREE

1

It was a room of about fifteen by ten feet. The walls were peeling from a greenish wetness that covered the dark brown corners like a mossy cloth. At the back of the room there was a window that had been covered with boards nailed haphazardly across it from outside. The remains of dried-up newspapers stuck to the plywood disguised the fact that they were rotting through. Iron bars prevented their removal. Exactly opposite that wall was the door. Made of wood covered in chipped paint, it was much thicker than many modern doors. It had three locks that made a frightening screech whenever it was opened.

The bed was narrow and sagged grotesquely, as if the springs had been crushed with unspeakable practices or unnatural acts. The yellowed mattress had designs of reddish flowers interspersed with humidity stains and other indelible marks that served to disrupt the chilling monotony. An equally narrow desk was located below the covered window, but it served more to make access to the window difficult than to actually be used. There was also an old wooden chair and a very old chiffonier.

Tom Wright was seated on the bed. His shirt and pants were wrinkled and covered with grease stains. His jaw showed evidence of at least one day without having shaved. His dry lips were about to split open in the middle, and there were small white pustules at the corners of his mouth. Having his is hands tied behind his back made the greenish veins of his arms protrude. A black cloth covered his eyes.

Suddenly Wright hear the unmistakable shriek of the door locks being opened. Two men wearing ski masks entered the room and turned on the light. They took the blindfold off his eyes and untied the ropes from his arms. The restraints had scarcely left his wrists when he began to massage them where the knots had cut off his circulation, leaving incisions on his skin surrounded by bruises.

"Just so you know, we just came from killing that traitor Manuel Fuentes Color."

Tom Wright almost let his lower jaw drop in spite of his effort not to show any kind of emotion. He felt a damp congestion in his head that came over him like a grayish ocean mist hanging in deformed angles over the Tulane Campus. As he rubbed his wrists, he let out a whistle.

"The presidential candidate? What for?" The other man did not let him finish his question:

"Silence! You only have permission to ask when..." But now it was the second man who saw himself interrupted by the first one who waved his palm at him with authority.

"Without a doubt the death of Fuentes Color is a blow. The elections will be canceled. This will infuriate the people, who will be in an excellent position to rebel against the army..."

"But you're crazy! Fuentes Color was one of your strongest allies, a fellow traveler..."

"We don't have allies. Only interests."

The first man retreated abruptly, followed by the second. It was a tiny gesture, but Wright intuited that the man felt uncomfortable playing his role.

"Of course. Changing topics, can I speak with Kukulkán?"

"Not yet. He's very busy. However, he promised that as soon as he gets back, he'll speak to you."

"Obviously he has a lot of things to deal with. First Gray, now Fuentes Color. That's not bad for someone who isn't even the Commander-in-Chief of his organization."

The first man twisted his mouth in displeasure, fighting back the urge to smack him.

"He's commander of the urban front. That gives him a very wide jurisdiction. Let's not talk about that anymore. I wanted to let you know something. We're going to leave you untied. But remember, no 'fuckin' around.' We don't want any funny little games. We've got all the angles covered."

"I don't doubt it."

"So be good. You'll be out of here soon enough." He smiled.

They exited the room, leaving the light on. He could hear the shrick of the lock. After that, the footsteps disappeared into the distance. When he could no longer hear any sound, he quickly took off his shoes and put them under the bed. In his socks he tiptoed to the window. He observed the headlines from the papers plastering the opening: "'No one dies in the evening,' says Father Chemita, after being threatened." He didn't know who Father Chemita was. "Two days after he was kidnaped, the Departmental Administrator of Internal Revenue is found assassinated in the Quiché." "Wave of assaults in the capital: three guards killed." "Three insurgents die in Comalapa." "Bombs hit the diplomatic headquarters of Israel, Argentina and Haiti." He picked off a piece of newspaper but could not see beyond the plywood that covered the window from the outside. He gave a half turn. He walked toward the door and put his ear against it.

He almost stopped breathing. He heard the voices of the men that had been in his room moments before. He almost wished his heart would stop beating so he could hear better. The first one said, "I don't have anything against it but I always end up playing the same role; I no longer know what is reality and what is fantasy."

The second commented:

"If he only knew..." He laughed with a sharp and prolonged buzz.

The first gave another opinion:

"It's just that they don't understand all the sacrifices we've made. That's why they just don't *get us*; it's all nonsense to them."

There was a pause. The second man spoke up:

"What should we do now?"

"Just wait. They said they would call as soon as the operation was underway. But we're not supposed to mistreat him in any way."

"And if he does something?"

"He's not going to. You'll see." Their footsteps faded away.

Tom Wright straightened up. The door's smell of cheap pine penetrated to the back of his neck. He began to doubt everything. *"Alas! He is betrayed and I undone."* He knew he wasn't a prisoner of the EGP. He knew it from the moment he was kidnaped. However, the rest was confusing. They wanted him to believe that the EGP had him. Everything was so topsy-turvy. Could Kukulkán exist? Maybe he was nothing more than a simulacrum, one more case in this hallucinating world that he was discovering a little at a time as he peeled it layer by layer in search of its elusive center. He was living an intolerable paradox, a monstrous ritual hidden under the most sophisticated of social graces. Guatemala was the object of dark desires that needed to be brought into the light. Where was that simple scene that he had learned? They were breaking all the rules on him. Would he himself end up on the wrong side of the tracks as well? At that moment there was nothing he would have liked more than a shot of Scotch to refresh his thoughts. He began to pace back and forth. He made numerical calculations to regain his calm. 144 was equal to three times 48 and also 6 times 24 and 12 times 12.

"Shit. I've been had from start to finish..."

A sharp twinge beginning in his stomach began to overtake him. Not because of what might happen to him. He felt strangely calm about the remote possibility that something could actually happen to him. No. It was, more than anything, discovering that everything he thought before was wrong. It was the terror of feeling that everyone close to him, from his bosses to Sandra, had tricked him. It was the fear of losing his faith in the system. It was the anguish of not knowing whom he could trust, of not knowing who was on which side. He was lost in a deep and dark loneliness, in a horrendous torrent of savage despair. He was living only an illusion, a macabre illusion. He had confused the dream with reality.

Outside, the phone rang. He was startled to hear it. He hurriedly placed his ear against the door. The phone rang four times. Nobody answered. He was about to return to his pondering when he heard the distinctive "click" of an answering machine. There was no recorded greeting, but there was space where a caller could leave a message. It was then that he got one of the worst surprises of his life. It was Sandra's voice. He was so confused that he doubted it at first. But no. It couldn't be any other voice. If there was ever a voice ingrained in his mind, it was that one. A spectral voice. He could be fooled about anything except that voice. It was Sandra. It couldn't be anyone else.

"Coral Snake two. Rattlesnake here. It's six o' clock. Prepare the transfer as planned. Confirm in ten minutes at the latest, or we'll have to use the reserve plan."

He doubled over in two as if they had kicked him in the stomach. He had heard only a few words, and, yet, they were clear scribblings on the margins of a nightmare. He felt fear at his vulnerability, which he hated to acknowledge, childlike fear, the stark realization that he had lost his peace of mind forever. He had control over nothing. He knew then that he had lost the immense physical and psychological energy required to keep up the illusion that he was persevering in his profession. He looked up at the ceiling, and it appeared as nothing more than a specter of himself. Tears ran down his cheeks, dirtying his face as if someone had smudged it with coal. He remembered the words of his most admired football coach: "When you're afraid, you fumble the ball to the opponent." He had to remain faithful to this wisdom. He slowly stood up in front of the bed. He had to find his feet. Death was just a synonym for nothingness. The enemy was embedded within him. He sat down. With the utmost care he tried to fit his swollen feet back into his shoes.

2

It was an enormous bathroom with an entire wall covered with mirrors. The sun entered diagonally through the window, its lukewarm late-afternoon rays tenderly wrapping all the objects in the bathroom, from the luxurious to the bizarre, in a golden aura like a fond embrace. The light reflecting off the mirror created a supernatural clarity, as if contained within a crystalline bubble. In the corner, a piece of white *copal* burned discretely, giving the impression that the mirror was smoldering.

Captain Pacal stood in front of the sink contemplating himself in the mirror with an air of grotesque disquiet. His tenuous smile was barely offset by the harshness and grimace of his face muscles. Shirtless, he radiated a precarious and overbearing fastidiousness. His hairy chest was clearly visible in the mirror as he looked carefully to make sure that the line of his thin mustache was absolutely perfect. Nothing in the world infuriated him more than irregularity in the moustache line.

To his horror he noticed that some chest hairs had begun to turn white. The same thing was happening on his forearm. There was a tattoo about two inches long of the K God of the

Mayas, "Ah Bolon Dzacab," on his left arm As tradition dictated, there was a serpent in place of one of the legs of the figure, which also had a grotesquely large nose with the head of an ax protruding from it. Leaning over the sink, he splashed warm water into his armpits. When they were thoroughly soaked, he stood and allowed the water to run down his body. Then he wet his neck and let the water flow down to the floor.

Water always calmed Pacal's nerves. Ever since he was a boy, only warm water could really calm him down, especially after his father had given him a beating and the temptation to shoot him in the head was almost overwhelming. In those days, they did not have hot running water, but the maid—Esperanza was her name, a powerful woman with dauntless eyes, a ready smile and a shrill voice—used to heat it for him. She would mix it in the tiny shower stall with the freezing gush that poured out of a naked pipe with a missing shower head. There he would sit, in an aluminum cauldron of tepid water, calming himself down. Coming from Escuintla, the city of palm trees, he never got used to the cold weather of the misty capital. He couldn't go for long without a stuffy nose. Warm water was his only relief.

He took the bar of soap in his hands and scrubbed his armpits vigorously. He rubbed the soap in his right hand and caressed the back of his neck in a fruitless attempt to relax those same muscles that seemed to be made of steel. He needed a massage, but there wasn't time right now.

The life he enjoyed now had not come easy. Abandoned by his father, half starving in Escuintla, by pure miracle he arrived at the capital, where he won a scholarship to the Adolfo Hall Military Academy. He was thankful to Colonel Búcaro, who adopted him and pushed him, though he had a difficult character. It was a shame that Búcaro's uprising ended unsuccessfully, forcing him out of politics. Coups d'état were also an art, like the art of war. Somebody should write a manual about them, a type of Von Clausewitz for uprisings. Coups are a continuation of politics through other means. In order to have a successful coup it's also necessary to accumulate all of the moral and material forces possible, while keeping them compartmentalized.

Pacal stretched his right arm over the basin. Languorously, his left hand began to take water from the stream and throw it under his right armpit in order to wash away the soap. He immediately repeated this with the other arm.

He rose quickly. He had luck. Luck and slyness. Just like in soccer, you needed a degree of slyness to move the ball forward. Playing cleanly never guaranteed a victory. Nice guys finished last. Still, you couldn't let the referee see you deliberately making fouls. The key was to do it without being seen, little low blows, the little kicks on the foot that would suddenly immobilize the adversary, the malicious forward spree toward the goal. *"Hasta la victoria siempre,"* as the subversives always said. Always onward to victory.

With marvelous prodigality he allowed the water to run down his hairy forearms to remove all traces of soap, while the words uttered in his long march to that very day echoed in his mind. He had been the director of the immigration office. He had studied all the ways to enter and exit the country, and he was responsible for capturing a double-hitch trailer that came from Managua loaded with weapons. That was worth gold to him. He even came close to capturing one of the commanders when he left the country, but the crafty, sullen-looking individual, who spoke with a waspish authority, disappeared between his fingers like water. He had to recognize that they were also good in their line of work. All the same, he rose to Commander of the Special Forces. It was he who introduced the cry, "Who are we, who are we?" "We are jaguars, we are jaguars, masters of all men on Earth!"

He already felt clean and more relaxed. Stretching his arms and fingers in front of the mirror, he suddenly remembered that this was the gesture that Colonel Lucas

Caballeros used to make in his presidential ads: "I am the man with clean hands." There weren't any men with clean hands in this country. Nobody could have them and survive.

The only dirt left was under his fingernails. They weren't like those of mechanics after working all day under a car, but they were somewhat dirty. Greenish. He thought about looking for the nail clippers in the cabinet but changed his mind. It didn't matter. They weren't very dirty. Clean hands were faggot's hands anyway. He didn't have any reason to be ashamed of the shit he had scratched.

With theatrical suddenness he gave a half-turn and took a bulletproof vest from the chair. He put it on in front of the mirror with circumspection, watching himself carefully to see how it fit, as a woman might have done trying on a corset. He wrinkled his brow while contemplating the scars on his face and thought about her. A contemptuous shrillness came out of his mouth, as if he were interrogating a ghost or trying to unearth himself from some troublesome and obstinate memory which had slipped out of place. He put on a short-sleeved khaki shirt and buttoned it up with care. He unzipped his pants to tuck in the shirttails, zipped them up again, and checked in the mirror to see that the shirt lay perfectly flat. He couldn't stand wrinkles in his clothes. He didn't tolerate uniforms that weren't impeccably clean, ironed, with the crease of the pants perfectly marked.

Once satisfied with how he looked, he walked to the room next door with a stiff, proud step. The sun was flooding the room with the same impalpable softness, breaking into luminous geometrical forms. He had a large double bed against the wall and flowers in all four corners of the room, beautiful begonias planted in wooden grenade boxes. To create a rustic effect, he had left the boxes unfinished. Black letters could still be discerned, announcing the old contents. The serial numbers were equally visible. He took a small red watering can discretely hung in a corner and began to water the plants. He would dip the can over the plants until a small stream of water glided out. He checked to see if the watering can needed more water. Refilling it in the bathroom, he moved to the next box, repeating the same casual movements. He began to think about her again, as if awakening from a sleep that had lasted centuries.

After watering the plants, he walked to the night table. He opened it with a small silver-plated key that he kept in the moneybag of his pants and took out a nine-millimeter Luger while his lips twitched in a would-be ironical smile, feeling, hovering over him, the breath of a new self-possession. He observed it meticulously as if coming out of a deep meditation, with great patience and care, before sitting on the bed. Taking a box of bullets out of the same drawer, he placed it next to the gun. He opened it and took the bullets out, catching the light on them in what seemed an enforced stillness, a moment laden with that perverse significance of bad dreams. He opened the chamber and proceeded to load it. Inspecting the bullets one by one, he would first roll them between his thumb and index finger, as if showing his dexterity to a fascinated audience. He pushed each one inside with as much care as a nanny changing a baby, and then he repeated the delicate ritual.

Once the pistol was loaded, he looked for a rag to shine his shoes. He was obsessed with making them shine as if they were made of patent leather. This was part of that singular personal neatness that he demanded of himself to futilely try to erase the uncouth image which he abhorred, that of an excessively Indian-looking face whose reflection in the mirror always tortured his distressed eyes. He couldn't overcome the reality that because of the traits in his face, people like her would never love him. Plastic surgery on his lips and nose wouldn't do him any harm. This would be in addition to fixing the deformation of his foot. It wouldn't be too hard. It wasn't that big of an issue. He'd heard that they did a good job with plastic surgery in Brazil. The only thing he wouldn't be able to repair was his height. He detested the fact that people could look down on him.

Finding the rag that he stored in the lower drawer of his closet, he began to shine his shoes. He had just finished brushing the left one when a uniformed soldier entered unexpectedly with a message for the Captain, but, upon seeing the eyes that struck him like lightning upon entering, he stopped and acquired a cowed expression as he gazed around him, doubting the orders he had received. Pacal would have killed him right there. He didn't tolerate anyone, anyone, violating the privacy of his bedroom. For any reason whatsoever.

"And who in the hell gave you permission to enter?"

The soldier stopped, frozen in mid-step, wishing he could bite the knuckle of his index finger. His mouth stayed open, his eyes widened, displaying an idiotic expression, waiting for the evil to hatch from Captain Pacal and head right for him.

"Um, I…"

"Nothing! You have no right! What's your name?"

"Soldier Halcón, sir!"

The soldier tried to turn around and walk away, get out, do something to stop Captain Pacal. He felt cornered and wished to flee from the mustached face that lunged at him. But this was no longer possible.

"Come here!"

The order was adamant and scared him even more. He did not want to get any closer. However, with all of the fingers on his hand wriggling like a spider, Pacal commanded him to move right next to him. His pupils had become so small that they now appeared as two little black dots, so black that they almost glowed. He began to walk towards him, twitching and throttling, like a man condemned to death.

"Shine my shoes!"

The soldier got down on his knees. He grabbed the rag and began to shine the right shoe without much energy. Pacal looked at him unflinchingly, with a slight, crooked smile. A drop of saliva escaped from the corner of his mouth. The soldier noticed that the right shoe had a thicker heel compared to the left.

"Do it harder! As if you were a man!"

He began to shine with more vigor. He spit a little on the surface of the leather in order to make it shine more and rubbed with all of the energy he could muster, evoking his days as a mistreated child wondering throughout the threatening city streets.

"*U nen cab, u nen cah*," whispered Pacal. Now he felt like a true Ah Bolon Dzacab.

3

"So what's up? What're you thinking about, man?"

Vallejo asked the question with an excess of energy that conveyed an abyss of misery and confusion.

"Think. Why the *Gringo*? And then Fuentes Color. There's some logic behind that, and we have to find out what it is."

Kukulkán repeated these facts with an offhand air, an indifference belied by the tension in the muscles of a face used to displaying an expressionless calm in public. He had an intuitive sense that the iron doors of some gigantic trap were closing in around him, and he hesitated to ascribe to it any particular meaning. Nonetheless, he felt the coldness of the iron. He could smell it.

"After that little speech he gave, it's normal he got fucked. Who said that in our country the tongue isn't the main enemy of one's own neck?"

It was a small, gloomy room with a tall wooden ceiling where, without paying much attention, you could hear the scurrying of the rats, as happy as if they were in their own playground. Ariadne rested on a cot covered by so many blankets that she seemed to have gained several pounds. The men walked from one side to the other, almost running into the yellowish lamp-globe that hung from an exposed wire, turning slowly like a pendulum in an eternal circle of light.

Vallejo had forgotten the elemental rule about speaking quietly at that late hour. Kukulkán's back had been hurting all night. Looking thoughtful and nodding slowly, he quickly drank little sips of bitter coffee that nearly spilled while he moved around in that small space. Fighting off the headache that had crept in behind his eyebrows, he let the lines of a tender poem float into his mind like a memory of youth, while remembering the jacaranda trees blooming as if they were never to bloom again: "It is you by my side, you are the shadow, it is you in my head who sleeps in the day, in my vagabond heart, in my tears, in my hand, in my pain."

"No, Vallejo. The operation was too well-planned to have been spontaneous. They decided to kill him well before. But, why yesterday...? Why after kidnaping the *Gringo*...? Of course! What time is it?"

"Whatever time your heart wills it to be."

"Don't screw around; this is serious."

"Six in the morning. Why?"

"Turn on the radio. Turn on the radio immediately!"

Reacting to the frantic shouting, Vallejo ran for the dusty transistor radio abandoned in a corner of the room. He turned it on right away. The unmistakable notes of the ragged Mariscal Zavala Brigade Band jumped out immediately, playing woefully out of key the Radetzky March. He changed the station. On the next one, the same tune blared out, the same metallic melody echoing a funereal air. He continued searching down the rest of the radio dial. On all the stations, the music was the same.

"They're on all of the stations...!"

Kukulkán looked at him with enormous eyes.

"A coup d'état!"

Vallejo sighed as if this were a bad joke. A half-asleep Ariadne tried to prop herself up on one of her elbows.

"We have to reestablish contact immediately. Our militants are all going to get confused."

"But, man, we can't go out now, don't lose it!"

"Yes we can. The coup, and the kidnaping of the *Gringo*. Think. This is starting to smell like a brutal offensive against us. And on top of it, we're stuck with Gray. The organization is going through one of its worst moments. At this point we have no alternative."

4

The house was only half-lit. A rosy, silk-flounced lampshade crowned the light. Sandra was seated across from Alvaro in a large club chair covered with embroidered upholstery. In the corner, the ashes of an old fire still glowed. A glass table with mahogany edges held a large number of dirty glasses and cigarette butts in a pentagon-shaped ashtray. She was flooded with the joys of a new self-possession, which pushed her to exploit her charm to the full. The sweetness of her affable smile reflected an abandon that could melt an entire column of tanks. With the incipient roundness of his face, Alvaro, sporting a day-old beard and displaying his careless diet in his expanding waistline, contemplated her benevolently, with a half-open mouth, bloodshot eyes, and a tinge of desire. She was wearing a large Brazilian-style cotton shirt with creases everywhere.

"You came home late."

He wistfully alluded to it, without irony or reproach.

"I needed to know what they thought in Washington."

Open-mouthed, quivering, he added, with a honey-coated voice that he only employed when he was being spontaneous and not making any political calculations:

"You work too hard."

"Tonight, it's anticlimactic to say that. Where's your sense of dramatic tension?"

The tenderness was replaced by a more perturbed tone. His ears perked up as if detecting danger. He stood up, violently grabbing her with fierce relish:

"No, don't go, please..."

She let herself fall, grinning, until she sank into the club chair. Her eyes vanished in the half-light as if they had traveled elsewhere. Scratching his balls, Alvaro charged back with an avid look directed at her:

"I've got nothing against masturbation. It lets me make love to the person I love the most but hardly ever see."

"What an elegant way of complaining about the fact that we hardly ever sleep together anymore. You poor thing, how you suffer!"

She gave him a deliberately quizzical look, noting his body half-falling from the chair, his feet on the table about to knock over the ashtray. His white linen pants were stained with ash and the remnants of a drink. He seemed to be a dirty rag mistakenly left behind by the cleaning lady. Overtaken by a feeling of maternal tenderness she rarely felt, Sandra embarrassed herself by speaking aloud in a philosophical tone.

"Sometimes we all feel very alone. But if you pursue that angle, the professional tone ingrained in me by my father will come out and bore you to death. I'll talk pompously about the search for serenity, about how a woman's continual self-questioning is something that can't be explained with words, about the passion we all have inside our little souls, and about reclaiming for ourselves everything that we hate about others. But after putting up with that heavy nonsense, not even your well-oiled sex vices would allow you to masturbate, because you'd be snoring like a happy pig."

Something about her tone rubbed Alvaro the wrong way, and, magnified by the Scotch, her words slapped him in the face. Grabbing her by the wrists, he squeezed hard. She groaned and shook like an angry snake caught by surprise behind the head. During their struggle several glasses fell, and they spilled the ashtray on the floor. Suddenly she stopped resisting.

"If you like…go ahead."

He stared at her. She held his gaze while her lips turned downwards, into a slightly mocking smile. He let her go. Her smile rebuked him like a poorly-behaved child.

"How did those lines go? Let's see if I remember. Yes. You don't have to act with me, Alvaro. You don't have to say anything and you don't have to do anything. Not a thing. Oh, maybe just whistle. You know how to whistle, don't you, Alvaro? You just put your lips together and blow."

"Good. Great memory! But how about if, while you talk about whistling, you say something like, 'Come here, come here honey. Drive me crazy, make me go wild. Suck, suck…. But what are you doing? Why do you blow? Suck, my dear.'"

"Excellent!" She clapped. "What are you thinking about?"

"Well, if you keep looking at me like that, I just might build up the courage to tell you."

"Very good!" She applauded again. "Have the courage."

"I would love to hit you."

The words had barely left his mouth and he already felt an unusual tension in his testicles and the smell of sweat under his arms.

"Let's see. We're getting away from the script. Explain how."

Her voice was daring, provocative. She brought her hands to her head and shook her hair as much as she could, while her pupils contracted.

"I would like to see you sprawled out on the bed, tied to the headboard, half-nude, dead with fear."

"That sounds good. As if I were a defenseless little girl."

"Yes. And then take out a hose and hit you with it on the

legs, on the back…Hit you and hear you yell that you like it, you like it."

Sandra closed her eyes and visualized the fantasy with unconnected images that incited the indestructible mosaic of desire. Her right hand traced a circle on her abdomen. Her left one slapped the thigh on the same side of her body.

"I like it…I like it…even if it's not in the script."

"And hit you more, and more, soaked in sweat. And tie up your hands and feet. I would want to see the ropes around your wrists."

She twisted herself while touching her breasts, her arms, her sex, leaning her head to one side and then the other in a single liquid lament that comically evoked a character from a romantic bolero.

"Now I understand why love at first sight saves so much time, and why, when she tries to decide between two evils, Mae West always picks the one she's never tried before."

"Caress your thighs with the hoses, feel your trembling and your attempt to move your leg away."

She put her leg on the table in such a way that her skirt ended up halfway up her thigh. In frank provocation, she began to caress her sex under her skirt while looking fixedly at him with a comically exaggerated ardor.

"The arms and tips of your feet asleep, like a convent girl who accepts the mysteries."

She twisted against the chair. Rubbing her shoulder with the palm of her hand, she lowered the strap of her dress, making faces with her lips as if she were drinking him entirely without leaving a single drop. Her mouth melted as if her lipstick had magically run in all directions from a myriad of invisible kisses.

"And hit you, time and time again, let me go, let go of me, see how the purple bruises show up on your skin, see the agonizing grin on your mouth with each blow, until I make you cry…"

"Me, cry? I don't cry."

The sensual expression vanished. She froze, then coiled, before turning and slowly walking away. He tried to stand up as best he could. Hitting his knee against the coffee table, he spilled another glass before accidentally kicking one of the legs, jerking the table forward several inches and producing a cacophony of broken glass.

"Wait! Now I know that it has been worth it to suffer so much, so much, and that the joy bought with sorrow is sweeter."

"I no longer have a heart, you arrived too late. No matter how much I…"

"So then it is better to die… I can't remember any other lyrics. Damn."

"Improvise, it doesn't matter. You were talking about dying?"

"Well, yes. Dying, because your love for me was fleeting…"

"And I exchanged your kisses for money, thus poisoning my heart. Maybe I will die tomorrow, but, tonight, I want to live!"

"Excellent memory for the boleros as well! In movies and boleros, we're even. Explain just one thing to me."

She threw her arms above her head in a melodramatic gesture. He felt a light pain in his knee.

"Why was it necessary to kidnap the CIA agent?"

It surprised her that he would come out with this question at that particular point in time. However she understood that such an out-of-place detail was the only thing that still created a sense of permanence in the couple, a complicity more relevant than love, kind of like the staunch friendship between two thieves. Their political conspiracies were the only rush that justified the pathetic nature of their kisses and the few hugs that they still gave each other.

"In order to force the hand of the *Gringos*…but also…"
"Yes?"

She paused as if she feared to say something that wasn't

completely clear to her either. She feared that the game would stop being one and simply turn into a forlorn chase in which she would lose her own skin like the *ixiptla,* the personification of god in the carnival called *Ochpaniztli* that so well represented the inhuman conditions of existence.

"So that the EGP wouldn't be destroyed."

Sandra smiled. She thought that she would no longer be able to get away from serious thoughts. Life was too contradictory and most of the time tasted like castor oil. In spite of that, people redeemed themselves by facing it with courage tinged with craziness. That's why one couldn't predict how long it would last, other than the axiom that it couldn't be too long in the country that was their lot, and that the end would inevitably be violent. She lived it with a bizarre touch of happiness. It was right up her alley. She had been an inspiration and her music pierced his heart, like the bolero said, even if she now invoked it with a sense of irony.

Sandra slowly walked away. Alvaro stayed behind in the living room, watching her appetizing bottom recede. The jiggling movement provoked a burning desire in him, but he held himself back. Feeling suddenly tired, Sandra began thinking about things that she usually denied entry to her head, because letting them in for even a few seconds could generate nightmares for weeks, months, years.

She thought about Alvaro and Don Leonel. She should have been told that the kidnaping of her savory *Gringo,* who had brought her back so many succulent memories of her idealist adolescence, and whom she hated for that very reason, was necessary to save his father's business, Tom Wright. His kidnaping and the uprising were the only way to conceal the fraud. So many times she had said to Don Leonel, "Be careful; they can screw us with that stuff." And he'd cynically reply, "Don't worry, honey, this old man knows how far he can push it." That old fart, he never knew how far to push it until he got stuck like a dog.

Such thoughts only crept out on those uncertain, rainy

nights, when dreams fluttered in her head, and, sobbing, she longed to expel the bats, until the droning sound of the rain pounding against the window glass would mercifully let her fall asleep and drown her sadness. Only then would the chain of nights plagued with insomnia finally be broken, freeing her to float in the momentary fantasy of tender, amber-tinted arms hugging her, familiarly warm bodies rubbing hard against her own as if the world were coming to an end, fleeting glimpses of soft and joyfully- tender caresses, angular sweet mouths, intimately wet, flooding her lips with ardent kisses from every corner while she let herself go like soft, bubbly foam from a calm sea.

CHAPTER FOUR

1

It was still dark outside. The night's coolness had captured the humidity in the air and compressed it into dew drops clinging transparently to the timid leaves on the deceptively strong trees. The fog hung low, covering with gray the moist, flat surfaces. The ghostly atmosphere was barely mitigated by the first few rays of sunlight that timidly dared to show themselves on the horizon. The seemingly peaceful environment of dawn in a mountainous corner of the world was rudely broken by gross vibrations resembling small earthquakes.

Many people already up at such an early hour ran into the streets, some because they feared it was an earthquake, and others simply because they were curious to find out what the monstrous noise was. What they saw was a huge tank advancing up the main road toward the city center. Like a gigantic, metal armadillo it worked its way slowly up the highway, making everything shake in its path. No sooner had it passed than another one came from behind, and, then, still another, until there was a long line of tanks shaking everything along their spasmodic path.

In the room that doubled as his cell, Tom Wright woke up with the vibrations. He couldn't see anything, but he knew it was a column of tanks. He got dressed in a hurry and immediately considered the possibilities. He went over them, but there were only two realistic ones: either a greater offensive against the guerrilla (although that would be like killing a fly with a cannon), or a coup d'état.

He didn't have time to speculate much. The noises made by the guards, combined with the unending jiggling of keys, alerted him that they were coming. He waited patiently. The circumstances indicated a new twist in his situation. He knew he was in Pacal's hands. But Pacal was a mid-ranking officer. He couldn't act with impunity without the complicity of a superior. Could it be the Minister of Defense? It was logical. Could the coup be led by him? Would Pacal be his operations liaison? What was Sandra's role? The men came in. They were wearing leather jackets.

"We're leaving."

"Where to?"

"A ride in the countryside. You have a meeting there."

"Wonderful. Finally!"

He felt like an actor in a third-rate play. He knew he wasn't going to meet anyone, and the other men knew it as well. They weren't even mentioning the tanks, as if they didn't feel the vibrations at that very moment. Where were they taking him? And for what purpose? The whole process seemed like a series of unknown cancers sprouting all over at once, making him feel as if all the people who seemed to be on his side turned out to be against him, and all the values that made up his identity were falling one by one, leaving him with nothing but the naked essence of cynicism barely protected by a confused heart.

"What about the tanks?"

"They're just drills."

"They're from Mariscal Zavala."

"Shut up, asshole, don't give him any information..."

"Oh, forgive me, my..."

"And we're going to leave in the middle of the drill?"

"That's the best time. When they can't even smell you on the street. You won't need to worry about them."

The second man blindfolded him with a black rag and

held his elbow with his hand. They led him out of the room and instructed him to head left for about fifteen feet and then turn to the right and continue for a similar distance. He felt the fresh air when he came out. He stumbled on the uneven floor. They held him firmly to keep him from falling. Not more than a couple of yards away he heard a car start with difficulty due to the early morning cold. They took him to the vehicle and told him to raise his left leg high. He raised it as high as he could, and they placed it on top of a metallic surface. They picked him up and he realized what was happening. They were stuffing him inside the trunk. He felt around him and touched a thick layer of rubber over a cold metal surface.

"We're going to leave your hands untied because it's a dirt road, and there are a lot of potholes. So, try to protect your head with your hands when you feel the bumps."

Wright nodded. They lowered his head carefully so they wouldn't hit it when they closed the trunk. He felt the air pressure and the noise when they locked him in the cramped space. The car started moving. They were indeed traveling on a dirt road. They moved slowly, but the endless holes gave him the impression he was on a roller coaster.

He removed his blindfold. He felt he was too important for them to punish him for that. Once he had it off, he let his eyes get used to the new darkness until he recognized the corners of the space that held him prisoner He could clearly see the metal supports of the trunk lid, the slightly slanting surface that separated him from the back seat, the spare tire under the metal plate on which he lay. He began poking everywhere with his right hand, looking for some object while he protected his head with his other arm.

The car reached pavement and started to move faster. He had trouble rummaging under the metal plate, since it meant he had to press himself to the top of the trunk in order to barely be able to lift it, but his fingers found a piece that moved. He fumbled around and was finally able to grab it. It was a large type of screwdriver that served as a handle on the jack used to change the tire. With that piece he started forcing the lock.

Wright sensed that the car had now reached the city. It moved forward and stopped, moved forward and stopped. He kept trying to force the lock. The long and tedious training he'd had more than ten years ago was paying off. Little by little the things he'd learned, the cunning and bossy voice of his trainer, came back to him as if they'd been carefully tucked away in a delicate box inside his mind, where they had gone unnoticed for years. Now they resurfaced and shook up memories from his past that he began to ponder anew as if they'd taken place the day before.

Wright tried forcing the lock from one side to the other and failed, and then tried again in the opposite direction. Just when he started to worry that his efforts were in vain, he heard that longed-for "click" that revealed his success in the endeavor. He used the same tool to hold the lid of the trunk in place until the car slowed down. He tensed up, his entire body bathed in a rancid sweat that smelled like garlic. He felt unkempt, forlorn, as though he had pneumonia. His heart was beating so hard that it resembled the deafening savagery of a bass drum. His fists gripped the iron tool with such force that they were becoming numb. The car stopped. At that moment Wright pushed the trunk open and jumped out.

After landing awkwardly on his right ankle and almost falling, he hunched low so the trunk would shield him and ran in a zigzag fashion, hoping not to be betrayed by his rubbery knees. He didn't even know how he kept his balance. He scratched his left hand and felt a piercing pain in his right ankle. He ran as much as he could in the opposite direction from the car. He didn't feel that he was making much headway. The car was only a few yards away. He felt shivers run up his spine where he figured the shots would hit him. The air shook him as though trying to slow his escape. It felt very cold, as though he were without a coat in the midst of a full American winter.

It took the men a few decisive seconds to realize what was happening. When they finally understood, they jumped out the car doors brandishing their Uzis. He would have been an easy target, but the first man had the presence of mind to scream to the other one:

"Don't shoot him!"

Weapons in hand, they left the car in the middle of the street and started running after him. Tom Wright heard the men's steps on the moist asphalt as they shot into the air. Each time they did, he felt the shots perforating his back, the shivers up his spine, his halted breathing, the choking of his beating heart. He could see himself as though in a carnival frenzy: losing his strength, slipping, hitting the wet asphalt; an imitation of a cadaver. However, his legs kept moving automatically. His heaving was that of an asthmatic, but he was still alive, intact, running, running. The shots rang in his ears as if they were just a few inches away. Each gust would burst his eardrum and fill his head with water like the rising tide, another dark whim of the sea. He didn't know whether they were catching up to him, or whether he was getting away from them. He simply ran, more tired than ever, confused and close to tears. He heard the shots and breathed laboriously, making guttural sounds like those of a scared goat.

He got to the corner. There was a bar next to a crumbling house, with men coming and going in various stages of inebriation. The stench of cheap booze, urine and feces filled his nose. They were the type of men who normally filled him with dread. In front of the bar was a bus stop, and a bus was just arriving. It was very old, with a long, purple body and recapped tires, and it was screeching as if its engine was an old espresso machine about to explode. Day was breaking over the horizon, but the bus was packed.

Without stopping for a second, he jumped inside it. Sweating, dirty, and unshaven, he was fighting hopelessly for breath. Only by taking a hard look could anybody figure out he was a *Gringo*. Rolling his head, the driver stared at him. He was a very dark man with thick eyebrows, a bushy mustache and an unfriendly face. At that moment Wright realized his tragic mistake: he didn't have a penny in his pockets. Shaking uncontrollably, his muscles turned to Jell-O. Fighting to regain use of his tongue, and making a series of contortions that better expressed his predicament, he finally dared to stammer softly:

"Please, the army's following me."

The driver lifted a thick, calloused hand and, cursing under his breath, directed him with his thumb and a short grunt to the back. With a mortal paleness and the vague expression of someone suffering from malaria, he headed to the reckless dark middle of the vehicle. It was full of people standing, and he couldn't find a seat. He bent over so as not to stand out and almost fell when the bus started violently with a blast of diesel, screeched harshly, and slowly, slowly, started moving, generating an infernal sound from its engine in a wake of oil and compressed air.

From between a man's elbow and a fat woman's waist, expressionless and yet with twitching lips, he managed to look for only a moment out the window and saw how his pursuers lost track of him. One went into the bar with his gun in the air, waking everyone still floating in an alcoholic stupor and giving them an adrenaline rush that rudely sobered them up. The other one kept running, checking the empty doorways of the houses on the block. He was safe. Closing his eyes, he took a deep breath and the world started to spin, while in his back, elbows, neck, calves, buttocks, he felt the lingering tension of his little adventure. Moisture appeared on his cheeks. He wiped it off with his shirt sleeve and realized he was crying.

The bus advanced amid screeches, slamming of breaks,

shaking; it went around and people got in and out, lunging slyly, weighed down by their possessions. In spite of the early morning hour, the enclosed atmosphere was charged with the unflinchingly pungent stink of human sweat. In other circumstances he would have been sickened by it. However, now he felt protected in the middle of that foul breath, and he didn't recoil from the sweaty people getting ready to begin their morning tasks. The warmth of the bus was giving him back his life and slowing down his pulse, even if it didn't offer him much fresh air. The bodies wedged against his own calmed his nerves, enabled him to regain a sense of himself, kept him standing until he was able to do so on his own.

Nevertheless, he couldn't very well stay on the bus forever. He had to muster the little strength he had left and abandon all that welcoming warmth to return to the hotel and reestablish contact. He wasn't familiar with the bus route, or with the city itself. As it got lighter, he noticed they were coming from the outskirts, from a poor neighborhood of dilapidated homes. They were gradually getting closer to downtown. At some point where he thought he recognized a familiar landmark, he moved forward and got off without giving it much thought. The driver turned to him and twisted his thick mustache upward in a smile. He murmured softly:

"Good luck, *compañero*."

2

Not far from where Tom Wright got off the bus, and more or less making an equilateral triangle between him and the tanks, Kukulkán, Ariadne, and Vallejo were riding in a small car on a deserted street. In the back seat, Kukulkán and Ariadne were embracing like lovers heading home just before sunrise. Vallejo drove like a voyeur obsessed with seeing what was going on in the back seat. His rough movements allowed him to turn his head around and carefully scrutinize any obstacles on his planned route, both in front and behind them.

In the cool sunrise it looked like a ghostly dance of theatrical ostriches occupying the only vehicle rolling along a sleepy street. The narrow twists and turns of the oldest part of the city lent themselves to this finale in which armadillos, ostriches and a scared mouse gradually converged toward the same point where a dangerous snake awaited them, coiled on a cabaret stage.

3

Still half asleep, the man answered the phone reluctantly. He felt colder than usual and looked around for a t-shirt. The voice on the other end didn't give him time to achieve his goal.

"Hello, yeth? Oh, Mr. Thecretary, how are you?...No, it'th a bad time. The Ambathador can't be disturbed. Do you realize what time it ith?...I underthtand it's an emergency, but all the methages have to be routed through me....I underthtand. I athume full rethponthibility. Whatever it ith. Do you understand, ath well?...Yeth. Try calling him exactly at eight, no matter what...Okay? Goodbye, then. Good luck and I'll thee you later."

Hanging up the receiver, Behemoth made a gesture of disgust. He hated those calls. Besides, there was nothing to be done. His orders were clear. Nobody could talk to the Ambassador until everything came to its conclusion, whichever way it ended. He found an old t-shirt displaying the logo of the university attended by one of the kids of the Ambassador's private secretary, then lit up a cigarette. He felt exhausted, but he had to stay awake. There would be more calls. The whole thing was just getting started. He was placing the smoldering, half-lit cigarette down on the ashtray when the phone rang again.

"Hello? Yeth?...Hi, what a thurprithe...Of courthe I know what's happening...Yeth, I know...Tom Wright escaped? Holy shit!...How did you find out?...And where ith he now?...Oh, shit. Holy Shit...Yeth. Thanks...Bye."

He hung up, feeling a sharp pain in his stomach. A sudden pain of heartburn made him immediately visualize a bottle of Maalox. He hunched over, shivering, eyes slowly sinking out of focus, tears bright on his cheeks. He lit up another cigarette and inhaled deeply. His bones felt like heavy blocks of cement that pulled him downward, sinking him in a sea of murky water. All he needed was for somebody to kill one of his own agents. Then the world would really come crashing down on him. Goodbye to his promotions, goodbye to all his business deals, goodbye to everything. He kicked the wastebasket in anger. It rolled around the room in a half moon curve, leaving behind a wake of white paper balls that scattered loosely around the room with incredible speed, as though someone had just opened the door of a rabbit cage.

Behemoth got up. His muddled brain even pondered calling Pacal before reconsidering. This was the worst possible time. Besides, it had been expressly forbidden. It would directly implicate the Embassy. But, what if they killed his agent? He couldn't bear the heartburn in his stomach. Maybe he'd die from a herniated ulcer. He bowed his head, feeling a heavy deadness. He inhaled deeply once more and dropped down onto the couch like a limp doll.

4

Walking the city streets made Wright anxious. He searched for a public phone but couldn't find one. In this dirty, unpainted city, riddled with peeling posters, one on top of the other, there was not a single phone booth. It was very early in the morning, and the sun still hadn't warmed things up, but the city was already bustling like an anthill punctured by a stick. His steps echoed with haste on the asphalt, where he was assaulted by baffled ghosts at every corner: Beggars consumed by indescribable diseases, sallow people without arms or legs dragging themselves on the sidewalk, seeking some burrow to hide their deformities now that the sun had begun to appear. The squeals of invisible children crossed the air, itself impregnated with the reeking stench of rot. The narrow and muddy streets formed a strange geometry, projecting a horror, a unique and suffocating sadness. Only the melancholy reflected on the faces blended in with a city devoid of beauty, order and a sense of rhythm; a city ashamed of its bodies, its color, its smell, of everything except its uncanny isolation and its crimes.

Wright started to look for a taxi. He wanted to survive this gigantic urban garbage can, whose cracking, dirty walls seemed to imitate the twisted souls of its scorched inhabitants. He turned the corner. He seemed to recall that there was a taxi stand at the central park. If he was in the city center, it would be the closest one. He thought of asking some pedestrian how to get there, but then he remembered the column of tanks. The National Palace was across the street. He had to find another way.

He crossed the next street. A small car was approaching with a couple necking. Wright looked back. There was no one else on the block. He decided to keep going as if nothing was happening. The car approached him. Inside, Kukulkán and Ariadne kept up their necking pantomime. Vallejo had already disregarded the ragged character making his way up the sidewalk and was about to keep going. Ariadne suddenly raised her eyebrows.

"Look, the *Gringo!*"

Kukulkán instinctively looked up and saw a dirty figure on the sidewalk. It was the foreigner whose photo he had studied carefully, and about whom Harlequin had given him three or four interesting pieces of information.

"He's the one who saved me in Antigua."

"He must have escaped. Stop, Vallejo. Stop! And you, get out and greet him. Life's full of unexpected surprises."

"Are you nuts?"

"Look at the way he looks. He must be on the run. This is our chance."

The car braked suddenly. As soon as it did, Ariadne jumped out in front of Wright. She timidly lifted the palm of her sweaty hand and waved it in the air while forcing a smile on her face. Tom Wright was startled. Then he recognized the woman waving at him. There was no doubt about it. It was the EGP agent from Antigua. Another of life's ironies.

The woman moved up to him without any hint of aggression. The car engine was still running and the door was ajar. Inside, he could make out the most normal faces he'd seen all morning. She looked pale and thinner, shivering on that lonely sidewalk as if she were a vulnerable teenager.

"Where are you headed?"

"I'm looking for a taxi."

"There aren't any around here. And if you keep going that way, they'll catch you."

The voice belonged to the man who had been embracing her inside the car.

"Where can I find one?"

"There aren't any around here." It was her again.

"Come with us. We'll take you wherever you're going."

Kukulkán's words surprised even Ariadne, and she wrinkled her nose awkwardly in ardent disapproval. The driver also seemed to be taken aback, and began mumbling discontentedly. Tom Wright thought quickly and realized that he had no other option.

"Let's go. We have pending business, anyway."

5

The bed was a mess. The sheets were twisted like a group of rattlers in the desert sun. Sandra had tried to sleep but spent the whole night restlessly turning over and over. Through the open window, the raw, reddish tones of the rising sun began to glow over the hill protecting that flanked the house, before turning to golden rays and then projecting a brimming white radiance across the ceiling of the room. By the time its light reached her cool room, the relentless sun was already melting the city center.

The sensual image conveyed by the veil of her carelessly tied gown, which opened in the middle and flowed freely behind her like the flapping of sails, was betrayed by the tense look on her face. She walked from one end of the room to the other with her hands behind her back. The phone rang. She rushed to her night stand with inordinate speed, lifted the receiver, and, foregoing her usual prudence, answered, without even waiting to find out who was calling.

"Fer-de-Lance!"

Her blood froze as she heard a voice she did not expect at all on the other end amid the electric static.

"No, Rattlesnake. It's the stupid *Gringo*."

He was calling her Rattlesnake. She made a note of that vital piece of data. Besides, he was calling her at a number that only three other people knew about. She felt a sudden urge to pee. She thought that, in the most sordid manner, her past was merging with an obscure and unpredictable present that felt, at that moment, like it was suddenly plummeting and about to break in pieces as if rattled by an earthquake. She stood there swaying awkwardly and trying to catch her breath.

"For God's sake, Tom, where are you?"

"With Kukulkán, my dear. Didn't he kidnap me, after all?"

"Tom, be serious!"

"I've never been more serious in my life, Rattlesnake. Dig?"

She ignored the irony and did her best to adopt a feminine attitude. The key to every situation was to be in control.

"I don't know what you're talking about, Tom."

"Oh, cut the shit! You know perfectly well what I'm talking about. Don't act dumb. You thought I was Fer-de-Lance."

"Tom, you're crazy!"

"Yes, but not that crazy."

Her head was boiling. A fine film formed in front of her eyes. It transformed the brightness of the dawn into prismatic colored lights that bounced off the walls like a net formed by diamonds that wrapped and imprisoned her.

"Where are you, Tom? Give me your number...I'll call you right back."

"Do you still think I'm a fool? If what you want is to confirm that I escaped, the answer is yes, dear. I escaped."

She could not help losing a few uncontrollable drops of pee. If he really had bolted and had access to this number, then everything was lost. Her efforts of many years, her dreams, all unpredictably ruined by her first illusive love.

"You're confusing me again, Tom."

"Stop acting, Sandra. I know you're a great actress, but now I know everything."

Could he possibly know everything? He knew something. He was hinting it, and he was not the kind whose silence could be bought, or who could be counted on to remain quiet. All her nightmares, her hidden fears, were becoming a reality. She realized that she wasn't living in a palatial mansion but in a dirty cave full of hungry rats willing to gnaw her sad bones. Drawing strength from within, and mindless of the fine stream of urine running warmly down her left thigh, she said:

"Don't you know me well enough to know I wouldn't fall for that old trick? Tell me where you are and that's it."

"You ought to know me well enough to know where I am."

Wright hung up. Sandra stood, holding the receiver in her hand, listening to the monotonous dial tone. Squeezing the receiver as if she could crush it with her hand, she let out a terrible, hoarse cry like the scream of a prehistoric bird. She held back, shivering, her teeth chattering. The broad band of muscle trembled in her back as though she was suffering from malaria.

She ran to the bathroom. After releasing her kidneys and allowing her intestines to run loose, she cried quietly while thinking about what to do. She hurriedly put on a pair of pants and a sweater. She didn't bother to shower, or put on makeup. She simply splashed some cold water on her face to wake herself up and wash off the tears, and then she put on the first pair of shoes she could find while searching nervously for her purse and keys. She ran out of the room, and was crossing the enormous living room and heading for the door, when an startling, fragile voice stopped her in her tracks.

"Where are you going at this hour, Sandrita? With the danger that must be lurking out there..."

The unexpectedness of it shook her like a ghost. She turned around and saw Don Leonel sitting on the sofa. He looked exceedingly tired but calm. In front of him, the small table was full of overflowing ashtrays and glasses with dirty water that undoubtedly had once been ice. There was a bottle of Chivas Regal lying on the floor next to him.

"I'm waiting for the Minister of Defense to call. I asked him to name me Minister of Agriculture. I always dreamed of being Minister of Agriculture. After that, I can die in peace."

Don Leonel looked at his watch. He closed his eyes,

satisfied, and placed his hands across his belly. Sandra felt a sudden wave of disgust turning to nausea and ran to the door.

"Don't go out, Sandrita. I feel it in my heart."

She barely managed to contain her sprint and, holding her breath to avoid the rancid odor of leftover whisky, said:

"There's no choice, Don Leonel. We got into trouble because of you, and now I have no choice. It's because of you that I'm running out at this hour."

Surprised, he straightened up and stared at her with a pathetic animal devotion.

"For God's sake, if women wrote history, they would say the sun comes up in the west and that the moon lights up the day."

"You don't even remember everything you've done. This isn't the time to talk about it, but, believe me, I'm not trying to provoke you. I've always swept the dirt under the rug and never complained. I admit it was also to my advantage. But now, I'm a little scared. Remember that a human being is neither angel nor beast, and misfortune would have whoever pretends to be an angel turned out to be a beast instead."

"Go on, my dear. I'm not reproaching you for anything. Just be careful. Remember that we're always looking for other qualities because we don't know how to use our own, and we step out of character because we don't yet know how to stay inside our own. Even if we wear stilts, we still have to use our own legs, and remember the added height is just a mirage. Sooner or later we have to get off them. And even on the world's highest throne, we're still sitting on our asses."

Sandra smiled and immediately headed out. As a last reflex, she added:

"Give my regards to the Minister."

She left. Impatiently, she asked for her car and then turned it on while taking a quick swig from the bottle she kept in the glove compartment. She turned on the inside light so that she could be recognized and placed a firefighter's helmet on the dashboard. The car with her bodyguards took off right behind hers, and both cars sped off en route to the city. The pale yellow lights on the public lamp posts were still on. They were so weak that they barely created a vague sickly sensation that couldn't overpower the morning fog generated by the hill's clammy humidity.

From the time Sandra reached the very first intersection, she noticed there were grunting, red-eyed soldiers on alert, wearing full combat gear. Where there were no guard posts, they were entrenched on a strategic corner like deadly lizards waiting to strike.

The two vehicles moved rapidly, heading toward the modern part of the city. Driving that morning was an unheard-of audacity, an unthinkable risk. If it hadn't been for what happened she'd never be out on the ludicrously-deserted streets covered with dead leaves flying around in the cool wind until they got stuck in brownish puddles. There was nobody on the sidewalks. Not a soul. Only Jeeps. Jeeps full of rumpled soldiers with 50-caliber machine guns pointing to the back, scurrying along the pavement like cockroaches. Raising her quick eyes, she noticed anti-aircraft machine guns protected by sand bags on the roofs of some buildings. Where there were no Jeeps on the streets, the mournful silence was frightening. Everything looked sketchy, as when you look through foggy lenses or see the timorous faces in a laborious nightmare.

After what felt like an eternity, they reached the hotel. She headed straight to the main entrance. She ran, literally ran, to the front desk.

"Room 312, please."

"Mr. Wright?"

"Yes..."

"He just left. He rented a car and told us that, in case of any problem, he was on his way to the American Embassy."

"Thank you."

She ran out again, her breast heaving, shouting at the attendant not to take her car to the parking lot. Jumping inside in a very crude imitation of film cowboys mounting their horses in a chase, she turned at full speed to reach Reforma Avenue as soon as possible. Once there, she accelerated even more.

Her last hope was Bald Eagle. But, what then? Tom Wright would talk. She had to find a way out. She had reached the most critical moment in her life, and she couldn't afford to hesitate. It was all or nothing, and the one who blinked first would lose. It would be enough if he didn't talk to anybody else at the Embassy. Even if just for a few hours. That was the only thing she needed, the only thing she was asking for. She'd take care of the rest later.

It was ironic for her to have to think that way about her first love, the one whose neck she'd childishly kissed with tiny bites that left blue marks before grazing his teeth with her lips in silent appeal as his head began to yield. The one whom she'd grabbed by the hair and confronted eye to eye until she felt her own penetrating his and both becoming one in the depths of their retinas where everything was mixed liquids, fused, impossible to separate. The one with whom she hysterically cried the first night after making love, asking him at dawn, in that bleak dorm room lost in the South of the U.S., to take her home immediately to Guatemala, that she wanted to sleep with her mommy, that, what would her mother think of her?

And now, here she was, with that nostalgic desire to be innocent once again, to be a small girl again, to be pampered again, to be able to sleep at night and stretch out in the morning with a smile on her face and the desire to live flooding her veins. She had lost all of that. She couldn't stop shaking without a sip of Scotch. She had to take pills in the morning to have the strength to get out of bed. She didn't love anyone. She couldn't have an orgasm. She was bored even when she was masturbating. She was alone. Everything was about politics; everything was calculated; everything was work; everything was rigid, about having an iron discipline;

everything was about being in control of your passions and having a clear mind; everything was about protecting yourself from your enemies. She didn't even know what it meant to be alive anymore.

She only cared about wealth in terms of power, and power was a drug that overwhelmed her with its fatal attraction. It dominated her like an enraged sea that kept her from reaching the shore, the waves would take her out farther, and she was floating like a cork on a surface she couldn't control. She'd never emerge, and the only thing she desired was for the moment to be over so that she could rest and sleep again like when she was a little girl; sleep.

Tears were streaming down her cheeks. To be born in Guatemala was an atrocious punishment that twisted her soul like a braid. Even her brother, the most lucid person she had ever known, the living example of mental health and good feelings, would get killed one of these days. But that anarchy gave life meaning as well.

She heard a noise and opened the window to look. They were jet fighters, coming from the airport at a low altitude in the direction of the National Palace, with rockets under their wings.

She made it to the Embassy. She took a quick swig from the flask to warm her throat. The Embassy was surrounded by sand bags, with marines and military police swarming everywhere. They stopped her immediately.

Now that the time had come for her to act, she regained her composure at once, quickly wiping her face, smiled and pulling out the special ID that Bald Eagle had given her for situations just like this. As soon she showed them the magical card, they let her park and enter the building. As she walked to the main door, not a single soldier could resist watching her move as she walked swaying her hips without the slightest inhibition, her hair loose and floating behind her like a starry waterfall. Now she was Sandra the invincible, the conqueror, the one who devoured anyone in her path.

Part Three

The Dragon's Teeth

CHAPTER ONE

1

Tom Wright was pacing from one end of the office to the other, beckoning Behemoth with his fingers, with his whole curving arm, beckoning like the cartoon image of an Italian on the verge of a nervous breakdown. Behemoth listened from the safety of his desk, rubbing his thumbs together and stretching the corners of his mouth.

"I don't want uth to thtop uthing ptheudonyms!"

"Well I do! It doesn't make any difference! What matters is that I was kidnaped by the Minister of Defense's people!"

"Leviathan!"

"All right, Leviathan's people! And you're telling me that there's nothing my country or the company can do about it?"

"Try to underthtand for once. It'th a matter of priorities."

"Pacal was with me! They were his people!"

"Athuming that'th so, ith Pacal working for Leviathan?"

"He's his right hand man! He doesn't even breathe without his permission!"

Behemoth lost himself in a confusing explanation about the importance of keeping a margin of influence over an army that increasingly considered itself autonomous from them and leaned dangerously to alternative sources for purchasing hardware.

Wright closed his eyes. Being there was unbearable. Kukulkán had treated him better. They took him to a white clapboard house with peeling paint and promised that later they would take him any place he wanted. At best, he expected to become the unwitting lodger of a new prison, similar to the one he'd just left. In the back of his mind, he still had preconceived notions that they would mistreat him or interrogate him about the company. They could get away with it. He was supposedly in Leviathan's hands. They didn't have to pay a political price for his disappearance, especially in the chaos generated by the coup. Nevertheless, they caught him off guard by offering him solidarity.

"There'th no unity in the army, Wright. It'th divided. We thupport one faction. That faction ith willing to collaborate in our effortth on a regional level, in El Thalvador, in Nicaragua. The other one ithn't. They're nationalithtic. They don't like uth. They resent uth becauthe Carter cut off their military aid, alleging human rightth violations."

Like a lone shivering prowler in that whitewashed office, Behemoth explained to Wright that this last faction was buying arms from Israel. It had the backing of the Chamber of Commerce, which represented the lobby behind the purchase of weapons and equipment. That support was due more to the large kickback they got from the transaction than to any patriotic purpose or useful military strategy. The pro-American faction was headed by mid-level officers seeking to reestablish the military chain of command because the war needed a political solution to transform it into a strategic victory.

Wright saw Behemoth's explanation as just a lot of talk to disguise the embarrassing situation and avoid sanctioning Leviathan. His illicit behavior was inadmissible and demanded an immediate and severe response that Behemoth simply was not willing to give. Incredulous about his colleague's reaction, Wright reviewed in his mind the roving images of his conversation with Kukulkán. Wright had taken the offensive by asking arrogantly:

"Why does the EGP favor terrorism?" He expected an answer that could place his safety in jeopardy, but didn't get one. Kukulkán gave him a calm, detailed explanation of the organization's view of things:

"The army has kept itself in power by means of electoral fraud. This has discredited democratic alternatives in the eyes of the people." Calmly, but with clear expertise, he described the country's history since the fall of the Arbenz government in 1954, then he added:

"So, think about it. Twenty-two years after Commander Turcios started the armed struggle in the northeastern part of the country, the understanding that you guys have of the historical roots of our political process is still incredibly superficial."

Kukulkán said this like a professor or a lawyer gathering scattered evidence to prove his case. He was looking Wright straight in the eye without any sign of hatred whatsoever, controlling his breathing, brushing the palm of his hand over his scalp without losing his professorial composure. It was a look that pierced him, generating in him a hypnotic sensation of vertigo. Kukulkán seemed uncannily familiar, somehow, and Wright assumed it was because he had seen his picture so many times.

"So, look. Religion, nationalism and ethnic consciousness are important issues to contemporary societies. Many people thought they would disappear with the cosmopolitanism and positivism inherent to industrial growth. Nevertheless, there they are, stronger than ever. In some cases, they're an expression of backwardness and confusion, but I can assure you that they're also an intuitive defense mechanism, a sort of lifesaver in the face of both individual alienation and the crude materialism that dominate First World countries today."

Wright could hardly believe that a guerrilla was capable of articulating such things. The subdued tone in Kukulkán's voice generated trust.

It was the opposite case with Behemoth. Everything about him was coarse. As he spoke, his whitish, pasty, wilted, moon-face grew rounder and rounder and his freckled breast heaved. He drooled from his fluted mouth in the midst of a waterfall of vague and inconsistent words, his eyes slowly sinking out of focus. His ugly baldness, his yellow, nicotine stained fingers, it all made Wright feel like grabbing him by the lapels and shaking him roughly. At that very moment, just as in a comical sequence of a soapy operetta, the phone rang with a shrill, piercing blast

"Yeth!...She'th here?...Sure. Have her come in right away."

He hung up the receiver. Arrogantly using some sheets of paper from his desk to fan his face, Behemoth glanced up at Wright.

"She'th here."

"She is?! Here? How did she manage to make it past security...?"

"There are many thingth that you don't know. Many."

There was no time for further exchanges. Just then the office bell rang. Behemoth pressed a button under his desk, and the door opened automatically.

"So, I finally found you, Tom."

Her presence made him feel as though he'd been punched in the stomach. Taking a few steps back, he glared at her with barely-contained fury, and foresaw, in an almost *deja vu* sense, not only what had really happened, but also what would happen in about an hour or so.

"You bitch...*Puta!*"

She stiffened. Ignoring him like a diva and using her entire bodily repertoire, she addressed Behemoth instead, with discernable mockery in her voice.

"You ought to hire agents with better manners."

Tom Wright grabbed her by the shoulder. Even though she raised her hands against the unexpected attack, he managed to pull her with such force that he spun her around on her heels. Her hair swung in a wide dark arch like a fan, filtering the pale institutional light inside the office.

Arturo Arias

"Both of you! Thtop it immediately!"

Sandra whirred menacingly with an almost unnatural cry of rage, trying to escape Wright's grasp. He shielded himself, squinted his eyes and shouted. As they struggled, their bodies sagged forward, backs bowed, shoulders drawn tightly, elbows sharply bent. It seemed like a mechanical dance, where the greetings and reverences were done in slow motion and with an overabundant accumulation of gestural clichés.

"Rattlesnake!"

"I thaid, enough!"

Wright threw his arms up in the air melodramatically, recalling Ariadne's words, her weak voice, like a wilted flower muted by the exhaustion of a recent injury, transparent as a ghost, with the color of the world shining through her eyes: "Don't worry," she had told him, "I've gone through worse things. Once I was left alone in a house without any weapons. We only had one, and the *compañero*, who later deserted, insisted on taking it with him, arguing that, when there was only one weapon to be had, it was the man's right and duty to hold it..." The dimples on the sides of her mouth had deepened as she said this. "The *compa* did not return. That night they attacked the house, and I escaped only because I stayed awake and there was a ladder in the backyard. But the worst part was the following day. The army caught my boyfriend in another operation. I never saw him again..."

Fighting to regain his normal rhythm of breathing, as well as a composure that he was far from feeling, Wright began to mutter with an amnesiac's air:

"Why was I kidnaped? Why was I told I was being held by Kukulkán? Why? Why? Why?"

"Oh, God, your innocence is touching."

Sandra's reply got on his nerves. Theirs was a horror story, not a love story. He couldn't go on being naive. He remembered Vallejo's quixotic figure, skinny and twisted like a wire, talking nonstop while he chain-smoked: "I got to the

205

southern area of the Quiché and saw that they were all mid-level peasants who owned fields full of apples. I started talking to them and noticed that their condition was relatively O.K. However, they were welcoming me as a representative of the EGP. Then I asked them why they were joining the fight. 'Because we're Indians,' they responded. 'And no matter how much money we make, Ladinos discriminate against us, and we're tired of being discriminated against in spite of having money. We want equality with Ladinos. A more decent society.' And when it comes to it, that's what it's all about. It's a war of decent people against corruption, more than a class struggle or an ideological conflict." When Vallejo had finished, Wright had looked at him with greater understanding than he thought he would feel for someone in his position.

Behemoth's voice brought him back to the present:

"You mutht underthtand, Tom. You don't have acceth to certain information. Our operationth are complecth."

"Does she work for us or not?"

"Tom, I can't anthwer that."

"I can. I work for my own interests, for myself," she interjected.

"Shut up, Thandra! And ath for you, Tom..."

Wright couldn't manage to say what he wanted. He wasn't able to organize the ideas that bubbled in his brain. He continued uttering phrases with contorted features and wet eyelashes.

"You listen first! They told me they had kidnaped a banker! I was coming to rescue him..."

"What a baby you are, Tom. You still believe in Santa Claus."

"At least I have principles...!"

"I don't need a map to find my way, let alone to think."

There was an instant of melancholy silence. They stood facing each other, breathing with the rhythm of palpitating arpeggios. Sandra opened her mouth slightly. Wright clearly

saw the pointy tip of her tongue, and recalled the last time they had embraced, her familiar warmth, how she would extend her arms smelling of burnt leaves, those listless looks that always made him feel as if he were in a swaying bed of flower petals awakening the paradise of passion. As so often happens, those images clung to his intimate recollection, becoming parasites of his sadness as he wondered how they could have sunk to such depths.

"That'th enough from the two of you! Thtop quarreling!"

Wright thought that war consumed people from the inside, leaving them without ethical substance; it reduced them to blurry and dusty scarecrows who simply repeated gestures learned at an earlier age of the universe. The blindness of conflict left them like trees riddled by termites. Their feelings became atrophied. They were caged in a tiny space where it was impossible to see the truth, and all they could do was beat themselves up masochistically. Their instincts acquired the strength of a wet firecracker.

"Thandra, Tom, thtop it! I don't want to hear either one of your voiceth. Shit!"

Right then the phone rang again. The sudden rupture of the stifling atmosphere froze them momentarily, as if the screeching sound could paralyze the thick entangled currents of this overacted drama staging their unpredictable, serpentine passions.

2

The big house had gotten brighter as the morning sun obliquely penetrated into its musty corners, like silvery water spreading over the surface, flooding furniture, rugs, and dirty dishes. It seeped between the gaps of the Venetian blinds and took advantage of the space left by the open curtains to spread enthusiastically across the living room. Don Leonel slept on the sofa. The sun had begun to cover him and, as it warmed him up, it generated in him a series of unconscious gestures.

The doorbell rang. Don Leonel felt as though a crystal grenade had exploded inside his head. He half awoke and touched his surroundings to orient himself. Squinting, he noticed that Jonás was going to the door. As if his head had been submerged in water all that time and he was barely regaining his functions, he began to remember what time and day it was.

"I hope nothing happened to Sandrita."

Feeling agitated by disorderly sensations, he had a vision of himself as a child, riding at his parents' ranch. The Indians would bow their heads and remove their hats before the majestic prancing of his Arabian stallion. Almost like a Greek chorus they would say in unison, "Good morning, little master, how are you, little master." The horse would dance with its front legs, decorated with bells. After he passed, the hats would go back on, and the workers would return to their tasks. He felt embarrassed for them each time this happened. That day they were approaching a patch of overgrown coffee trees that had lain abandoned for years. His father dismounted. He and the plantation caretaker followed suit. His father said nothing but was meticulously checking everything. He was afraid of his own father but obsessively studied his gestures, sensing the need to repeat them in the future.

Suddenly the caretaker fell on him like a jaguar lunging from a tree and shouted, "Careful little master!" He fell face down. Just a few yards away the caretaker struck a small bush with a stick over and over again, hitting it repeatedly until spent. His father watched expressionless. When the caretaker finally stopped swinging, he was pale, heaving in a hopeless sweat.

"What was it?"

"A rattler."

His father walked over to the caretaker.

"Did it bite you?"

"Yes, boss."

"Let's go back, then."

They got back on their horses and started on the long road back to the plantation house. The caretaker arrived with glassy eyes and overcome by an intense fever that could not be broken with the small quantity of anti-venom they kept in the house. He died a few hours later. The only comment his father made was:

"We're going to have to hire another caretaker."

Dozing still, Don Leonel thought with the faint exhalation of a low moan that he should be presentable just in case they came to offer him the job as Minister of Agriculture, while wondering why he had remembered just now that old episode from his childhood. He'd always felt that peoples' heads worked in strange ways. Then he heard Jonás' voice. It wasn't his usual tone: Sharp, it conveyed a whimpering panic, a lack of control.

"Don Leonel!"

The shout, lacking any touch of elegance or grace as it disintegrated into a profound desperation, finally woke him up. He opened his eyes and blinked. He couldn't believe what he was seeing. He felt around for his glasses. A group of soldiers armed to the teeth was inside his living room. The door was still open. The movement of men and vehicles outside was clearly visible and their clumsy metallic noise grated in his ears. Jonás was pressed against the wall like a sticker, making superhuman efforts to disappear inside the wall.

"What's going on? How dare you come in like this?"

The soldiers seemed deaf and dumb. They refused to speak to him, as they spread to every corner of the house. From his position, Don Leonel watched as they walked over to the small desk next to the living room and threw his papers up in the air, looking for God knows what. He couldn't believe it. He felt like a hundred thousand scorpions were stinging him.

"Hold it there! What's happening? How dare you?! Alvarito!"

In a matter of seconds Alvaro was running down the stairs with an Uzi in his right hand as if portraying the role of a psychopath in a bad movie. He was incredibly lucky that he didn't shoot and that no one shot him. When they saw him, the soldiers kneeled and aimed their weapons at him. Both Alvaro and the soldiers froze in that position. They looked like decorative porcelain statues just out of the oven. Don Leonel, his heart floating in a dark sea, was making frenzied gestures from the sofa.

"Nobody move! Somebody, explain what's going on!"

Just then a sergeant came in. Dressed in his full battle regalia, he looked like a miniature dragon that smelled of mildewed cardboard. Walking at a normal pace, he went directly to Don Leonel.

"Mr. Leonel Herrera?"

"At your service."

"You are under arrest for conspiring against the government of the Republic."

3

The door was ajar. Sandra was already standing outside the office, pacing up and down. She refused to leave until she knew the content of the conversation. Behemoth got progressively whiter as the seconds passed.

"Yeth...I underthtand...I will thpeak to the Ambathador immediately...I know what the options are, thir. Thank you very much."

He hung the phone up as if he wanted to decapitate it. The blood had completely drained from his face.

"There wath a counter-coup. The Minithter of Defenthe wath arrested. Tho were Don Leonel and Alvaro."

"Who staged it?"

The coldness in Sandra's voice cut like a knife.

"Thandra, don't..."

"Who staged it?"

"Pacal."

"Goddamned son of a bitch."

She stretched out the phrase, accenting it as if with a sharp cutting instrument, with a very long "i" that summarized what she wanted to do to him. By the time she finished enunciating, she was already running down the narrow stairs with a bursting, thirsty impatience, and only a vague echo of her presence was left, the aura of an invisible perfumed cloud in the men's nostrils.

"Thandra, don't!"

Behemoth reacted with utter panic at her rashness.

"Where's she going? Tell me!"

Behemoth's paleness increased, smearing his face with a handkerchief. Imitating the gestures of a young girl disenchanted with love, he bit his lips, as if sealing himself more and more tightly into some sort of desperate honeycomb of dead time. Tom Wright gasped for air, feeling a pressure on his chest as if his bronchial tubes were tightening up on him. Behemoth looked up and scrutinized him as if he had suddenly discovered a repulsive object that had invaded his very guarded intimacy.

"It ith evident, Tom. Don't be thtupid. She went to confront Pacal."

"And what's going to happen?"

"They're going to kill her."

Sweat in his eyes, hands dangling like dead hamsters, Tom Wright felt like he was having an epileptic seizure. With a great deal of strain, he suppressed a cough. His back was sweating. His tongue seemed to have grown, and it no longer fit inside his mouth. Shutting his eyes, he sagged, gasped, then spun around.

"Wait, Tom! You can't! It ith not American jurithdiction!"

Behemoth jumped from his desk trying to stop him, but Wright was already running down the stairs.

"Tom, pleathe!"

Overwhelmed and exasperated, Behemoth damned Wright's asinine petulance. It was absurd to have to deal with valiant princes from the movies that tried to rescue the heroine they loved from the claws of the monstrous enemy. He forcibly hit the dark blue wall in the corridor, making the paint flake off.

"Thandra ith right, Tom! You're thentimental! You won't get far in thith profession!"

4

Growling obscenities, Sandra told her men to follow her, then muttered something else without turning her head. She jumped into her car, pulled out with the engine all revved up, ramming the clutch pedal in and out impatiently, and almost ran over two marines that barely had time to remove the barrier that prevented access to the Embassy. As if sucking on a cough drop, she licked repeatedly with her tongue the list of insults she'd like to yell spitefully to Pacal's face, while at the same time pulling out the Scotch and rinsing her mouth with one swallow, keeping one hand on the wheel.

Was it possible that her longed-for day of triumph would turn out to be the unlucky one of her defeat? She, who had calculated every single thing so carefully through the years as if coldly plotting a chess move, as if embroidering a *huipil* of many colors in which she paid special attention to each single thread, to each one of the rows, as if she were the reincarnation of the goddess Ixchel?

Sandra was convinced of her triumph. As Harlequin liked to repeat, it was the inevitable outcome for those who knew how to pick the winning horse. Of course, she smiled coyly; they both expected different endings to that story. The logic was the same, though. In the crazy race the country had embarked upon in a hallucinatory way, every person's logic was the same. They all invested everything, up to their last gasp, in winning. For the first time in many years she longed for a human being who could understand her, a person with whom to speak. She shifted gears, then her hands moved around aimlessly around the steering wheel before picking up the telephone next to the gearshift, and, holding once more the steering wheel with one hand, she dialed a number from memory.

Sandra was laughing now, a low, mannish laugh full of scorn, and self confidence. She wanted to walk naked on the beach, listening to the rhythmic violence of the crashing waves, to feel the wet sand between her toes standing the nerves in her legs on end and flowing into the soft suede of her sex. Escape from everything, deal only with her body, feel the breeze molding her curves, the irruption of her nipples like headlights in the air's freshness, her hair floating ethereally like the light wings of a fleeting seagull. She wanted to run along the beach looking for an embrace, licked by the sun and the heat, and lose herself in the bluish sky like a dew drop that slides on the tongue of the handsomest of men.

"Hello...this is Harlequin. Pierrot please. Pierrot? Harlequin. Yes. I know. I used this number because it is indeed an extreme emergency. There was a counter-coup. Pacal overthrew the Minister of Defense....I know it for a fact....Gray's the joker in this deck of cards. Release him. He's no longer useful to you. Myself, I'm going to try to fuck Pacal big time....You can count on your Harlequin, my dear Pierrot. Lots of kisses and watch out for people like me..."

She let out one brief, intense, somewhat shrill yet contained sob. Pierrot was the only person, life's uncanny paradox, who truly understood her. Her pained expression melted her harshness. A longing for life escaped through that slight crack, even as grief began to overtake her.

"That's enough. Don't fuck with me. Remember that all of this is the social cost of the revolution, that we must be tough enough to bear our historical moment, and all that other rhetorical nonsense you're always throwing around that not even our grandmother would believe....And, just in case we never see each other ever again, I want you to know that I always loved and respected you, and tried to be faithful in my own way, and that those few times I screwed you over were, because, after all, we played on different teams... I am not melodramatic, bastard. Goodbye."

Scowling, she hung up. She bit her lips hard until she cut them.

"Pacal, damn bastard."

As she approached the Ministry of Defense, a column of tanks blocked the road. She honked while lowering the car window and impatiently waived an identification badge, muttering, grunting, cursing and yelling all at the same time. She turned the wheel and drove with her left tires on the grassy median that separated the wide avenue, waving the tanks contemptuously aside with her left hand out the window. The impression she made was so authoritative that the tanks moved as much as they could over to the right, to allow her to pass and be rid of her. Behind her zoomed the bodyguards' car. After the blockade, the avenue was wide open, clear, with bright tree shadows lining it. She took the diagonal in front of the Reforma movie theater and the Yurrita Church. It brought back memories of her first communion, dressed in ruffled white, with gigantic candles illuminating all the nooks of the dark domes, pressing toward the cross while the bells tinkled, the first shy adolescent kisses in the theater's cavernous darkness while fearing being discovered by the man with the flashlight and the unhappy face like the tortured roots of a dead cypress tree, illuminating her sin with mock contempt and wet black eyes fixed on her. She felt as if she were a fraud, naïve, pursuing a country that was never found, that escaped her like chaotic smoke detaching itself from a pale fire.

Continuing along a thoroughly deserted Seventh Avenue, she saw the dirty brownish buildings, some owned by her in-laws, and others where they had interests or businesses. She had never paid attention to them. Their ugly architecture did not make them worthy of even a glance, and the deafening noise of broken-down buses that normally hissed and clattered down the crowded avenue while all those people with plum-like faces ran around like scattered ants on their narrow sidewalks, discouraged her away from ever walking around places like that. Now there were no buses though. Everything was empty. Only the filth accumulated at the edge of the sidewalk remained, glistening in the sun.

Sandra entered the old downtown area. The unhappily claustrophobic streets anguished her, as did the gloomy, gray dilapidated castle copied from some god-forsaken farcical fairy tale, that tried to pass for National Police Headquarters. She was close to "the big guacamole," the popular nickname of the National Palace because of its color. It was a space she believed she had conquered, but it now spit her out like the unwanted pulp of a dried fruit. But she would not allow it. In the distance, movement could be seen in the park. People joined the already large group of onlookers as if it were a carnival spectacle, a macabre carnival that was lived daily and never stopped. At its center the wheel of fortune turned, turned.

She got to the park. It was surrounded by tanks, jeeps, troops armed to the teeth in full combat gear, reporters and television cameras. Everyone ran in one direction, then the other, like the long Chinese New Year's dragons, whose bodies always snaked in opposite directions. She went as far as she could. The television cameras ran to film her. A toad-faced sergeant approached as well.

"No one can come through!"

With her customary speed, she pulled out a badge from her purse and waved it in front of the astonished sergeant. Once the surprise was over, he grabbed it from her hands and examined it backwards and forwards, as if he did not believe what he was seeing. The only thing he didn't do was bite it to ensure its authenticity. With an expression of total confusion, he took out his walkie-talkie and started to ask for instructions.

"Green triangle here... I have a G-2-411 pass answering to Black Falcon. Do I authorize access? Right. Over and out."

He turned off the walkie-talkie, lowered the antenna and put it back, delaying his response to the absolute maximum to underline his authority while generating suspense. Like a repressed guard dog, he finally barked between growls:

"You can go through. But the men stay."

"Agreed."

She whispered quick instructions to them, before exposing her long legs as she walked towards the main entrance to the palace. The television cameras filmed her movements from all possible angles until the sergeant ended it with a strong growl that scattered them like roaches when light floods a dark room.

5

A third vehicle crossed the tree-lined avenue at top speed, also racing in the direction of the palace. His face remorseful, Tom Wright's mouth squirted specks of saliva without thinking if they would drip on to his shirt as he accelerated even more. He saw Ariadne, Vallejo and Kukulkán prowling like misty ghosts, poking him, whispering words that shone on each other and made him dizzy, making him feel as if he were eleven. Despite the sun, his hands were freezing. Suddenly he let out the answer to an inconclusive dialogue with one of his superiors:

"You were so right, sir. I don't know who the good guys are and who the bad guys are. I don't know if my first love works for us, the Guatemalan army, or for the EGP. Or for all of them."

The trees on the edge of the median passed by the car like sinister cartoon giants foreboding tragedies in some enchanted forest. In line with the operatic melodrama that he had begun to live against his will, Wright let Vallejo's voice drift inside his head. With a nasal tone full of comic touches, he talked and talked endlessly and almost as fast as Wright was now driving. "...When I was clandestine, my son lived with my mother. One day I visited him; I took him out for ice cream. We sat on the small tables outside, and we had just started eating when a car full of agents drove slowly by. There were three in front, and two in back. And in the middle, in the back seat, was my ex-wife. We both saw her, and she looked at us. It was an eternal instant when everyone's tormented eyes met. She immediately looked straight ahead, so they wouldn't notice she had recognized us. I was afraid that my son would yell out 'mom' or something like that. He was only eight. He didn't say anything, though. We saw the car move slowly forward with her looking forward, unmoving. We didn't budge either. We never saw her again."

Wright took the diagonal that led to the wide, grayish avenue. Out of the corner of his eye, he caught the sight of a pinkish, baroque, excessively ugly church with unsymmetrical lines. That excess of a building, melted like a half-baked cake, became a symbol of the city for him. There was an enormous movie theater on one side and a modern building on the other. Further on there were ugly square houses, buildings half finished, an infinity of steel rods pointing forlornly into the sky, all buildings and houses urgently needing a coat of paint. He entered the old part of town while thinking that people really lived only to fight, even when they disguised it with the metaphysical ghosts of unreachable utopias that sought to justify their most primitive need to destroy their neighbors.

Wright accelerated still more. At a distance, he could see the disfigured movement in front of the palace. Like a mirage, it vibrated full of colors before a whitish sun that forced everyone to squint. He reached the park, recognized Sandra's car and pulled up next to it. A toad-faced sergeant was already blocking his path. The television cameras surrounded them. The sergeant examined his badge and furrowed his brow.

"You can't come through. Orders from above."

He spun back around, assuming the matter was settled. The television cameras continued to focus on Wright. An overweight man with black hair and a fine moustache asked him:

"Do you work for the Embassy, sir?"

"I'm a private citizen..."

"And you came to see the overthrow of our government as a sort of tourist attraction?"

"I had business affairs inside... Excuse me."

He walked away. The reporter laughed mockingly and commented into the microphone:

"The evident presence of United States government officers in the vicinity of the palace leads us to assume that the U.S. was either supporting the overthrow of the government, or fully aware that a coup would take place and approved the operation."

CHAPTER TWO

1

Despite the size and elegance of the building, the inside of the National Palace was dark and intimidating. Its small, inner patios, obliquely illuminated by the skylights alone, created a sensation of pale, impersonal luminescence, amidst the vaguely greenish impersonality and humid blackness. Only the asthmatic neon lights kept the building from being confused with crumbling colonial ruins full of bat nests. From the thick carpet, the smell of urine overwhelmed passersby, a deplorable residue of the previous night's occupation. Armed soldiers came and went down the hallways. They entered and exited the many offices at their disposal, opening and closing doors, carrying piles of papers, moving typewriters, making telephone calls. At the end of the hallway, a middle-aged man in camouflage nervously read aloud a bunch of papers he held in his freckled hands. As he read, his whitish moustache moved up and down like a buzzard's wings.

Pacal materialized around a corner of the corridor, surrounded by soldiers who looked like barefaced adolescents playing war games. In a chaotically surreal scene, everyone was handing him papers and asking him questions simultaneously. Pacal waved his arms energetically and approved or nixed whatever he was being told by nodding or shaking his head. When he saw the lone man talking to himself, he approached him.

"Have you memorized the speech, General?"

"Calm down, Captain. It's hard. But with God's help..."

"Yes, General, but remember. In..." He looked quickly at his Rolex. "...20 minutes, you have to be in front of the TV cameras. Make sure we don't lose face. After all, we picked you for a reason."

"Don't worry, Captain. Everything's going to work out the way you want it to."

Another soldier came up running. He opened up his way through the circle and, leaning over, whispered something in Pacal's ear.

"Take her to the Minister's office."

The soldier saluted and ran back.

"Excuse me, General. I have a little business matter to take care of."

"As you say, Captain. And, don't worry about me. My memory has improved since I stopped drinking and accepted Christ as my Savior."

"I don't have the slightest doubt, General. As long as you don't screw it up. Take note that it is us, the young officers, who are giving you your last chance..."

"The Lord wanted me to be reborn..."

"Well, make sure He keeps you kicking. Excuse me."

He walked away with a hurried step. The soldiers that surrounded him looked like a beehive in perpetual movement.

Sandra was led to the Minister's office. She looked around, as if assuring herself that everything was still in its place. She went over to the desk. Noticing the television behind the desk, she turned it on. It snapped and crackled as if the glass was cracking. The screen filled with colors so intense that they made her squint her eyes. Central park appeared under an intense, dank, summer sunlight as if it had been painted recently with vibrant primary colors. In the background, a small figure came closer as the camera closed-up on him. It was Tom Wright, slightly deformed due to the camera's lack of depth. The reporter's voice said, "...or fully aware that a coup would take place and approved the operation." Upon hearing the phrase, she almost burst out laughing, exhaling a burst of air from the rigid lopsided square of her mouth.

"It's funny how rumors start, isn't it?"

She turned and found herself face to face with Pacal. She had not heard him come in, and that worried her. Her shoulders shook against her will for a barely noticeable instant.

"Motherfucking bastard!"

"Calm down. That's no language for a beautiful and fine lady."

"Don't give me that lady bullshit!"

Pacal's eyes narrowed as he let out his typically obnoxious laughter of the stereotypical tropical tough guy. Sandra became rigid. Pacal's heavy neck became contused by a blush of annoyance. Sandra's eyes were as firm as mahogany. She trivially played with her long hair, pulling over one shoulder and then the other. He noticed the dark circles under her black eyes, her uncombed hair, her white face. She shook her head, walked quickly towards him and gave him a tremendous slap in the face. Drops of blood sprouted immediately from Pacal's lip.

"You ruined everything!"

"Too bad. But what do you expect? It's *my* coup."

"Since when does a captain..."

"When a captain gives an order, the sailors obey. Besides, I'm not doing it for myself. The new Chief of State is General Lagos Cerro."

Her mouth gaped in a slight ironic smile. She started playing with her hair again, twisting loose strands in her fingers. And then her lips moved, her mouth quivering:

"He's been retired for years. Did you find him in a bar?"

"No. In an evangelical church. Same thing."

Sandra caressed her chin, half thrusting her head at him, computing the information.

"Minister of Defense?"

"Me."

"And you'll be promoted to colonel in a few days, I suppose."

"That's right."

"In this country the Ministers of Defense have always been the ones who rule anyway."

"That's true. But I can't control history."

Sandra started to walk in a circle around Pacal, who spun around himself as she walked, both of them wearing a grotesque half-smile that ineffectively masked a reciprocal distaste.

"I came to negotiate."

"There's nothing to negotiate."

"I don't want the family touched...and don't stick your hands in you-know-what. The percentage of the previous Minister is yours now..."

"Don Leonel and Alvaro are already in jail."

"Anyone can spend a night in jail in this country."

"General Lagos Cerro is very firm. You know that he's a Protestant. He's talking about no lying, no stealing..."

"I couldn't care less about General Lagos Cerro. Tell me, yes or no?"

"You don't have anything to offer me."

Looking at his watch, thereby displaying his well-manicured fingers, he suddenly added in a cold tone:

"...and I have more important things to do. The TV..."

"I have the channels and the contacts, which is no small thing. I have the relationship with the North..."

They looked at one another with a ghostly antipathy, conscious of the sorry mediocrity of their fabulous encounter, whose details would undoubtedly be exaggerated in the fantastic recountings of the coup as time passed. Sandra showed a serene smile that contrasted sharply with Pacal's aloof, porcine aspect. Winking an eye, she added with the boldness of an old dealer:

"...and I have Kukulkán."

"Not even your grandmother believes that."

Then began one of those staring battles that can last for hours without anyone blinking, while everything seems to move in slow motion and, in the background, the prolonged sobbing of violins increases. He moved his hand, humbly, to where the slap had parted his lip.

"You used to treat me like a servant. Now you want me as a partner."

"That's the miracle of democracy."

Pacal stretched his lips bitterly into an arch expression. The violins' lament would have increased at this point. He felt insignificant, ugly, lacking the appropriate mannerisms in the presence of someone who made him lose control, and with whom he could never have the thing he wanted most. He noticed that under the blouse she was naked. Although he was in power now, he knew he was just a usurper, and that produced a tingling of disgust in him that burned slowly in his mind until it became a sense of social resentment. Shrugging his shoulders with obvious pique, Pacal joined his fingers into a gesture reminiscent of a pout. Wanting to taunt her, he replied sarcastically.

"The problem is that when you start to ascend socially, you don't know when to stop and don't want to."

"Until someone stops him."

Pacal closed his eyes confusedly, meditating upon the twists and turns of his destiny. As he struggled to define the moment, he wrote off words like "satisfaction" or "happiness."

"You could be right. But no one's stopping me right now. I'm the one stopping all of you, watching your precious assets go up in smoke...and I like it."

"The only thing going up is your dick, Pacal. Stop jacking off and get back to your place."

He jumped as if stung by a bee. Those words stripped her of the veil of mystery and revealed her as just a vulgar woman who should be punished for rubbing shit in his face as if he were a nobody. If he was ever to claim the world of action as his rightful due, he had to begin somewhere. Trembling in anger, he closed his eyes like a jail cell door. There was nothing to be done. He licked his lips.

"No deal. I'm not interested in your merchandise."

He turned with exaggerated purposefulness and, tripping slightly, walked to the door awkwardly with his slight limp, trying to find the solemnity that the circumstances required. Swallowing quietly, his eyes fixed on the corridor, he waved his arm in a gesture of theatrical farewell.

"You didn't even offer me a drink to celebrate."

"I thought you came here on business. Besides, I only drink at night."

"Who knows what you might stick in your mouth at night. As for drinks, I know you."

"Get out! That's an order!"

She realized that she had lost everything. Fifteen years of work and her whole future were evaporating in the blink of an eye. Blind with fury, she melodramatically let out, like an engorged turkey, the most provocative of all insults one could make in Guatemala with all the rage with which Jehovah threatened Job.

"Lame Indian full of shit, who do you think you are?"

He stood deathly still, almost surprised by an absurd disposition to let some tears flow out of sheer anger. He could not believe it. Those words touched his most vulnerable point. It was as if she had torn up a cherished picture of his mother. He spun around to face her. At that instant, he received a second smack in the face. He closed his eyes tightly as the intense burning penetrated all his pores like *chile*.

"You'll learn to respect old money one of these days."

She left the room, slamming the door as hard as possible to cement their rupture. Pacal stared furiously at her, his cheeks inflated, his eyes bulging. He snapped his fingers.

Two soldiers approached him immediately, eager to follow orders.

2

The iridescent shimmer of heat melted the park. The vendors had lost their initial fear and were now taking advantage of the crowd to sell potato chips, peanuts, popcorn and sodas to kill their thirst. The spectacle resembled a country fair or a parade day. The cathedral towers floated high in the blue and white sky as if levitating from sheer warmth above the colorful multitude of gloomy, blurry faces smelling of rancid sweat that stood idly about, discussing feverishly the events around them in a fervent hubbub of high-pitched voices.

Tom Wright walked from one end of the park to the other. In the middle of the crowd, he looked like a hunting dog separated from his master. He observed all the movements carefully. If the jeeps moved, if a new car with officers carrying briefcases arrived, if someone got too close to him or stopped to check him out. In the middle of the drunken spectacle, he noticed a dead bird lying in the middle of the glittering pavement, before he caught a more important detail: the sergeant that had kept him from entering was now pulling out his walkie-talkie, speaking on it, and pointing to Sandra's bodyguards. Wright ran over to him, elbowing aside everyone in his way.

"Sergeant, what's going on?"

"Nothing. It's just that they've just called these men in."

Tom Wright smiled, smacking his arm with his hand, soothed by the jealous thought that Sandra would end up smelling like a rose, as always, if not literally in bed with Pacal. He was an idiot for worrying. He shouldn't have listened to Behemoth. He sighed, berating himself for always falling into the same old patterns of behavior, conditioned by the internal voices of his comfortable Anglo-Saxon childhood laden with the ancient familiarity of Protestant guilt and rigid, simplistic notions about good and evil. This country would never stop surprising him. It was as if all the particles, all matter, functioned in a way contrary to the laws of physics and determinism to which he was accustomed. It confused him so much that he had begun to suspect his basic instincts. At the same time, he feared that if he penetrated the Guatemalans' absurd logic, he would be disabled like a tennis ball soaked by a gush of water, without any way to make sense of his life. Walking with his head down, like someone who has finally made the painful decision to separate from the woman he has loved for years, he returned to his car in the midst of constant shoving and elbowing. He was just getting in, when the television reporter came up to him again.

"Look, *Gringo*. You're missing it."

The reporter had a tiny monitor where they were showing General Lagos Cerro coming into a press conference with Pacal leading him by the arm. Lagos Cerro was in the center, Pacal to his right whispering words in the General's ear, and a fat-bellied officer with a big butt stood rigidly on the left. Everyone was wearing camouflage. The General began to speak with a metallic voice that, despite its haughtiness and humming bossy tone, betrayed a speech recently memorized.

"...The Army's high command, and those others who sign this document, military commanders of the air, sea and land forces, gathered in council through God's graces, with a high sense of patriotism and with the professional sense of duty that always accompanies all movements of the glorious national army, fully aware of the critical historic moment that Guatemala presently faces, in the midst of a difficult juncture for the entire Central American region, and also to protect and safeguard the Army's honor and dignity, announce to the people of Guatemala..."

Wright felt a crushing stomachache that stretched and shrunk his guts like springs, reducing him to a shivering pain-racked ghost of himself. With a nod, he thanked the reporter and got into his car. Honking to scatter the crowd around the car that was slowing him down to a crawl, he began to cruise away, weaving rhythmically to escape that place as soon as possible.

3

The first thing he noticed when he woke up was that he had a terrible hangover. A wet stain on the sheet marked the place where he had been lying. The brutal whiteness of the sun felt like a knife perforating his eyes. He felt the sweat pouring down his chest, tickling him. Gagging, he realized that to get up and close the blinds required energy he did not possess. His mixed dismay and alarm translated themselves into queasiness. His dry mouth annoyed him; it was so dry that he could count the scarce saliva drops that he still had left. His head felt as if someone had drilled a hole in it and drained the fluid out, so that his brain seemed to hit the cranial wall every time he moved. The mere thought of eating made him nauseous. He lay there without moving, grunting, submerged in a state of half-sleep from which he returned startled every so often, thrashing around and doing his best to buck. With great difficulty he put his hand on his forehead and tried to give himself a massage, but he couldn't even stand the pressure of his hand. He tried to sit up when he felt the room move like a boat, but fell back on the bed. "Only the winners have the right to live." There was no air flowing in the room.

He thought he heard some knocking on the door. He sat up again with the scarce reflexes left from an old efficiency on its way to extinction. He tried to stand, but the shaking in his legs forced him to opt for prudence. He was able to make himself out on the mirror on the inside of the closet door. He was wearing a tee shirt and pants, but he had not shaved. His eyes were bloodshot. He perspired in streams. Someone knocked again. He heard it distinctly. It was no illusion, no fantasy. But who was it?

"*No estar*! *Váyase!*"

The knocking became more persistent. Maybe he should report to the Embassy and get out as fast as possible under diplomatic immunity. No. He didn't have the right to live. His mission had failed. The knocks continued, but they weren't violent. It wasn't Pacal's people. He made an effort to stand.

"OK, OK, *voy*."

He ran his hand through his hair. He walked as if he'd just finished a long horse ride. Feeling the solid ground under his feet, he drew a sigh of relief. The floor was almost hotter than the bed. With an enormous effort, he was able to remove the chain that preserved his intimacy.

"May I come in?"

His mouth hung open. Ariadne was on the other side.

"Is that a question or an order?"

"I wish I could give you orders."

Of all the possible scenarios, this one had not even remotely occurred to him. He became dizzy with the smell of perfume. Ariadne noticed his state, read his indecision, and pushed the door gently.

"Don't worry. Nothing's going to happen…my God you're in bad shape."

The room reeked of alcohol. Empty or half-empty bottles rolled everywhere. Like a slightly offended motherly lady bringing the comfort of familiarity, she rushed to the window to air out the room. Then she picked up the bottles and arranged them on the desk.

Wright asked her:

"Would you like a drink?"

"I'd prefer arsenic. But you need one. From miles away one can see that you're hung over."

"I'll die if I have one more."

"You're not used to drinking this much. You'll come back to life if you have a hair of the dog. You'll see."

She poured him a drink. Taking ice out from the refrigerator, she placed it in the glass, then deposited the drink in his hand. He did not protest. Tightening his eyes and opening his nose, he gulped it down like a laxative. He roared immediately afterwards like an injured lion, feeling as if he had drunk acid that was now corroding his esophagus. The sudden, intense heat expanded his lungs. Sure enough, the headache began to subside slightly.

"See? You're going to have to drink another later. Beer is better. That always had a better effect on my father because it would rehydrate him. I learned from him."

"To take care of drunken men?"

Ariadne lowered her eyes.

"Forgive me..."

He came closer and gave her a couple of pats on the shoulder. She accepted the gesture as a sign of peace.

"This will be a short visit. It's not good for me to stay long."

"I know."

"Do you think you can understand me?"

"Perfectly. I'm coming to my senses."

Trapped between embarrassment and torment, he looked at her with the eyes of a trapped goat. Ariadne looked different. She wore a light brown summer dress, high heels. She had changed her hairstyle, putting her hair up. With her face made up to disguise her recent injury, the makeup produced a floury effect that made her look older than she was. For the first time, he thought that, with her nervous, little doe-like gestures and big eyes, she could actually be an attractive woman.

"I just came to tell you...to give you a message."

He nodded without saying anything, thinking she was right: he urgently needed another drink.

"We're going to release Gray. The national picture has

changed. Now the conditions are such that he's no longer useful for us."

She paused. He didn't say anything. He walked over to the table and served himself another drink. The only remaining trace of shaking left in his body was in his hands. He dropped two of the ice cubes that he tried to put in the glass. She watched him and picked them up automatically, dumping them in an ashtray. He smiled gratefully.

"Now you can go home."

"What?

"We've let Gray go. You can go home."

"And injured as you are, you risked coming here only to tell me that?"

"No. I'm no sister of charity. There's more. Kukulkán thinks your life's in danger."

"And since when does the *Comandante* worry about my health?"

"Since you became a political problem for us. If you were to disappear, they would blame us, and then everything that's happened up to now would look like child's play in comparison to what they would do."

"A military intervention? A greater military presence?"

"Maybe. Those possibilities can't be excluded. Although I don't think it's what Pacal wants. The Maya calendar will decide."

Wright remained thoughtful. Wanting to imitate Bogart's steely harshness, he let his fiery eyes focus on the window and smacked his lips in a melancholy grin of disdain.

"Don't worry about me. I have friends in high places."

"I'm afraid you're wrong again. You…knew a woman named Sandra de Herrera, right?"

The sole mention of her name made him crazy, producing a slow steady fatigue with his last spent cry of pain. He felt the sharpness of the headache coming back. He did not say anything, just nodded.

"Well, they arrested her husband and father-in-law, accusing them of drug trafficking and corruption..."

He shivered, and tried to smile evoking Sandra like a forlorn memory on a distant shore. He had thought that there were some people in this world who were so far above ordinary mortals that they could never be splattered by the daily filth of politics.

"...but the worst is that Señora de Herrera has disappeared."

"She's what?

"Disappeared."

Now he was truly dumbfounded. His eyes were totally out of focus. His throat closed up, and he lost all pretension of any Bogardian airs. The control over his sphincters reached a precarious level. Wright put his head in his hands. Ariadnee tossed her coldness aside and leaned down to console him. Helping him stand, she led him gingerly to his bed as if she were teaching him to walk. He fell on it like a heavy lump of metal and started to cry like a baby.

4

The peeling, rotted walls of the small, windowless, dark room with its cracked masonry, warped beams and swaybacked floor, smelled of humidity and pesticide, that seemed to emanate from the green sludge scattered across the ceiling. Her feet and hands were bound to a narrow rusted steel spring bed pushed up against a wall, her body covered only by a sort of semi-transparent nightgown. A tape player at an exaggeratedly high volume created an environment of blurred unreality in such an asphyxiating space, as if what was happening in the room were some sort of theatrical gesture or mythical rite.

A man with a woolen ski cap beat her thigh a little bit above the knee with a plastic baton.

"Do you like it, baby, do you like it?"

He struck another blow slightly higher, halfway up her thigh. She felt as if her femur had split in two neat pieces. The third blow was already on the upper part of her leg, and it stung as if an acetylene torch had burned her skin. Each blow was faster and harder than the one before. At first, he would give them with a chillness that slowly melted until it turned into real passion.

"That's how we kill snakes in my town. We hit them in the middle, crack, so they can't lift their heads, and then we hit them again, crack, and again, crack."

The red-hot, burning blows were now a crazed torrent. They fell completely on the middle part of her body, abdomen, breasts, kidneys, threatening to eviscerate her with a cruel and implacable rhythm. They appeared to submerge her in a wan purplish dance played at high speed. All her bones cracked. Her body was an out of tune marimba keyboard facing the intense stroke of the mallets.

The man paused to raise the volume of the music. Even though he was no longer hitting her, Sandra' body continued to shake with agitated, convulsive movements, like a wind-up toy left behind by a distracted child. Her muscles were out of control, contracting automatically like those of dissected laboratory frogs. Everything raged under her skin, as if someone had thrown melted lead inside her body, her stomach boiling over like an overheated car radiator. The man tottered back to her side and halted to stare at her elongated body with a dazed sigh. With his free hand, he radiantly caressed her up and down with tame, delicate, slow movements as if afraid to touch her invisible life, barely making contact with the velvety tips of his fat fingers. Immediately, he gave a quick, excruciating blow to the center of her abdomen. Sandra groaned and contracted sharply in the fatalist desperation of a drowning man who fights to cough up water from his lungs. She made hoarse, tremulous sounds as she tried to take air in gurgles. Her tingling face shrunk like the twisted grimace in a funhouse mirror. The wet nightgown was already in shreds. Its color became indistinguishable from the white skin lacquered in scratches and bruises as if both, nightgown and skin, were a modernist collage unified by the same coat of shellac. The man stopped beating her.

"That's how snakes are killed in my town," he said. He left the room.

During a brief moment that could very well have been minutes or hours, she was left only with the music that engulfed her and that cut her off further from any sense of reality. Rock-and- roll music, pre-historical echoes and unconscious words.

That death's unnatural that kills for loving.
Some bloody passion shakes your very frame.
These are portents; but yet I hope, I hope
They do not point on me, on me.

Her body slowly adapted itself to the feverish, numbing stupor of unconsciousness, mixing visual and aural primary sensations with disconnected memories. Then a swaying Pacal entered, glanced once about the room, his hair unkempt, unshaven. His bloodshot eyes saw the poked and prodded body with the same delicacy of one who studies a dog's cadaver in the middle of the road, as if trying to memorize each shattered line of it.

"I'm going to tell you what the shoeshine boy told General Lucas when he went out to get his shoes shined in the central park..."

Slowly he removed his clothes. One by one, he graciously took off each garment, greatly exaggerating expressions and ostentatious gestures of false modesty, until only the bulletproof vest remained. He looked like a grotesque hairy faun with short, thick legs and plump, tyrannosaurus arms madly flinging about in excitement. He walked to her side and leaned toward her face, blowing his fetid breath into her nose as if deliberately trying to stage a parodic imitation of Leda and the swan. Then he kissed her neck.

"He said, 'Do you know the latest joke about General Lucas?' 'Stupid kid,' the General answered, 'I am Lucas.'"

He walked back to where he had cast the precarious pile of wrinkled clothes. It looked to her as if he was drinking a reddish liquid from a stone vase carved in the shape of a python. He searched among his clothes until he found his pants. Taking out a Swiss army knife, he threw the garment in one of the corners of the shabby room.

"'Don't worry about it,' the shoeshine boy told him, 'I'll speak extra slowly for you.'"

Laughing, he opened the army knife. Pacal went back to her side and with the same enthusiasm that naughty children display when they draw pictures on blank walls, he sunk the blade into Sandra's thigh. The intense, acute burning was worse than the pure liquid iodine her father put on her cuts when she was a child. Pacal began to trace lines. When blood began to sprout on the whitish skin that bordered the cuts, an equilateral triangle emerged. He immediately designed a circle around it. He repeated the gestures, the wild tracings, on the other thigh and then on her stomach, until the abundance of blood distorted the neat harmony, the purity of the designs. His breathing became heavier as the blood increased.

"Rattlesnake. Here is your Fer-de-Lance."

Pacal leaned in to lick the blood. The salty taste on his tongue excited him even more. With nervous, jumpy gestures, he lowered his mouth to her sex. He traced a fine line with the army knife around her vaginal lips, dazzled by the optical effect produced by the blood bubbles mixing in with the saliva. His legs shook so much that his knees were almost hitting one another. He pulled some toothpicks out of the bulletproof vest. With great precision, he incised the outer lips of her vagina with the sharp, pointed tip of his knife, then pushed the toothpicks through the recently-opened holes.

With the awkwardness of a wide-eyed, midget tightrope-walker, he got on the bed, clearing his throat, gasping, fumbling, and scraping the ankle of his deformed, shorter, lame foot on the iron bed. The difficulty was highlighted by the breathless desperation of his capricious desire. Euphoric, he mounted her with the same aura of a general on his purebred horse about to head his triumphant parade. His body had an acid smell, a lingering sensation like that of a stinking dead dog, emanating from all his pores.

5

"*Fuera*! Get the hell out of thith country! Gray ith free!"

Behemoth was apoplectic. His face contracted like a prune, making his shiny nose even more prominent, like the bulging belly-button of a corpse, crowned by a gray moustache that had acquired with that gesture the appearance of a gigantic decoration. As he yelled, elbow shaking, he blew tobacco smoke in Wright's face.

"I'll say what I want! My career doesn't matter to me!"

"I can dethtroy you! Tho, watch out, buthter! *No jugar conmigo*!"

Tom Wright leaned back slightly, rolled his eyes, pretending that he misunderstood, then repeated the phrase as if it were a joke in bad taste.

"And who do you think you are to threaten me? Aren't there laws in our country...?"

"There are national thecurity issueth at thtake!"

"I could resign from the company."

"That ith your right...and your rithk."

"Others have done it."

"And have they lived happily ever after?"

Wright stood there looking at Behemoth with clear, providential eyes, like the *femme fatale* in a famous melodrama. Everything was like a sinister costume ball, a carnival slowly turning into a terrifying nightmare as people removed their masks and there was no face behind them. Behemoth lit another cigarette, hands shaking. The piles of paper almost leaning against each other had grown even more. Even so, it was still possible to spot the gallery of posters on the wall. Wright recognized Vallejo. He had seen the poster the first time he visited that place. There were no posters of Ariadne and Kukulkán. Everything was like a snail soup in which the ingredients are mixed together so thoroughly that it's impossible to tell apart. He looked at his smooth, white hands and stretched his fingers. They seemed to stretch more than normal. In his imagination, he saw them as if they had been lopped off. They were not fingers at al; they were five decapitated serpents from the Medusa's head. The serpents, rattlers all of them, danced and twisted against each other as if an invisible flutist incited them with peculiarly intense music only they could hear. He observed the serpents of his shaking fingers and had an unexpected vision of what he would do in an unpredictable future.

Suddenly there was a loud blast as if a bomb had exploded. A scream simultaneously caught in their throats as they both jumped up, open-mouthed. The bulging piles of paper had finally lost their precarious balance and fell to the floor with a terrible noise that seemed to never end. Papers and yellowish dust flew all over the place, freely following the curves the rarified air dictated to them as if they were thousands and thousands of tiny, floating skydivers. Tom Wright smiled. He stood up and, without saying anything, walked out of the office.

CHAPTER THREE

1

The airport had the same mixture of colors and scents as a farmer's market. Everywhere voluminous women in bright-colored dresses moved around with enormous suitcases weighing a ton. They yelled with high-pitched voices as if what they had to say concerned the whole world, with no trace whatsoever of shame. The space was too small. Movement was limited because of security measures. You had to get in line just to get into the building. Once you got to your airline counter, they inspected everything manually and with X-rays, so slowly that the line snaked back all the way to the street. Waiting impatiently, Tom Wright saw them bring in a casket through a side door and take it directly to an airplane.

"I'm glad I'm not the one going home like that."

The bald, middle-aged man of medium height smiled and made a gesture as if wiping his forehead. He had the good physical shape of one who has lived a healthy lifestyle and exercises daily. Only the crow's feet on the sides of his eyes gave away his age or recent experience.

"That's true, Mr. Gray."

"You know that they treated me well, really. Logic told me it was not politically convenient for them to harm me. But when you're the one being held prisoner, logic is not much of a comfort."

"I can imagine. It must be terrible."

"You've never lived anything like that, I'll bet."

"Never."

Tom Wright indicated with his hand that it was Gray's turn. His job was to escort him to the plane. Once in it, he was a free man. After the thorough inspection, he left Gray sunk in a straight-backed waiting chair while he went through his own check-in at the counter. He made his way through by pushing a group of teenage girls wearing cutting-edge clothes with a combination of shyness and exhibitionism in, a nasty flicker of false appearances. He looked around to see if he was being watched, if people's hands adopted suspicious poses, if they carried packages where weapons could be concealed. Even the furniture and the inanimate objects seemed to gesture to him. The funniest thing was that the only ones who clearly wanted him to leave the country with his health intact were the members of the EGP. Nothing was as it seemed. Guatemala was a macabre movie set. The world was completely upside down.

Wright finished the paperwork with the airline. He fought his way back through the crowd, getting stepped on by a child chasing another. He arrived where he had left Gray. He wasn't there. He double-checked that he wasn't at the wrong place. It was indeed the right one. Gray just wasn't there. Terrified, he flew around, looking everywhere. He pushed past a woman blocking his path, who insulted him in Spanish in return. He saw heads of all types, shapes and sizes, side by side, like a disturbing mirage dancing in the bright sunlight coming through every window until his ears and eyes throbbed. But not one of them was the man he was looking for. He walked instinctively to the entrance leading to the boarding gates, pushing two other people aside in the process. Everyone quickly went around him, dizzying him with their continuous movement and the smell of perspiration mixing badly with starched outfits. He did not pay attention to the whisperings behind him. Suddenly a strong hand took him by the arm. He felt his world had come to an end.

"Shoeshine, mister?"

It was a little, ungainly boy about ten years old offering

to shine his shoes. He was wearing shorts; his legs were thin and long, twig-like, with and he had a wooden box hanging from his shoulder. Large scrofulous blotches stained his face. He had the most mischievous smile he had ever seen in his life. His fear dissolved at its magic effect.

"Did you see a *gringo*, like me, come through here? A bald man that was sitting in that chair?"

"Maybe..."

The boy shrugged his shoulders and showed a set of enormous teeth with gaps between them. Wright pulled out two quetzal bills and extended them to him. The boy's eyes grew in size. He took them and made them disappear in his pants pocket.

"He went to the drug store."

He pointed his finger in the appropriate direction, shrugged his shoulders, smiled again, crossed and re-crossed his legs, and ran off into the crowd with his shoeshine box.

Wright walked towards the drug store. Indeed, he saw Gray coming out at that moment. To his surprise, he had *Time* magazine, rolled up with the cover on the outside, in his left hand. All he needs is the carnation in the lapel, Wright thought. When Gray saw him, he smiled pleasantly and walked rapidly in his direction.

"Do you like to read *Time*? It's my favorite."

"No. I prefer *Newsweek*."

It was unbearable. He couldn't take it for one more second. The simplest movements were burdened with a macabre symbolism that he wanted to immediately vanish from his head.

"Oh well. They don't have it. I looked for it as well."

"It doesn't matter. I don't feel like reading right now."

Gray smiled. Wright let the air in his lungs escape. Was it a coincidence? Or was it punishment for his lack of faith, for his demands for rationality and order? What had he actually done to deserve this?"

"I generally read on planes. Today I'm unable to."

"Sure. I imagine you won't relax until we're inside."

"You won't either."

"I *am* calm. With you here, I've nothing to fear. You don't know how much I appreciate your going all the way to Washington with me."

"Think nothing of it, Mr. Gray. Business as usual."

At that merciful instant the call to go through passport control was made. Wright felt that it was his last obstacle. If it didn't happen there, he was safe. A rude man with a thick moustache and curly hair asked for his passport and for the international boarding card. He opened a huge binder with thousands of handwritten names and looked for Wright's with his index finger.

"You can go through."

That was it. As he moved down the wide hall that led to his plane, he felt lighter. He saw the Anacafé counter as if for the first time. From that side of the barrier, everything seemed more American, safer. In front of Anacafé, there were toys, magazines in English, the last Maya fabrics for sale. Everything was cleaner, more orderly, more accessible. The rancid signs of hostility had dissipated, like a language too difficult to pronounce whose syllables disappear from the muscular tongue movement after they're enunciated. For the first time he felt that it was not too late to cleanse himself of his guilt as one who undresses under a virgin waterfall and the fresh torrent takes away the remnants of bitterness in its white foam.

2

Tom Wright saw his face in front of the other man's. It was a stylized image in which both men's expressions had that air of strange distance manifested by those who have seen death up close, and are not quite convinced that its threat has disappeared. It was a sort of faraway, ethereal confrontation with comedic airs, in which the dialogue seemed to have been written for a vaudeville act. Kukulkán reprimanded him once again.

"...It may surprise you, but we love and feel life, we contemplate the ocean and dissolve its foam between our fingers, we caress the soil that generates corn and the hips of dark-skinned women. We're not beasts nor rocks, but human beings with warm flesh and an insatiable soul..."

Kukulkán circled around him, staring at his feet while waving his hands with histrionic dexterity. Wright felt the conversation was a river of words fluttering like nocturnal butterflies in a spiral that descended to chaos. The outlandish exchange was like an incantation, a recital in which Kukulkán's words charred him like branding irons. Wright saw Kukulkán's face in front of his own, in the light, as if surrounded by diminutive rainbows full of warmth. The points of light grew, dazing him, making him feel as if he were falling in a dark, bottomless void. Then the face came forward, but it was no longer Kukulkán's. It was Sandra's, superimposed over the first, unfolding itself from the first, two faces from the same substance. Wright heard his own cry of desperation like an echo reaching him from an opposite shore. He opened his eyes to see where it had come from, and again saw Sandra's face, heavy like the world, about to crush him with the awesome speed of a gigantic. Only it was not her face. It was the triangular head of a rattler with its mouth wide open, its fine tongue dancing in front of him with its two fork-like points, the enormous fangs about to penetrate his throat.

"Sandra!"

He opened his eyes. He was drenched in sweat. The tie was choking him and the shirt collar scratched his neck. All eyes converged on him. He was in his airplane seat, his head resting on a small, mangy pillow that had sunken into the hollow of the window through which one could see a sky so violently blue that it paralyzed the imagination with its thick, paste-like solidity. There was nobody else in his row of seats. Gray must have gotten up at some point. Around him, passengers looked at him with an air of perplexity. He must have screamed in his dreams. Smiling stupidly, he indicated with his hand that nothing was wrong and, looking for a napkin to dry off the perspiration, he headed for the aisle.

3

"Daddy!"

Wright's daughter, bright pudding-face, ran to him with birdlike hops in her spotlessly clean white shoes. Her red hair was pulled up in two pigtails floating over her ears. Behind her came his wife and son, walking quickly to keep pace. The girl arrived giggling, her arms extended, moving excitedly like a top. He bent down, opened his own arms, and lifted her up by her armpits, looking at her face intently, as if he had just discovered the freckles around her nose. She smiled a toothless grin. She had lost her two front teeth. He pressed her against his chest so hard the girl complained:

"Daddy, you're hurting me!"

Two steps later, his wife and oldest son fell all over him. Buried by so many hugs, he felt trapped by a giant octopus. He looked at his wife's face. It was a plain face, as milky as if it had been sculpted in spotless white marble. She wore no lipstick. Not a trace of makeup. Her blond hair fell neatly to each side of her forehead without sophistication. Her ice-blue, almost transparent eyes, lacking in malice, only became moistened when an involuntary teardrop filled them. Her long legs were covered by canary yellow slacks. He was her entire world. No. He and the children were her entire world. The small Virginia suburb full of trees and gardens with perfectly-mowed, shiny green lawns were her world. The fresh, white, wooden house with perfectly-polished, spotless hardwood floors, iridescent, pastel walls so luminous they blinded everyone with their cleanliness when the sun shot through the translucent glass of the windows and quivered on its surface, was her world. The white walls of the immaculate kitchen, smelling of freshly-made coffee and of all the spices in the world, perimeter cabinets in an antique-white enamel finish, the island with a Cherry Hill stain, stacked molding with a painted layer that matched the burgundy Viking oven, the white aprons hanging neatly behind the door, all of that was her world. The church where she would meet the neighbors wearing their Sunday best was her world.

Those eyes had not seen what he had seen. He no longer wanted his life to disintegrate in his fingers like a wet sugar cube. Now he wanted to be able to control events. To be an active agent of his destiny, not a passive victim of other peoples' wills. After all, everything is always coherent and simple on television. Harmonious. On TV you could miraculously touch the other side, the one we always see shining in the distance without ever reaching it. Not like in real life, but in life as he wanted it. He closed his own eyes forcefully, as hard as a bank vault. They all hugged him harder, bursting with love.

The days passed. Wright's wife asked no questions. She knew his work was classified. Every day at dinner time, they watched the news together on TV. An old habit that he had picked up again since his return. One of those evenings, they returned home late because the checkout lines at the supermarket were longer than usual. His wife was irritated. The previous night he had dreamt that the sun darkened. He told her they were on a tropical island when it started to dim. Everything went dark. As it got shadowy, ominously black, he felt as if a gigantic hand compressed his chest and cut off his breathing, a thick serpent crowding his dreams. He woke up screaming, sweating profusely as suffering from a malaria attack.

When he turned on the set, a familiar road was clearly visible on the screen. A sun-dipped mountainous sierra that took your breath away with its dramatic beauty, previously dark green but now devoid of trees, turning cinnamon and rouge, ran along the side of the narrow stretch of asphalt. The camera focused on a group of men carrying a bundle whose shape was impossible to discern in the far-off distance of the image. A plump man with black hair and fine moustache appeared on screen speaking Spanish with an unmistakable Guatemalan accent. It was the same reporter who had let him see Lagos Cerro's speech on his TV monitor in the central park of Guatemala City.

"The mutilated corpse of Señora Sandra de Herrera, wife of wealthy entrepreneur Don Alvaro Herrera, was found today..." He did not say more. His lips continued to move, but his voice was gone. His gestures were melodramatically accentuated by that muteness. Less than a second later, the image was displaced by the nasal voice of the popular American anchor man whose gray-haired face filled the screen with elegance, stature and optimistic confidence.

"The disappearance of this important Guatemalan high-society figure has been attributed to a terrorist organization, the EGP, Spanish acronym for Guerrilla Army of the Poor. General Lagos Cerro's government promised to do everything in its power to capture the perpetrators of this heinous crime and ratified that they were willing to fight Communists to the end by any means necessary. He also stated that this terrorist organization finances its operations by smuggling cocaine into the United States. Spokespersons from both the State Department and the DEA congratulated General Lagos Cerro's government for its quick response, and the White House promised to support him in his titanic crusade on behalf of the free world. In other news today..."

The screen of the TV seemed to explode just before it went black, and the sound decreased gradually like the pained howling of a dying dog hit by a car. Tom Wright was still aiming at the TV with the remote control as if it were a gray hand gun, closing one of the squinting eyes to aim better at an imaginary target. He nervously clenched and unclenched his right hand. His wife cozily laid her head on his shoulder.

All he saw in front of him was the head of a poisonous snake that formed an equilateral triangle surrounded by a red circle with the caption in black letters: *"Only the winners have the right to live."*

Austin / Rio de Janeiro / San Francisco / Madrid
1990 - 1997

ARTURO ARIAS is Director of Latin American Studies at the University of Redlands. Co-writer for the screenplay for the film *El Norte* (1984), his most recent novel in English is titled *After the Bombs* (Curbstone Press,1990). Author of five novels in Spanish—*Despues de las bombas* (1979), *Itzam Na* (1981), *Jaguar en Llamas* (1989), *Los caminos de Paxil* (1991) and *Cascabel* (1998)—he is the winner of the Casa de las Américas Award and the Anna Seghers Scholarship for two of them. In 1998 he published two books of criticism, one on Guatemalan 20th Century fiction, *La identidad de la palabra*, (The Identity of the Word), and another on contemporary Central American fiction, *Gestos ceremoniales* (Ceremonial Gestures). His most recent novel is *Sopa de caracol* (Alfaguara, 2002). In 2000 he edited two books, the critical edition of Miguel Angel Asturias's *Mulata,* and *The Rigoberta Menchú Controversy*, dealing with the recent polemic about the Menchú's testimonial. An article on this same topic also appeared in the January 2001 edition of the *PMLA*. He recently served as president of the Latin American Studies Association (LASA).

SEÁN HIGGINS is a bilingual resource teacher at Grant Elementary School in the San Jose Unified School District. His translations of fiction have appeared in a variety of publications, including *Index on Censorship*, *City Lights Review*, and *Columbia Translation Review*.

JILL ROBBINS is an Associate Professor of Contemporary Spanish Literature and Culture at the University of California-Irvine. She is at present working on a book-length study on the representations of the "feminine" and the nation in the poetry of 20th century Spanish women.

CURBSTONE PRESS, INC.

is a non-profit publishing house dedicated to literature that reflects a
commitment to social change, with an emphasis on contemporary writing
from Latino, Latin American and Vietnamese cultures. Curbstone presents
writers who give voice to the unheard in a language that goes beyond
denunciation to celebrate, honor and teach. Curbstone builds bridges
between its writers and the public – from inner-city to rural areas, colleges
to community centers, children to adults. Curbstone seeks out the highest
aesthetic expression of the dedication to human rights and intercultural
understanding: poetry, testimonies, novels, stories,
and children's books.

This mission requires more than just producing books. It requires ensuring
that as many people as possible learn about these books and read them. To
achieve this, a large portion of Curbstone's schedule is dedicated to
arranging tours and programs for its authors, working with public school
and university teachers to enrich curricula, reaching out to underserved
audiences by donating books and conducting readings and community
programs, and promoting discussion in the media. It is only through these
combined efforts that literature can truly make a difference.

Curbstone Press, like all non-profit presses, depends on the support of
individuals, foundations, and government agencies to bring you, the reader,
works of literary merit and social significance which might not find a place
in profit-driven publishing channels, and to bring the authors and their
books into communities across the country. Our sincere thanks to the many
individuals, foundations, and government agencies who support this
endeavor: J. Walton Bissell Foundation, Connecticut Commission on the
Arts, Connecticut Humanities Council, Daphne Seybolt Culpeper
Foundation, Fisher Foundation, Greater Hartford Arts Council, Hartford
Courant Foundation, J. M. Kaplan Fund, Eric Mathieu King Fund, Lannan
Foundation, John D. and Catherine T. MacArthur Foundation, National
Endowment for the Arts, Open Society Institute, Puffin Foundation, and the
Woodrow Wilson National Fellowship Foundation.

Please help to support Curbstone's efforts to present the diverse voices and
views that make our culture richer. Tax-deductible donations can be made by
check or credit card to:
Curbstone Press, 321 Jackson Street, Willimantic, CT 06226
phone: (860) 423-5110   fax: (860) 423-9242
www.curbstone.org

IF YOU WOULD LIKE TO BE A MAJOR SPONSOR OF A
CURBSTONE BOOK, PLEASE CONTACT US.

La casa del árbol #1

Dinosaurios
al atardecer

Mary Pope Osborne
Ilustrado por Sal Murdocca
Traducido por Marcela Brovelli

LECTORUM
PUBLICATIONS, INC.

Para Linda y Mallory,
quienes me acompañaron en mi viaje.

DINOSAURIOS AL ATARDECER

Published by arrangement with Random House Children's Books,
a division of Random House, Inc., 1745 Broadway, New York, NY 10019.

MAGIC TREE HOUSE ®
Is a registered trademark of Mary Pope Osborne, used under license.

978-1-930332-49-2
Printed in the U.S.A.
CWMO 10 9 8

Library of Congress Cataloging-in-Publication Data
Osborne, Mary Pope.
          [Dinosaurs before dark. Spanish]
          Dinosaurios al atardecer / Mary Pope Osborne ; ilustrado por Sal
Murdocca ; traducido por Marcela Brovelli.
               p. cm. – (La casa del árbol ; #1)
Summary: Eight-year-old Jack and his younger sister Annie find a magic
treehouse, which whisks them back to an ancient time zone where they see
live dinosaurs.
          ISBN 1-930332-49-1 (pbk.)
          [1. Dinosaurs–Fiction. 2. Time travel–Fiction. 3. Magic–Fiction.
4.Tree houses–Fiction. 5. Spanish language materials.] I. Murdocca, Sal,
ill. II. Brovelli, Marcela. III. Title.
          PZ73.0746 2003
          [Fic]—dc21
                                        2003005594

Índice

Dinosaurios
al atardecer

1

En el bosque

—¡Socorro! ¡Un monstruo! —gritó Annie.

—Sí, claro —dijo Jack—. Un monstruo en Frog Creek, Pensilvania.

—¡Apresúrate, Jack! —dijo Annie mientras corría por la calle.

—¡Vaya!

Esto le pasaba a Jack por juntarse con su hermana de siete años.

Annie adoraba dar rienda suelta a su mundo imaginario. En cambio Jack, tenía ocho años y medio y prefería el mundo *real*.

—¡Cuidado, Jack! ¡El monstruo se acerca! ¡Está a punto de alcanzarte!

—Bueno, que me atrape.

Annie se alejó corriendo hacia el bosque.

Jack miró el cielo. El sol estaba por esconderse.

—¡Vamos, Annie! ¡Es hora de ir a casa!

Pero Annie había desaparecido.

Jack se quedó esperando.

¡Oh! Annie, ¿dónde estás?

—¡Annie! —Jack la llamó otra vez.

—¡Jack! ¡Jack! ¡Ven aquí!

—Espero que no sea una tontería —dijo enojado. Cruzó la calle y se dirigió hacia el bosque. El sol del atardecer hacía brillar las hojas de los árboles.

—Ven aquí —insistió Annie, parada debajo de un enorme roble.

—¡Mira! —dijo, señalando una escalera hecha de soga y madera.

Era la escalera más larga que Jack había visto en su vida.

—¡Guau! —susurró al verla.

La escalera era casi tan alta como el árbol. Y, allí, en el medio de dos grandes ramas, había una casa de madera.

—Debe de ser la casa más alta del mundo —dijo Annie.

—¿Quién la habrá construido? —preguntó Jack—. Es la primera vez que la veo.

—No lo sé. Pero voy a subir —agregó Annie.

—¡No! No sabemos quién es el dueño —dijo Jack.

—Sólo por un minuto —agregó Annie trepando por la escalera.

—¡Annie, regresa!

Pero ella siguió trepando e ignoró el llamado de Jack.

—¡Annie! Ya casi es de noche. Tenemos que regresar.

Annie entró en la casa haciendo oídos sordos a las palabras de Jack.

—¡Annie!

Jack esperó un momento. Estaba a punto de llamarla otra vez cuando ella asomó la cabeza por la ventana.

—¡Hay libros! —gritó Annie.

—¿Qué?

—¡Está llena de libros!

—¡Genial! —Jack amaba los libros.

De inmediato, se acomodó los lentes, se agarró de ambos lados de la escalera y comenzó a subir.

2
El monstruo

Jack atravesó el agujero de la entrada y entró en la casa.

¡Guau! Era verdad, la casa estaba llena de libros. Cientos de ellos. Por todos lados. Algunos eran muy viejos y tenían la tapa llena de polvo. Otros, eran nuevos, con la tapa de colores muy brillantes.

—¡Ven! Desde aquí se puede ver todo —dijo Annie mirando por la ventana.

Jack se puso a observar el paisaje junto a su hermana. Desde allí podían ver la copa de otros árboles más pequeños. A lo lejos se divisaba la biblioteca de Frog Creek.

También se veía la escuela primaria y el parque.

Annie señaló hacia otra dirección.

—Ahí está nuestra casa —dijo.

Estaba en lo cierto. Aquella casa de madera blanca con la galería verde era su hogar. En el jardín de la casa contigua estaba Henry, el perro del vecino, que se veía como una pequeña mancha negra.

—¡Hola, Henry! —gritó Annie.

—¡Sssh! Se supone que no debemos estar aquí.

Jack se alejó de la ventana y echó un ligero vistazo al interior de la casa del árbol.

—Me pregunto de quién serán todos estos libros —dijo. De pronto, notó que muchos de ellos tenían un marcador dentro.

—Me gusta éste —dijo Annie mientras le mostraba a Jack un libro con un castillo en la portada.

—Aquí hay un libro sobre Pensilvania —dijo Jack dando vuelta a la página con el marcador.

—¡Uy! Aquí hay un dibujo de Frog Creek. ¡Mira! ¡Es *igual* a este bosque! —agregó Jack.

—Mira, aquí hay un libro para ti, Jack —dijo Annie, con un libro de dinosaurios en la mano, que tenía un marcador de seda azul.

—Déjame verlo —dijo Jack. Puso la mochila en el suelo y tomó el libro.

—Tú mira ése y yo miraré el de los castillos —dijo Annie.

—No. Creo que esto no está bien. Estos libros no son nuestros —contestó Jack. Pero mientras hablaba con Annie abrió el libro de dinosaurios en la página del marcador. La curiosidad lo devoraba.

Se detuvo en el dibujo de un milenario reptil volador. Era un Pterodáctilo.

Mientras lo observaba, Jack recorría con el dedo las enormes alas de murciélago del animal.

—¡Guau! —susurró—. Ojalá pudiera ver un Pterodáctilo de verdad.

8

Jack se quedó estudiando el dibujo de la extraña criatura que volaba en el cielo.

—¡Ay! —gritó Annie.

—¿Qué sucede? —preguntó Jack.

—¡Un monstruo! —gritó Annie mientras señalaba la ventana.

—Deja de imaginar cosas, Annie —insistió Jack.

—¡De verdad! ¡Mira!

Jack miró por la ventana. Vio una criatura gigante planeando sobre la copa de los árboles. Tenía una cresta larga y muy extraña sobre la cabeza. Un pico muy fino y dos enormes alas parecidas a las de los murciélagos.

¡Era un Pterodáctilo de verdad!

La criatura se acercaba a la casa del árbol dando enormes volteretas.

¡Parecía un planeador!

En ese momento, el viento comenzó a soplar.

Las hojas temblaban enloquecidas. Y, de
repente, la criatura volvió a remontarse en
el cielo. Muy alto. Tan alto que Jack casi se
cae por la ventana por no perderla de vista.

El viento sopló con más fuerza aún,
dejando oír su feroz silbido.

En ese instante, la casa del árbol comenzó a girar sobre sí misma.

—¿Qué pasa? —preguntó Jack exaltado.

—¡Aléjate de la ventana! —gritó Annie
asustada.

11

Annie tiró a Jack hacia atrás para que se alejara de la ventana.

La casa giraba cada vez con más y más fuerza.

Jack cerró los ojos apretándolos fuertemente, y se abrazó a su hermana.

Más tarde, todo quedó en silencio. Un silencio absoluto.

Jack abrió los ojos. La débil luz del sol se colaba por la ventana.

Annie continuaba junto a Jack. Los libros y la mochila de Jack seguían en el mismo lugar.

La casa del árbol continuaba en la copa del roble.

Pero, aquel, ya no era el mismo árbol.

3
¿Dónde estamos?

Jack miró por la ventana.

Observó el dibujo del libro. Y volvió a mirar por la ventana.

El mundo exterior y el dibujo del libro eran exactamente iguales.

El Pterodáctilo remontándose en el cielo, el suelo cubierto de helechos y de hierba, el arroyo ondulante, la ladera empinada, y los volcanes que se veían a lo lejos.

—¿Dó- dónde estamos? —preguntó Jack.

El Pterodáctilo se abalanzó planeando hacia el roble, aterrizó en el suelo y se quedó quieto.

—¿Qué nos pasó? —preguntó Annie mirando fijamente a su hermano. Jack la miraba sin entender.

—No lo sé —contestó él—, yo sólo miré el dibujo del libro.

—Sí. Y luego dijiste: ¡Ojalá pudiera ver un Pterodáctilo de verdad!

—¡Sí! Y después pude verlo con mis propios ojos, y en pleno bosque de Frog Creek —dijo Jack.

—Después, el viento empezó a soplar y la casa comenzó a dar vueltas como un trompo —agregó Annie.

—Y aparecimos aquí —dijo Jack.

—Sí. Después aparecimos aquí —dijo Annie.

—Entonces, quiere decir que... —agregó Jack.

—Quiere decir...¿qué?... —preguntó Annie.

—Nada —contestó Jack y, sacudiendo la cabeza, dijo: —Nada de esto puede ser real.

Annie volvió a mirar por la ventana y dijo:

—Pero, *la criatura* es real, es *de verdad*.

Jack asomó la cabeza por la ventana junto a su hermana. El Pterodáctilo estaba parado en el suelo, al lado del árbol, como un guardia atento y con las alas completamente desplegadas.

—¡Hola! —gritó Annie.

—¡Sssh! —se supone que no debemos estar aquí.

—Pero, ¿dónde es *aquí?* —preguntó Annie.

—No lo sé —respondió Jack.

—¡Holaaá! —Annie volvió a saludar a la criatura.

El Pterodáctilo levantó la cabeza y miró a los niños.

—¿Dónde es *aquí?* —insistió Annie, pero esta vez preguntándole a la criatura.

—¿Estás loca? Los Pterodáctilos no hablan —dijo Jack—. Espera, me fijaré en el libro. Tal vez encuentre la respuesta a tu pregunta.

Jack tomó el libro y comenzó a leer lo que estaba escrito debajo del dibujo:

15

**Este reptil volador vivió en el
período cretácico y se extinguió
hace 65 millones de años.**

No. No era posible ¿Cómo podía ser que
hubieran aterrizado 65 millones de años
atrás?

—Jack —dijo Annie—, parece amigable.

—¿Amigable?

—Sí, lo sé. Bajemos a hablar con él.

—¿Quieres hablar con él?

Annie comenzó a bajar por la escalera.

—¡Espera! —gritó Jack.

Pero Annie no le prestó atención.

—¿Te has vuelto loca? —preguntó Jack.

Annie dio un gran salto y se paró con
valentía delante del Pterodáctilo.

4
Henry

Jack se quedó observando a Annie con la boca abierta mientras ella alargaba el brazo en dirección al Pterodáctilo.

Annie adoraba hacerse amiga de los animales, pero éste no era como los demás.

—¡No te acerques demasiado, Annie!

Pero, haciendo oídos sordos, Annie comenzó a acariciarle la cresta y el cuello al Pterodáctilo mientras le hablaba.

¿Qué diablos le estaría diciendo?

Jack respiró profundo y pensó en bajar. Examinaría a la criatura y tomaría algunas notas. Como un verdadero científico.

Jack bajó por la escalera y se paró a pocos pies de la criatura.

El Pterodáctilo miró fijamente a Jack, con ojos brillantes y atentos.

—Tiene una piel muy suave, Jack. Es como si estuviera acariciando a Henry.

—No es un perro —dijo Jack enojado.

—Tócalo —le dijo Annie.

Jack no se movió.

—No lo pienses, sólo anímate y hazlo. Vamos, Jack.

Jack dio un paso adelante, estiró el brazo con precaución y acarició el cuello del Pterodáctilo.

¡Qué interesante! Una delgada capa vellosa cubría la piel de la extraña criatura.

—Qué suave es, ¿no? —preguntó Annie.

Jack buscó dentro de la mochilla, sacó un lápiz y un cuaderno. Y escribió:

Piel velluda

—¿Qué haces? —preguntó Annie.

—Estoy anotando algunas cosas —contestó Jack—. Tal vez seamos los primeros en el mundo en ver un Pterodáctilo vivo.

Jack volvió a mirar a la criatura. Tenía una cresta huesuda sobre la cabeza, más larga que su brazo.

—Me pregunto si será inteligente —dijo Jack.

—*Muy* inteligente —contestó Annie.

—No estés tan segura, tiene un cerebro más pequeño que un garbanzo.

—Es inteligente. Lo sé, lo presiento. Lo voy a llamar Henry —agregó Annie.

Jack volvió a escribir en su cuaderno:

¿Cerebro pequeño?

Jack volvió a observar al Pterodáctilo.

—Tal vez es un mutante —dijo.

La criatura levantó la cabeza bien alto.

—No, Jack, no es un mutante —dijo Annie riendo.

—Bueno, entonces, ¿qué hace aquí? ¿Dónde estamos? —preguntó Jack.

Annie se acercó a la criatura y, con voz serena, le preguntó:

—¿Sabes dónde estamos, Henry?

El Pterodáctilo la miró fijamente mientras abría y cerraba el pico sin cesar como un enorme par de tijeras.

—¿Tratas de decirme algo, Henry? —preguntó Annie.

—Olvídalo, Annie —dijo Jack. Y luego escribió:

¿Boca en forma de tijera?

—¿Hemos viajado a un tiempo muy lejano, Henry? —preguntó Annie—. ¿Está este lugar en el pasado?

De pronto, Annie abrió la boca asombrada y exclamó: —¡Jack!

Jack alzó la vista.

Annie señalaba hacia arriba. ¡En la cima de la colina había un enorme dinosaurio parado!

5
Oro en la hierba

—¡Vámonos de aquí! ¡Rápido! —dijo Jack. Metió el cuaderno dentro de la mochila y arrastró por la fuerza a Annie hasta la escalera.

—¡Adiós, Henry! —gritó ella.

—¡Apresúrate! —dijo Jack y le dio otro empujón para que se apurara.

—¡Déjame! —dijo Annie mientras subía por la escalera.

Ambos entraron en la casa con tanta prisa que se cayeron al suelo.

El corazón les latía a toda velocidad. Y casi sin aliento se asomaron a la ventana para ver al dinosaurio. Continuaba en el mismo lugar. Estaba parado en la cima de la colina, comiendo magnolias del árbol.

—¡Increíble! —susurró Jack—. *Estamos en la prehistoria.*

El dinosaurio parecía un rinoceronte, sólo que mucho más grande. Y, además, tenía tres cuernos en vez de uno. Dos en la frente y uno en la nariz. Detrás de la cabeza tenía una especie de coraza que sobresalía como una gran corona a punto de caerse.

—¡Es un Triceratops! —exclamó Jack.

—¿Se come a la gente? —preguntó Annie en voz baja.

—Lo voy a averiguar. Jack tomó el libro de dinosaurios y lo hojeó rápidamente.

—¡Aquí está! —dijo señalando el dibujo de un Triceratops. Y leyó con cuidado la dcfinición:

El Triceratops vivió cn cl período cretáclco. Se alimentaba de plantas y pesaba más de 12.000 libras.

Jack cerró el libro rápidamente y dijo:

—Sólo se alimenta de plantas. No come carne.

—Vayamos a verlo de cerca —sugirió Annie.

—¿Estás loca? —agregó Jack.

—¿No quieres escribir algo acerca de él? Tal vez seamos los primeros en el mundo en ver a un Triceratops vivo.

Jack suspiró resignado. Annie tenía razón.

—Bueno, vamos —dijo.

Guardó el libro en la mochila, se la acomodó en la espalda y comenzó a bajar por la escalera.

Mientras bajaba, Jack se detuvo para decirle algo a Annie.

—Prométeme que no lo tocarás.

—¡Lo prometo!

—Promete que no le darás besos.

—¡Te lo prometo!

—Prométeme que no le hablarás.

—¡Prometido!

—Promete que no vas a...

—¡Vamos! ¡Apúrate! —dijo Annie.

Jack continuó bajando. Annie lo seguía detrás.

Cuando los niños bajaron, el Pterodáctilo los miró amistosamente.

Annie le tiró un beso con la mano y, alegre, le dijo:

—Enseguida regresamos, Henry.

—¡Sssh! —exclamó Jack. Y, muy despacio y con cuidado, comenzó a abrirse camino entre los helechos.

Cuando llegó al pie de la colina, se escondió detrás de un arbusto muy frondoso.

Annie se arrodilló junto a Jack y comenzó a hablar.

—¡Sssh! – Jack hizo un ademán con la mano para que su hermana se callara.

Annie hizo una mueca.

Mientras tanto, Jack se quedó observando al Triceratops, que no paraba de comerse las magnolias del árbol. Aquel dinosaurio era increíblemente grande, casi tan grande como un camión.

Jack sacó el cuaderno de la mochila y escribió:

Se alimenta de flores.

Annie le dio a su hermano un suave codazo. Pero él la ignoró.

Jack continuó estudiando al Triceratops y haciendo anotaciones:

Come despacio.

Annie le dio otro codazo a Jack con más fuerza. Y, esta vez, él la miró.

Annie se tocó el pecho con el dedo índice, extendió el brazo señalando al dinosaurio y empezó a reírse.

¿Estaría bromeando?

De pronto, Annie le dijo adiós a su hermano y, aunque él trató de detenerla, ella se alejó a saltos riendo.

Apenas en unos segundos, quedó a la vista del Triceratops.

—¡Regresa! —dijo Jack ya casi sin voz.

Era demasiado tarde. El enorme dinosaurio había visto a Annie, y la observaba desde la cima de la colina mientras devoraba las magnolias.

—¡Oh, oh! —exclamó Annie.

—¡Regresa! —gritó Jack.

—Parece amigable, Jack.

—¿Amigable? Mira sus cuernos, Annie.

—Es amigable, Jack.

—¿Lo es?

El Triceratops permaneció en el mismo lugar, observando pacientemente a Annie. Luego se dio la vuelta y comenzó a bajar por la ladera de la colina.

—¡Adiós! —dijo Annie y se volvió hacia Jack—. ¿Ves que no es malo?

Jack refunfuñó. Pero al tomar el cuaderno escribió:

Es amigable.

—¡Vamos! Recorramos el bosque
—sugirió Annie.

Mientras Jack caminaba detrás de su hermana, vio algo que brillaba en la hierba. Se
agachó para recogerlo y vio que era un
medallón. Tenía grabada la letra M. Y era de
oro.

—¡Caramba! Alguien estuvo aquí antes que nosotros —dijo con voz serena.

6
El valle de los dinosaurios

—¡Annie! ¡Mira lo que encontré! —gritó Jack entusiasmado.

Ella estaba muy entretenida cortando magnolias del árbol, en la cima de la colina.

—¡Annie, mira! ¡Un medallón!

Pero su hermana no escuchaba. Observaba algo del otro lado de la colina.

—¡Guau! —exclamó Annie asombrada.

—¡Annie! —gritó Jack.

Annie descendió hacia el otro lado de la colina, con una magnolia fuertemente apretujada entre los dedos.

—¡Annie, regresa!

Pero ella siguió su camino hasta desaparecer.

—La voy a matar —murmuró Jack enojado. Y guardó el medallón en el bolsillo del pantalón.

Luego, Jack oyó gritar a Annie.

—¡Annie!

Jack volvió a oír otro ruido, sólo que mucho más potente. Similar al bufido de un toro enfurecido.

—¡Ven aquí, Jack!

—¡Annie! ¿Dónde estás?

Jack tomó la mochila, se la acomodó en la espalda y corrió a toda prisa hacia la cima.

Al llegar, se sorprendió tanto que casi no podía hablar.

El valle, del otro lado de la colina, estaba colmado de enormes nidos construidos con barro. ¡Y dentro de cada nido había decenas de dinosaurios recién nacidos!

Annie se agachó cuidadosamente y empezó a caminar en cuatro patas hacia uno de los nidos. Pero antes de llegar, se topó con un gigantesco dinosaurio con el cuerpo en forma de pato, que la observaba desde arriba.

—¡No te asustes! ¡Quédate quieta! —dijo Jack bajando por la ladera.

El enorme dinosaurio hembra estaba parado muy cerca de Annie, agitando los brazos y bramando enfurecido. Al lado de la pequeña parecía una torre gigante.

En ese momento, Jack se detuvo. No quería acercarse demasiado.

—Bueno, Annie, ahora ven hacia mí, pero muy despacio —sugirió Jack agachado en el suelo.

Annie intentó ponerse de pie muy lentamente.

—¡Quédate agachada! Trata de caminar en cuatro patas.

Con la magnolia aprisionada entre los dedos, Annie comenzó a gatear muy despacio hacia donde estaba Jack.

Al ver que Annie se movía, la madre de los dinosaurios bebés empezó a seguirla emitiendo un bramido ensordecedor.

Annie se quedó paralizada.

—¡No te detengas! —le dijo Jack con calma.

Al oír a su hermano, Annie se tranquilizó y siguió caminando en cuatro patas.

Jack se acercó un poco más a Annie, la tomó de la mano y la trajo hacia él.

—¡Quédate agachada! —le dijo mientras permanecía arrodillado en el suelo—. Inclina la cabeza hacia abajo y haz como si estuvieras comiendo algo.

—¿Qué? —preguntó Annie.

—¡Sí! Una vez leí que hay que actuar así si un perro callejero trata de atacarte.

—¡Pero ella no es un perro! —agregó Annie.

—¡Sólo haz como si masticaras algo!

Jack y Annie inclinaron la cabeza hacia abajo, fingiendo que comían.

Rápidamente, el dinosaurio comenzó a tranquilizarse.

Jack alzó la cabeza.

—Gracias por salvarme, Jack.

—Annie, usa el cerebro. No puedes correr hacia un nido así como así. Las madres de los dinosaurios recién nacidos siempre están cerca de sus crías.

Annie se puso de pie y se alejó.

—¡Annie! —gritó Jack.

Era demasiado tarde.

Annie estaba junto al dinosaurio ofreciéndole una magnolia.

—Perdóname si te hice preocupar por tus bebés —dijo.

El dinosaurio se acercó más a Annie estirándose para tomar la flor. Pero en vez de alejarse, se quedó esperando. Quería otra.

—No tengo más flores.

Al escuchar esto, el dinosaurio respondió con un desgarrador chillido de tristeza.

—No te preocupes. En la cima de la colina hay más flores —dijo Annie—. Te traeré algunas.

En ese instante el dinosaurio, que caminaba como un pato, comenzó a perseguir a Annie para no perderla de vista.

Sin perder tiempo, Jack comenzó a estudiar los dinosaurios recién nacidos. Algunos de ellos empezaban a trepar por las paredes del nido para salir.

¿Dónde estaba el resto de las madres?

Jack tomó el libro de dinosaurios y comenzó a hojearlo rápidamente.

Encontró un dibujo de unos dinosaurios con el cuerpo en forma dc pato y se detuvo a leer:

Los Anatosauros vivían en manadas. Mientras algunas madres cuidaban a los bebés, otras salían en busca de alimento.

Entonces las demás madres de los dinosaurios bebés debían de estar muy cerca.

—¡Oye Jack!

Jack alzó la mirada y vio a Annie en la cima de la colina. Alimentaba al Anatosauro con magnolias.

—Ella también es amigable —dijo Annie.

Pero de pronto, el Anatosauro produjo uno de sus aterradores bramidos. Al oírlo, Annie se agazapó en el suelo y fingió que masticaba algo.

En ese instante, el dinosaurio descendió de la colina con rapidez.

La madre de los recién nacidos parecía asustada por algo.

Jack guardó el libro en la mochila y subió rápidamente a la cima de la colina.

—Me pregunto por qué habrá huido —dijo Annie—. Nos estábamos haciendo amigas.

Jack miró a su alrededor y lo que vio a lo lejos casi lo hizo vomitar.

Una horrenda y gigantesca criatura avanzaba por la pradera caminando sobre dos grandes patas, agitando dos brazos diminutos y una gruesa y larga cola. Tenía una cabeza enorme, y abría y cerraba la boca constantemente.

Aunque la criatura estaba lejos, Jack podía distinguir sus dientes largos y brillantes.

—¡Un Tiranosaurio! —susurró Jack.

7

¡Preparados! ¡Listos! ¡Ya!

—¡Corre, Annie! ¡Corre hacia la casa del árbol! —gritó Jack asustado.

Ambos descendieron velozmente por la colina. Abriéndose paso entre la hierba y los helechos, dejaron atrás al Pterodáctilo, hasta llegar a la escalera.

Subieron a toda prisa y en unos pocos segundos entraron en la casa de un tropezón.

Annie se paró junto a la ventana de un salto y con voz agitada dijo:

—¡Se está alejando!

Jack se acomodó los lentes y se acercó a la ventana.

El Tiranosaurio se alejaba por el bosque.

Pero, en ese instante, detuvo su marcha y se dio la media vuelta en dirección a la casa.

—¡Al suelo! —gritó Jack.

Ambos se agacharon en un segundo. Y después de un rato, se asomaron a la ventana cuidadosamente para espiar.

—¡Tenemos el campo libre, Annie!

—¡Genial!

—Tenemos que marcharnos de aquí —dijo Jack.

—Antes pediste un deseo.

—Muy bien. ¡Deseo regresar a Frog Creek!

Todo seguía en el mismo lugar.

—Deseo...

—Espera, Jack. Cuando pediste el deseo, mirabas un dibujo en el libro de dinosaurios. ¿Recuerdas?

—¡Oh, el libro! —gruñó Jack—. Lo dejé en la colina, junto con la mochila.

—Olvídalo —contestó Annie.

—No puedo. El libro no es mío. Y, además, también olvidé el cuaderno con todas mis anotaciones.

—¡Apresúrate! —dijo Annie.

Jack bajó por la escalera de madera a toda velocidad. Dejando atrás al Pterodáctilo, atravesó el campo y los helechos hasta llegar a la cima de la colina.

Desde allí miró hacia el valle y divisó su mochila tirada en el suelo. Y encima de ella, el libro de dinosaurios.

Pero ahora, el valle se encontraba atestado de Anatosauros. Todos montaban guardia junto a los nidos.

¿Dónde se habían metido antes? ¿El miedo por el Tiranosaurio los había hecho esconderse en sus guaridas?

Jack respiró profundo.

—¡Preparados! ¡Listos! ¡Ya!

Jack descendió a toda prisa y recogió velozmente la mochila y el libro de dinosaurios.

En ese instante se oyó un potente bramido. Y luego, ¡otro! Y ¡otro más! Al notar la presencia de Jack, todos los Anatosauros empezaron a bramar con furia.

Jack retrocedió y, rápidamente, corrió hacia la cima de la colina para descender por la ladera.

Pero antes de lograrlo, tuvo que detenerse. ¡El Tiranosaurio había regresado! Estaba parado a mitad de camino entre Jack y la casa del árbol.

8
Una sombra gigante

Jack se escondió de un salto detrás del magnolio.

El corazón le latía tan fuerte que ni siquiera podía pensar.

Desde allí espiaba al gigantesco monstruo. La horrible criatura abría y cerraba la boca sin cesar, mostrando unos dientes enormes y afilados como cuchillos.

"Tranquilízate. Trata de pensar", se dijo Jack.

Desde su escondite, Jack podía espiar qué sucedía en el valle.

Todos los dinosaurios con cuerpo de pato permanecían en sus lugares junto a los nidos.

Jack volvió a espiar al Tiranosaurio. ¡Excelente! Al parecer, la criatura aún no se había enterado de que Jack estaba escondido allí.

"Ten calma. Trata de pensar. ¡Vamos, piensa! Tal vez en el libro haya más información", se dijo para sí Jack.

Jack abrió el libro y encontró un dibujo del Tiranosaurio. Más abajo decía:

El Tiranosaurio fue el animal carnívoro más grande de la Tierra y de todos los tiempos. Si hoy estuviera vivo, se comería a un ser humano de un solo bocado.

¡Rayos! El libro no decía nada que pudiera ayudar a Jack. No podía esconderse del otro lado de la colina. Los Anatosauros podrían huir en estampida.

Tampoco podía correr hacia la casa del árbol. Seguramente, el Tiranosaurio lo alcanzaría. De acuerdo. Tal vez la única opción era esperar hasta que el animal se marchara.

Jack volvió a mirar a su alrededor.

El Tiranosaurio estaba más *cerca* de la colina.

En ese instante algo llamó la atención de
Jack. ¡Annie bajaba por la escalera de
madera!

¿Se había vuelto loca? ¿Qué hacía?

Annie saltó de la escalera al suelo y se acercó al Pterodáctilo. Mientras le hablaba, sacudiendo los brazos como un par de alas, señalaba a su hermano, hacia arriba y hacia la casa del árbol. Jack continuó observándola.

¡Annie se había vuelto *loca*!

—¡Annie! ¡Sube a la casa! —dijo Jack en voz baja.

De pronto, Jack oyó un feroz rugido. El Tiranosaurio lo observaba.

Jack se echó al suelo de inmediato.

El Tiranosaurio comenzó a acercarse. Jack sintió cómo la tierra temblaba debajo de él.

¿Qué podía hacer? ¿Correr? ¿Regresar al valle de los dinosaurios? ¿Trepar al árbol de magnolias?

En ese instante, una sombra gigantesca lo cubrió por completo. Jack alzó la mirada.

El Pterodáctilo volaba por encima de Jack. Luego, la criatura aterrizó lentamente sobre la cima de la colina. Y se dirigió directamente hacia donde estaba Jack.

9
Un viaje inolvidable

El Pterodáctilo se acercó a Jack y lo miró con ojos brillantes y atentos.

¿Qué se suponía que debía hacer él? ¿Montar sobre el lomo de la criatura?

"Soy demasiado pesado", pensó Jack. "No lo pienses. Hazlo."

Jack observó al Tiranosaurio, que se dirigía hacia la cima de la colina. Los rayos del sol le hacían brillar los dientes.

"¡Vamos! ¡No lo pienses! ¡Hazlo!"

Jack guardó el libro en la mochila. Y, con cuidado, se sentó sobre el lomo del Pterodáctilo, y se agarró con firmeza a él.

La criatura se movió hacia adelante, desplegó las alas y despegó del suelo. Una vez en el aire comenzaron a balancearse juntos, de un lado para el otro. Tanto, que Jack estuvo a punto de caerse. El Pterodáctilo estabilizó su vuelo y se elevó más alto.

En ese momento, Jack miró hacia abajo. El Tiranosaurio lo observaba abriendo y cerrando la boca furioso, como si tratara de morder el aire.

El Pterodáctilo se alejó planeando con elegancia. Sobrevoló la cima de la colina. Y se desplazó en círculos sobre el valle y sobre los dinosaurios recién nacidos y sus madres.

El Pterodáctilo se remontó más alto aún sobre la planicie. Y sobre el Triceratops, que rugía entre los arbustos.

¡Qué grandioso! ¡Era un milagro!

Jack se sentía como un pájaro. Tan liviano como una pluma.

El viento le agitaba el cabello. El aire era suave y dulce. Gritaba de emoción y reía sin parar.

No podía creerlo. ¡Volaba montado sobre un reptil prehistórico!

El Pterodáctilo planeó sobre el arroyo, sobre los helechos y los arbustos. Luego se detuvo junto al roble y Jack descendió cuidadosamente.

Una vez que Jack estuvo en tierra firme la criatura desplegó las alas y levantó el vuelo.

—Adiós, Henry —susurró Jack.

—¿Estás bien? —le preguntó Annie desde la casa del árbol.

Jack se acomodó los lentes y se quedó mirando al Pterodáctilo mientras desaparecía en el cielo.

—¿Estás bien, Jack? —insistió Annie.

Jack miró a su hermana y le sonrió.

—Gracias por salvarme la vida. Esto sí que fue divertido.

—¡Sube, Jack!

Jack trató de mantenerse en pie, pero sintió que las piernas le temblaban.

Se sentía un poco mareado.

—¡Apúrate! Ahí viene —dijo Annie desde lo alto.

Jack miró a su alrededor. El Tiranosaurio se acercaba hacia él. ¡A toda velocidad!

Sin perder tiempo, Jack se agarró de la escalera y subió con rapidez.

—¡Vamos! ¡Apresúrate! —gritaba Annie desde arriba.

Jack entró en la casa de un salto.

—Viene directo hacia nuestro árbol —agregó Annie aterrada.

Hasta que, de pronto, algo hizo impacto contra el roble. La casa tembló como una hoja.

Annie y Jack cayeron asustados sobre los libros.

—¡Pide un deseo, Jack!

—Necesitamos el libro. ¡El que tiene el dibujo de Frog Creek! ¿Dónde está?

Jack buscó entre todos los libros de la casa. Tenía que encontrar el libro de Pensilvania.

—¡Aquí está! —dijo aliviado.

Tomó el libro y recorrió las páginas con rapidez en busca del dibujo de Frog Creek.

—¡Lo encontré! —dijo Jack señalando el dibujo.

—¡Deseo que regresemos a casa!

El viento empezó a soplar. Primero suavemente, y más fuerte después.

—¡Vamos! ¡Rápido! —gritó Jack.

El viento sopló más fuerte aún. La casa del árbol comenzó a girar más y más rápido.

Jack cerró los ojos. Y se abrazó con todas sus fuerzas a su hermana.

Más tarde todo quedó en silencio. Un silencio absoluto.

10

En casa antes del anochecer

Se oyó el canto de un pájaro.

Jack abrió los ojos. Todavía tenía el dedo apoyado sobre el dibujo de Frog Creek.

Miró por la ventana y vio el mismo paisaje del libro.

—Estamos en casa —dijo Annie en voz baja.

El bosque resplandecía con los últimos rayos del atardecer. El sol estaba a punto de ocultarse.

Desde el momento en que Annie y Jack se marcharon hasta que estuvieron de regreso no había transcurrido ni un solo segundo.

—¡Anniee! ¡Jaack! Una voz los llamó desde lo lejos.

—Es mamá —dijo Annie señalando hacia
su casa.

Jack se asomó por la ventana y vio a su
madre junto a la casa, se veía muy pequeña.

—¡Annieee! ¡Jaaack!

Annie asomó la cabeza por la ventana y gritó: —¡Ya vamos!

Jack continuaba maravillado. Miraba a Annie sin decir una sola palabra.

—¿Qué nos pasó? —preguntó.

—Viajamos a otro lugar en una casa encantada —dijo Annie con toda naturalidad.

—Pero desde que nos fuimos no transcurrió un solo minuto. Es la misma hora.

Annie se encogió de hombros

—¿Y cómo hicimos para llegar tan lejos y tan atrás en el tiempo? ¿Cómo hizo la casa para llevarnos? —preguntó Jack.

—Mirabas un dibujo en el libro y dijiste que te gustaría conocer ese lugar —dijo Annie—. Y la casa del árbol nos llevó hasta allí.

—Sí. Pero... ¿cómo? ¿Quién construyó esta casa? ¿Quién trajo todos estos libros?

—Un mago, creo —agregó Annie.

—Oh, mira. Casi me olvido de esto —comentó Jack mientras sacaba el medallón del bolsillo—. Se le debe de haber perdido a alguien allá... en la tierra de los dinosaurios. Mira tiene grabada la letra M.

A Annie se le salían los ojos de las órbitas.

—¿Tú piensas que el medallón tiene la letra M porque le pertenece a un mago?

—No lo sé —contestó Jack—. Lo único que sé es que alguien estuvo allí antes que nosotros.

—¡Annieee! ¡Jaaack! —se oyó de nuevo a lo lejos.

—¡Ya vamos! —contestó Annie en voz alta asomándose por la ventana.

Jack guardó el medallón de oro en el bolsillo. Sacó el libro de dinosaurios de la mochila y lo dejó junto a los otros libros.

Antes de marcharse, Annie y Jack echaron un último vistazo a la casa.

—Adiós, casa del árbol —susurró Annie.

Jack se acomodó la mochila sobre los hombros y se dirigió hacia la escalera.

Annie comenzó a descender con cuidado. Jack bajaba detrás de ella.

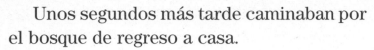

Unos segundos más tarde caminaban por el bosque de regreso a casa.

—Nadie va a creer lo que nos pasó —dijo Jack.

—No se lo contemos a nadie —agregó Annie.

—Papá no nos va a creer, Annie.

—Tienes razón. Nos va a decir que lo soñamos.

—Mamá tampoco nos va a creer. Va a decir que todo fue producto de nuestra imaginación —dijo Jack—. Y mi maestra tampoco me va a creer.

—Va a pensar que te volviste loco.

—Sí. Lo mejor es no contárselo a nadie —agregó Jack convencido.

—Ya te lo dije antes, Jack.

—Creo que ahora yo también empiezo a creer que todo fue un sueño.

Los niños salieron del bosque y tomaron la calle de regreso a su casa.

A medida que se acercaban al hogar caminando por aquella calle, dejando atrás las casas de la cuadra, el viaje a la tierra de los dinosaurios parecía cada vez menos *real*.

Sólo *este* mundo y *este* momento parecían verdaderamente reales.

Jack buscó en el bolsillo y apretó con fuerza el medallón de oro, recorriendo con entusiasmo el contorno de la letra M. Se sonrió.

De pronto, se sintió muy feliz. No podía explicarse lo que había vivido. Pero estaba completamente seguro de que el viaje en la casa encantada había sido real.

Completamente real.

—Mañana volveremos al bosque —dijo Jack en voz baja.

—¡Por supuesto! —agregó Annie.

—Y subiremos a la casa del árbol.

—¡Claro que sí, Jack!

—Y veremos qué sucede después —dijo Jack.

—Por supuesto —respondió Annie—. ¡Echemos una carrera! Y se marcharon corriendo juntos hacia la casa.

¿Quieres saber adónde puedes viajar en la casa del árbol?

La casa del árbol #1,
Dinosaurios al atardecer

Jack y Annie descubren una casa en un árbol
y al entrar viajan a la época de los dinosaurios.

La casa del árbol #2,
El caballero del alba

Annie y Jack viajan a la época de
los caballeros medievales y exploran
un castillo con un pasadizo secreto.

La casa del árbol #3,
Una momia al amanecer

Jack y Annie viajan al antiguo Egipto y se
pierden dentro de una pirámide al tratar de
ayudar al fantasma de una reina.

La casa del árbol #4,
Piratas después del mediodía

Annie y Jack viajan al pasado y se
encuentran con un grupo de piratas
muy hostiles que buscan un
tesoro enterrado.

Mary Pope Osborne ha recibido muchos premios por sus libros, que suman más de cuarenta. Mary Pope Osborne vive en la ciudad de Nueva York con Will, su esposo y con su perro Bailey, un norfolk terrier. También tiene una cabaña en Pensilvania.